Still Shining Bright

Emma Batten

First published in the UK by Emma Batten 2020

Printed and bound in the UK

A catalogue record of this book can be found in the British library

ISBN 978-1-9995820-8-1

Edited by Maud Matley and Michael Golding

Proofread and further editing by Rosemary Bartholomew

Cover painting by Zoe Beardsley

www.emmabattenauthor.com

In memory of those who were onboard the *Northfleet* on the night of 22nd January 1873

To Michael Golding, with thanks for the interest you have shown in my writing since we met in 2016 and for taking the time to give this latest Dungeness novel a thorough read through. Your on-going support and friendship are much appreciated.

About the Book

In the first of two prequels to *Secrets of the Shingle,* I take readers back to Dungeness and Ashford. The year is 1873 and we begin with a real shipping disaster – the loss of the *Northfleet.* In this fictional account, my survivors are brought ashore by lifeboat to Dungeness, whereas in reality all who were rescued were picked up by other ships and taken to Dover.

As always, I have tried to portray the area accurately while keeping the imaginary story in mind. All characters, including those on the ship, are entirely from my imagination. For those with a close eye on Dungeness details: references to a vicar and church services are fictional. It wasn't until later that a school was built and also used as a church. There was a curate to the coast, but no vicar based at Dungeness. The British Inn was known by that name until about 1890, and later renamed The Britannia. It was on a different site to the current pub. The lighthouse is not the black one seen today and open as a tourist attraction, but the previous one (dating from 1792), now marked by the ring of houses added later at the base.

Thank you to Michael Golding who has suffered random queries being thrown at him, and then agreed to read the whole book before it was published – and all for the price of a cream tea!

As always, my thanks to Maud Matley, a constant supporter of my writing, and to Rosemary Bartholomew for her excellent editing and proof reading.

I love this bright cover – thank you so much to Zoe Beardsley (www.greatstone-art.co.uk) for this fantastic design.

It has been a strange year. My previous novel was launched during lock-down and most retail outlets were closed for months. There have been no craft fairs or author events. I have been lucky to receive huge support from my readers and am grateful for every book sale which has enabled me to continue to write and publish.

Emma Batten – October 2020

Sources:
Life on Marsh Andy Holyer & Niko Miaoulis (2008)
A digital copy of the book *The Loss of the Ship 'Northfleet'*, originally printed in February 1873. Published by Waterlow and Sons, London.
Keith Swallow's *Nanny Goat Island, Dungeness Then and Now.* (2019)
www.magicmastsandsturdyboats.weebly.com
www.theromneymarsh.net
www.dungeness.org.uk
maps.nls.uk>geo>explore
The poem *One Seaside Grave* by Christina Rossetti was written in 1853 and published in 1884.

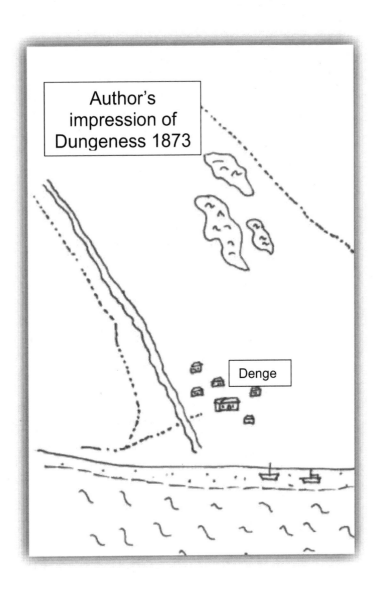

Author's impression of Dungeness 1873

Denge

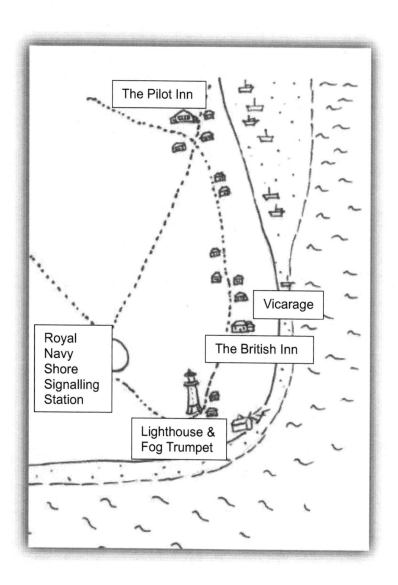

The Pilot Inn

Vicarage

Royal
Navy
Shore
Signalling
Station

The British Inn

Lighthouse &
Fog Trumpet

Chapter One
Gravesend, Kent. 1872

"Tasmania? What's got into you, Stan? Isn't life hard enough without another of your fancy ideas?" Cora looked down at her daughter who still sucked at a limp breast. "Get me a sack of coal for the range, and some flour to make bread, and I'm happy enough."

The young mother nudged the sleeping child and wiped a bead of milky dribble with a rag. She adjusted her light corset and fastened the buttons on her pleated blouse. Then, after placing Emily on the cushioned seat, Cora lifted her lips to Stan's, giving him a brief kiss.

"She's getting too old for your milk." Stan glanced at his daughter; with her pale skin and auburn hair Emily was already the image of her mother.

"I know, but if it stops me having another then I'll feed her till she's seven," Cora replied, flashing a quick grin at her husband.

"Fair enough." Stan lifted the lid from the pot bubbling on the range and sniffed the meaty aroma. Then he turned to Cora and tried again, "They're all talking about it since Ron got the letter from his cousin in Tasmania. It's paradise there, do you hear me? It's heaven compared with all this."

Cora scanned the living room of their flat-fronted terraced house. This was the best they could afford on Stan's wages. She had seen rows of new homes with bay windows and their own small back gardens. It wasn't much to aspire to: a front parlour with some lovely floral wallpaper and a lace cloth on the table. Cora didn't yearn for the stuff of fairy tales: a big house and servants. She would be happy with just enough coal in the grate, a room for Emily and the others who would eventually come, and some decent food in their stomachs. Not much to hope for, but more than she could dream of at the moment.

"Paradise doesn't exist." Cora rolled her eyes and turned to the loaf of bread on the table. "But I'm thankful for this and the bit of mutton I got today." Picking up the knife, she set about cutting one thick slice for Stan and, reluctantly, a thin one for herself.

"Listen, love." Stan stood behind her and wrapped his arms around her slender body. "Ron's cousin has written home and told him there's work in Tasmania, and sunshine, and little plots of land to build houses on. There's oranges growing on trees, and lemons too."

"Oranges!" scoffed Cora. "It's not for the likes of us to have a garden with an orange tree. Talk sense, Stan. That's for those who go over as the foreman, or more."

"It *is*, Cora," Stan persisted. "It's for everyone! They have plots for vegetables. Imagine that — me working on my own little garden and you cooking our home-grown food!"

"Tasmania. Tasmania. It might as well be the moon," Cora snapped. "In fact, I know where the moon is. I can see it from me window. I don't know where bleedin' Tasmania is, do I?"

"It's all the way across the world," Stan informed her. "Past Africa, and then Australia. It's like Australia, but smaller. I think."

"I don't want nothing to do with Australia and all them convicts."

"It's not Australia. But it's down that way and sunny too." Stan reached for the butter pot and spread a thin layer on his bread. "Have some of this, Cora. You need a bit of fat on your bones."

"No, I don't fancy it," she lied. "You have it."

Lifting the pot of stew onto the table, Stan continued, "There's no convicts. At least not anymore."

"I can't think what it would be like, seeing the sun." Cora's eyes narrowed as she imagined a golden ball in vast blue skies, not just a glow through the mist which rose from the Thames, or the lighter patch of sky amidst the smog of the industrial areas of Gravesend. The streets here by the docks were narrow, the houses packed tight, windows covered with a film of dirt. On a good day, Cora could enjoy an hour when a warm shaft of light shone through the small back window and, if she could spare the time, it was a treat to put the armchair in the soft sunlight for a while.

"I'm telling you, Cora, we could leave all this – the river mists, the cold winters, the rain and me working all day for nothing much." Stanley gestured to their one downstairs room, and continued, "It breaks my heart, love, not being able to provide more for you and our little girl. But it's all there waiting for us. I'm not sayin' it wouldn't be one hellish journey by boat – four months it takes – but Ron's cousin did it and he's got five little ones. Best get our Emily away from all this while she's still little and before you've got another nipper at your feet. It's Christmas in two days and then it will be 1873 – let's give ourselves something to look forward to?"

Cora looked down at Emily, sleeping in a ball on the tatty old armchair. She reached out and stroked her daughter's auburn ringlets; they were dull and a little greasy. Turning back to Stan, she questioned, "So he went, with his wife and family and he's living there in the sunshine, eating oranges and growing vegetables?"

"He is Cora. He really is." Stan's eyes were shining as he pictured the scene. "Now how about you dish up the stew, and we'll talk as we eat? I'm starving."

"Of course, you are! You had me all in a bother. I weren't thinking straight." Cora ladled the stew, containing a meagre amount of mutton, onto the plates and pushed Stan's across the table to him. She took a small amount and placed it in a tin bowl, then mashed it with a fork. Emily would soon wake, but for now they would enjoy their meal in peace.

Looking around the room, Cora despaired of ever keeping it warm and free of damp. *If only he didn't have to bring that stinking great overcoat home, then the place would smell a damned sight better. But there's nowhere else for it to go,* she thought. Stan worked in the boiler room of the *Earl of Essex* – the Gravesend to Tilbury ferry. His overalls were ingrained with soot and if he got wet walking home – which he had done every day that week – then they had to hang on the rack in front of the fire. Cora was sure the living room smelt just like the boiler room, but not half as warm.

The wallpaper was faded and peeling but the curtains, with a nice climbing rose, were new. Well, not new but they came from a charitable organisation which collected household goods and distributed them to the poor. The kitchen table was solid, but the upright chairs needed some repairs and the two armchairs had been re-covered recently. Cora had plenty of pots and pans in the cupboard next to the chimney breast and had kept the good teapot and carriage clock away from the pawn shop. It would be harder when young Emily had brothers and sisters. She was fully aware that she would fall for another child sooner or later and dreaded the moment when her monthly bleed was late.

While spooning the stew into her mouth, Cora imagined her daughter in a summer dress, sitting on a rug in a garden with orange juice dripping down her chin and her small hands full of the sweet sticky fruit. She visualised Stan with his hand on a garden fork, standing and looking over his well-stocked vegetable plot. *What would he grow?* J*ust imagine a plate with fresh peas, or purple sprouting broccoli or salad leaves...* For a moment Cora could almost feel the heat of the sun on her thin arms.

"Stan, is it really a better life out there? Is he spinning a yarn, that cousin of Ron's?"

"Well, love, it can't be perfect, but it's one hell of a better life than the one we have here," Stan replied. "I'm sure of it."

"And he's written about it… about his home and the fruit trees and the sunshine?"

"He has. I've seen it for myself."

"It must be awful," Cora reflected. "The journey, I mean. Would it be fair on Emily?"

"It would be bloody awful – all those months at sea. There's no denying it." Stan put the last of the bread in his mouth and chewed slowly. "But it would be worth it for a life in paradise and that's why Ron's going. He's leaving in three weeks; no more river mists and stinking mudflats for him. Eight shillings a week they'll pay for him to labour on the Hobart-Launceston railway. Imagine that – eight shillings a week! And only a pound to buy a nice plot of land to build a wooden bungalow on."

"Eight shillings," Cora repeated. "And that's for working on the railway? Building it, I mean. What about when it's built?"

"They'll need engine drivers and station staff and engineers," Stan informed her. "There's work for those who want it. No doubt about it."

Emily stirred and began to clamber out of the armchair. Cora scooped the child into her arms and tucked a cloth into the neckline of her dress before offering the mashed-up stew. "Are you thinking of us going there?" she asked. "Seriously thinking?"

"I'm more than thinking about it, love," Stan replied. "I've told Ron to hold the places for us. We'll leave in three weeks if you're agreeable."

"Three weeks!" Cora's voice was high. "What are you talkin' about? Surely there's things to be arranged like permissions and getting a job and..."

"It's all set up. Ron's brother was going but his little one has the scarlet fever and even if she survives, she'll not be strong enough to travel. We can have his places."

Cora tightened her grip on her young daughter. An infant's life was fragile, with one fifth of those born not reaching their fifth birthday. For people living as they did, in cramped, often damp conditions, amongst the terraced streets of Gravesend, the average life expectancy was just forty-four years. At low tide, the stench from the river mud wafted through the streets, infiltrating homes as it passed under doorways and seeped around the edges of window frames. Frequently, the smog from coal fires and factories hung low, blanketing the area, stifling the spirits of the town's people.

"I want better than this for Emily and the others that will come." Cora flashed a quick smile at her husband.

"You're not saying no?" A wide smile stretched across Stan's face, which still bore the smudges of coal dust.

"I'm saying let's sleep on it, and I'd like to see this letter from Ron's cousin," Cora replied. "I know what this means, Stan. We'll never see the family again and Emily will grow up without her cousins and with no memories of England. But if we can live a healthier life and you earn a better wage, well, I think it's worth it." And as she said those words, the young mother, who was only twenty-three years old, felt the burdens of her life wash away from her.

Cora was drawn to take the short walk to the river and view the *Northfleet* as soon as she heard the ship had arrived. Three weeks after she and Stan first discussed emigrating, she held Emily in her arms and stood on the riverbank, gazing in awe and trepidation at the clipper. The *Northfleet* was at anchor, not far from the Town Pier. Its three masts stood tall. *As tall as any of the factory chimneys,* Cora thought. *And the length of her – well, it's a wonder she can float. Especially when they say she's loaded with iron rails going all the way to Tasmania with us.* It made her head ache to wonder how a wooden ship could carry great metal bars, as well as hundreds of people and all the food and household goods they needed for three or four months at sea.

There was something majestic about the *Northfleet*. Even Emily, who was too young to understand, nestled soundlessly in her mother's arms and gazed at the ship rolling on the tidal river. She was an old-fashioned sailing vessel, with wooden sides and a great beam protruding from the bow. The sails were limp and gathered against the three masts, waiting for the wind and the voyage ahead. Cora could see cabins at either end of the ship; she imagined the captain's bunk and the huge table for his charts. For her and the steerage passengers, it would be a space in a shared room, not just under the decks, but also below the waterline. They were one better than the iron bars stored below them. Or did the iron have more value than the emigrant workers?

They stood at the riverside for ten minutes, absorbed by the activity on the water. The air had a vicious chill to it, cutting through Cora's coat and hat. She stamped her feet to keep them warm, then moved away. There was still so much to do before they all returned to the ship and it became their home for the next few months.

The following morning, Cora again gathered Emily close, and stood on the pavement looking up at the terraced cottage. The small family were turning their backs on Gravesend forever, to embark on a great voyage.

"Come on; we'd better get going," Stan said, gathering the three canvas bags into his strong arms. Over the past weeks the small collection of precious items that Cora had been determined to take with them – the carriage clock, a book containing a collection of nursery rhymes and pictures, an enamelled jewellery box and some watercolours painted by her mother – had been cast aside in favour of the clothing needed for the long voyage. The only treasure remaining was a cross-stitch sampler commemorating their marriage, and this had been removed from its frame before being stowed safely in the folds of a thick cardigan.

"I'm ready," Cora declared, with more gusto than she felt.

As the sun made a tentative attempt to shine upon the rooftops of the workers' cottages, Stanley and Cora took one last glance at their home before turning the corner and walking along the riverfront to the Town Pier.

Whatever scene Cora expected when she saw the *Northfleet* preparing to embark on the voyage, she was not prepared for what was before her: the whole of the pier and nearby riverfront was crowded with more people than she had seen in her whole life. *Surely, they're not all going to be travelling on the ship? It's enormous, bigger than I could have imagined, but not enough for all these people. No, there are too many.*

At first it seemed there was no order to the mass of people with their bags and young children clutched close to them. But on their approach, a ship's officer stepped forward and barked just two words: "Assisted emigrants?"

"That's right, sir," Stan replied.

"Steerage," was the response. "Over there." He pointed to the right-hand side of the already crowded pier. "Family groups in the middle."

The officer turned away before Stan could offer his thanks, and the small family filed through the gateway onto the pier. With officers keeping a pathway clear to the left, the rest of the area was for the waiting steerage passengers. They stood in their family groups: the wives wide-eyed and worried, children uncharacteristically silent and the men looking about, unable to offer any reassurance or protection. At that moment, Tasmania seemed further away than ever. Despite the sunshine, and the fresh food, this paradise land was unknown. *Life can't be that easy, not like Stan made it seem,* Cora thought. *Will we be all right when we get there or will it be just like home, but sunny?*

Somehow emigrants moved aside, and the family found their own small patch of pier to wait on. Cora lowered Emily to the floor and looked about, making eye-contact with the other steerage passengers and offering a brief smile. Emily clung to her mother's long skirt, her curls blowing about in the stiff breeze, coming straight up the Thames from the east.

"Do you see Ron?" Cora asked.

Stan was scanning the crowds. "I think he's over there." He nodded towards the far end and said, "We'll see them on board, I guess."

"Do you think we'll be standing about here for long?" Cora asked.

"I don't know, love, but I imagine the officers want to make a move like the rest of us do."

"'Ere, look at them!" A woman raised her voice and those nearby swivelled to look in the direction she pointed. A ship's officer marched along the left-hand side of the pier, with a cabin boy scurrying along beside him, a large case in each hand. They were followed by a man and woman, both wearing well-fitting coats and carrying small leather cases. As they walked, they looked straight ahead, avoiding the stares from the steerage passengers.

"Private cabin for them," a man remarked. "Above the waterline."

An hour passed, Emily fidgeted, and Stan gave her some plain biscuits to eat. Still more people were crammed onto the narrow pier. *At least they shield us from the wind*, Cora thought, as she attempted to entertain Emily with nursery rhymes. They watched the Gravesend-Tilbury ferry cross one way, and then the other. In Cora's head there came a scream: *Go back, Stan. Go back to the ferry and I'll take Emily home.* But the oranges and the extra two shillings a week beckoned them to Tasmania.

"Into groups now. Eight adults and their children." The words were barked by one of the ship's crew. "It doesn't matter who you're with. Get into groups."

Two sailors went amongst the families on the pier. They pushed people closer, urging them to stop dithering. Not knowing the reason for this, adults exchanged glances and raised eyebrows, fearful of what was to come next and frustrated by the delay in boarding.

"These are your mess groups," the member of crew announced. "John here will assign you a number and you'll quote it when you collect your rations for each meal. You'll be shown an area to cook and eat in."

He moved away. Cora glanced at the others who would become their family over the following months. They were number four. There were two other sets of young parents, with their children ranging in age from a baby to a girl of about eight years. The two remaining adults were a little older, with no children. The woman said, "I'm Ann and this is Bert. It's going to be strange at first, but we'll all have to make the best of things."

Cora gave a weak smile and nodded, unable to find the words to reply. And then there was no more time for the emigrants to whisper their fears or compare hopes, as all eyes were on the group of single women who were being escorted onto the *Northfleet*. There were not many of them: ten or twelve walked the plank bridge to the clipper, silent and nervous. Then it was the turn of the family groups and, looking back, they saw the largest group of them all, the single men, who would be the last to board.

"It's time," Cora murmured to Stan.

"It is, my love," he replied.

They moved slowly, across the walkway spanning the gap between pier and ship, and onto the main deck. Before they could become accustomed to the swell of the tidal river and the ship's continual movement, the passengers were ushered down two sets of stairs, passing a lower deck and then to the steerage accommodation. *It's true what I heard,* Cora thought. *We are to live below sea level.* And she tried not to let panic set in.

The second set of stairs led to a vast open area. The ceiling was low and supported by two lines of upright beams. Tables and benches filled the central space. But before they could fully take in the scene, they found themselves following the others through to another area on the left, running from bow to stern. This was lined with bunks, each one covered in a thin mattress and topped with two folded blankets. The far end was curtained off and, judging by the signs of movement in the hidden space, this is where the single women were to sleep for the duration of the voyage.

"Children sleep with a parent, or two per bunk," the officer advised.

"Come on, Cora, we'll take these." Stan dropped their canvas bags on the nearest set.

They sat with Emily between them on the lower one and watched as families claimed their spaces.

"It's all wood," Cora whispered. "The floor, the walls, the bunks."

23

"It is, love," Stan said, placing his arm around her slim shoulder.

"And just there, the other side of those bunks..." Cora pointed to the opposite row of beds. "That's the sea! Right there and all around us."

"It is," Stan agreed. "Makes your mind spin, doesn't it? And above us, the rooms for the crew, and the kitchens and the storerooms. Imagine the food they'll have to bring. I heard that they were loading the ship all day yesterday."

"And did you see... did you see the horses on deck? Blimey, Stan, horses on a boat goin' all the way across the world. I'd have never believed it. They've got their own stables!"

"I did," he replied. "They must need them as well as people and iron rails. Amazing, ain't it, Cora? To think of us travelling all the way to Tasmania!"

Chapter Two

By the 22nd January, the *Northfleet* had been at sea for nine days. "How can we ever reach the other side of the world, when all we see is the Kent coast?" Cora asked May, one of the other emigrants also living below the waterline.

"A hundred days they said it would take. At this rate we'll not reach Tasmania in a thousand," the other woman complained. She looked out to sea and scowled.

They were pegging out newly-washed nappies belonging to the children from their mess group. It was a job the pair of them did daily, while the other women kept an eye on the young ones. The men were cleaning the decks. At nine o'clock any child between the age of five and twelve attended the ship's school for three hours. As the adults went about their morning chores, they would pass the small group of pupils with their slates and chalks sitting before the central benches, or clustered on the floor listening to a story.

"I could have stepped on a train and come this far in a day," May remarked. It was true, there was no town or village in Kent they could not have reached within a few hours of Gravesend. Yet sailing around the coast had taken them no further than the White Cliffs of Dover in over a week.

"I know. My Stan was saying just the same last night," Cora replied.

"It's got to get better than this soon, because I don't think I can cope with another nine days and us no closer to Tasmania." The ship lurched and May put out an arm to steady herself. A crew member passed by and the young woman called out, "'Ere, can you tell us why it's taking so long? We'll never get to the other side of the world at this rate!"

"I know what you mean." The sailor gave a broad smile. "But we've got to go all along the south coast until we reach Plymouth, and then you'll say goodbye to England forever. The wind is the problem: it's not in our favour." He looked up at the vast white sails, and continued, "If we were going east then we'd all be a damned sight happier!"

It had been a miserable few days and morale was low throughout the ship. At first it had been fun to adapt to the routines set by the captain: watching the matron keeping a stern eye on the unmarried women, lest they become prey to one of the many single men; cooking in pairs for their mess and eating in a family group brought both new challenges and a sense of camaraderie; walking the decks with the children and gazing in surprise at the chickens and pigs in their pens, gave new interests and entertainment to the youngsters.

Barely a day had passed before the south-westerly breeze, already brisk, seemed stronger than ever and it was clear this great clipper was battling to make headway. The initial enthusiasm soon drained away as the emigrants took to their bunks, or hung over the sides of the ship, their skin grey and clammy. Sea sickness became a constant threat to them. It became almost impossible to cope with pans of hot food in the galley, and besides, no one wanted to eat the meal presented to them on a table which swayed before them.

Of all the jobs that needed attending to, the washing of nappies could not be avoided and in some ways it was better to be working above decks than trying to pacify fractious children below. Cora reached down to the basket and picked out the next wet nappy, then stretched up to the washing line to secure it with the crude wooden pegs provided. She repeated the process at least a dozen times.

That night, having struggled through another day at sea, yet with the Kent coast still in sight, the passengers were thankful when it was time to take to their bunks. With darkness falling early and use of candles limited, the adults went to bed with the children. Cora tucked blankets around herself and Emily on the lower bunk. Stan knelt and gave them both a kiss. "Goodnight my darlings, let's hope for a peaceful sleep. They say that the captain has anchored close to land for the night, in the hope we can shelter from the worst of the storm that's due."

"I'll be thankful when this bad weather passes," Cora replied. "I hope this is the end of it."

"Tasmania still seems far away," Stan reflected. "I hope we made the right choice."

Reaching out for Stan's hand, Cora gave it a squeeze. "We did, my love. Think of the fruit trees and our own plot of land."

"I will," Stan murmured. "I'll think of them as I go to sleep. And Emily with the sun on her skin, not the damp from those awful river mists. Sweet dreams."

"I love you, Stanley. You're a good husband."

Stan heaved himself up onto the bed above and Cora heard it flex as he shifted about, attempting to get comfortable. Lying below, with Emily in her arms, she tried to allow her body to relax with the rhythmic rise and fall of the water cocooning the steerage deck. She listened to the snores, the whispers and the shuffling about of the other emigrants. Pulling the thin blankets tight around her shoulder, Cora was glad of the warmth coming from her young daughter. Her thoughts began to drift away from the cramped living area to other times and places.

In her dreams Cora was back in Gravesend, with orange trees growing in the back yard, but the oranges never ripened. Then she found herself on the Gravesend-Tilbury ferry, but it was taking the family to Tasmania. Emily was playing on a stony beach. *It should be sandy*, was Cora's last thought before a deep dreamless sleep took hold.

The *Northfleet* slumbered at anchor, two or three miles off a shingle peninsula named Dungeness. It was in the company of several other ships who chose to shelter in the bay rather than brave the rough seas and strong winds of the open channel. The ship's boy huddled behind the bulwarks; his oilskin jacket kept the worst of the wind and rain from his body, but he thought of his bunk and the blanket he would wrap around himself when he was relieved of his duties

Nearby, the monotonous rumble coming from the belly of a steamship and the churning of water within its paddles went unnoticed. It mingled with his dreams, as his eyelids lowered and breaths deepened. The *Murillo*, seemingly ignorant of the volume of ships at anchor, ploughed steadily onwards, unaware of the *Northfleet* in her path.

The sounds of *Murillo's* iron bow piercing the port side of the wooden *Northfleet* reverberated through the whole ship. A cracking, splintering sound as it smashed through planks would live on in the memory of the survivors for the rest of their lives. The clipper was wrenched apart as planks split and iron nails released their grip. The *Murillo's* engines were put into reverse as she eased her nose from the side of her victim, pulling the *Northfleet* further apart in the process. The steamship changed course and continued her journey to Spain.

With her heart pounding, Cora woke abruptly, unaware of what had happened. An eerie light first caused confusion in that place between sleep and consciousness. It came as a hint of pale grey trickling through what she later realised was the rupture caused by the collision. The silence, as the emigrants began to understand what had happened, lasted seconds. Then the screams… the gasps… the unfinished sentences. Cora swung from her bunk, carrying Emily with her and reaching for the coat used as an extra bed covering.

Above the commotion, there came the sharp, disciplined tones of an officer. "There's been a collision. No need to panic. Move to the decks. Women and children first."

Cora steadied herself on Stan's bunk and grabbed at a cardigan for Emily. "Come on, sleepy. Help me put this on you. It will be cold, darling."

"You've got to go," Stan said, as he lowered himself from his bunk. "I'll be right behind you." He reached out and ran his fingers through Emily's hair.

"Our bags… Can you manage them?" Cora asked.

"I think we've got to leave them behind."

"Of course." Cora felt a little foolish now, and took a step away, allowing herself to join the flow of emigrants. "I'll see you soon, Stanley," she called out. If the words were said, then it would happen. "I'll see you soon."

"I'm right behind you…"

The water couldn't be seen on the dark planks, but already it had spread in a thin layer over the floor. Cora could feel the icy wetness lick around her bare toes; she hadn't even paused to push her feet into boots. *Should I go back for them?* she wondered and looked towards the bunk. *It's too late; I can't press past all these people and slow them down. No one can go back for anything.* An image of her treasured cross-stitch came into Cora's mind; it was the only precious item she had allowed to be taken in their luggage amongst their clothes and

29

toiletries. If they survived, it would be in their nightclothes, coats and cardigans; they would take nothing else with them to their new lives. Not even a pair of boots.

Having reached the open deck, there was no time to pause. With nearly four hundred people on board, Cora had to keep moving. The moon was full, casting a mottled light on the grey sea as clouds raced across its surface. The *Northfleet* was listing to the port-side, not in the way it rolled from one side to another, but as a constant lean. Women were ushered past horses in their temporary stables, chickens, and pigs. *What hope of rescue do the animals have? It can't be possible to lower a horse into a lifeboat. And there wouldn't be enough of the wooden dinghies.*

In the semi-darkness, with the decks so crowded, Cora found it hard to make sense of what was happening. It seemed that the crew were busy at the sides, lowering the lifeboats. All around people were calling out, screaming, panicking. The horses were stamping, and their shrill whinnies prompted Emily to put her hands over her ears. Officers and crew barked orders. Then amongst it all, as a lifeboat was lowered, there came another sound, shocking them all: a pistol fired. Just the one shot. Now the emigrants were silent. The horses still screamed their fear.

It was impossible to see the whole scene. The emigrants jostled and moved one way then another, unsure of where to turn. And through the crowds, Cora glimpsed snapshots of the larger picture. In the distance there were other ships at anchor on the waves, and a silver pathway created by the moon on the water seemed to beckon them to safety. At the bow, the captain was standing above them all, brandishing a pistol and barking orders, making it clear he would not hesitate to use it.

"Move forward!" A command came from nearby.

Cora moved with a group. *How strange. They said women and children, but I only see men here. It must mean Stan has been allowed up.* A few more steps and Cora stood at the edge of the boat, on the port-side tipped towards the writhing sea.

"You now, hand the child to someone."

"I can't..."

"She'll come next. Hurry up. Lift yourself over the edge."

Cora didn't even kiss Emily. It wasn't goodbye. She swung the little girl around and into the arms of a crewman. As she did so, and looked back through the crowds, she glimpsed another woman being pushed forward. And in the way some things become fixed in your mind, she wondered why this woman was wearing a hat, and what made her pause in the chaos to place it so neatly on her head.

"My husband?" Cora could hear the desperation in her own voice.

"He'll be all right. Come on..."

How Cora managed the ladder she never knew. Her bare feet somehow stayed firm on the hard rungs, and her hands gripped the rough rope while it flexed with every movement. She took a step down and then came the call: "Your little girl's waiting." With her left arm clamped onto the rope, Cora allowed herself to reach up and Emily was held over the side of the ship, screaming. And then came the most terrifying moment of all, when she took Emily's weight on her hip and wrapped her arm around the child, clutching onto the rope again. The ladder swung, and Cora's shoulder smacked into the plank side of the ship. She bore the pain without comment.

One step at a time, they descended the ladder. There was no choice but to keep moving, although it seemed almost impossible that they would reach safety. The lifeboat was so far away and the sea so wild. Cora knew there were hundreds of people to be saved and was aware of how many would die within the hour. Perhaps six or seven steps had been negotiated when the ladder began to twist with an urgency and, looking up, she saw the next person could wait no longer. Then hands gripped at her ankles, her thighs and waist, and Cora was being eased away from the ladder into the lifeboat. Emily was again taken from her mother's arms.

"Sit down and move along."

Cora followed the order and Emily was placed in her arms again. A man moved alongside, and she was sandwiched on both sides by men in rough overcoats. A distant voice in her head queried: *They said women…* Looking towards the ladder, Cora saw the woman in the hat, moving swiftly down the rungs, followed by a man – the last to step stumbling into the lifeboat. These two were seated at the bow. An oar reached out from the lifeboat and pushed at the *Northfleet*. With the oars in the hands of two burly sailors, they moved away from the stricken ship. In seconds, there was a safe distance of quite a few yards between the two vessels

Closing her eyes, Cora moved her hand in circles on Emily's back. The child had stopped screaming and now seemed to be rigid with fear. "We are safe… safe in a little boat," Cora told her, hardly believing the words herself.

All sense of time was lost. Locked in a private world, just herself and Emily, Cora's mind drifted to other times and places. First came memories of their damp cottage and the smell of Stan's skin, then a vision of their planned vegetable plot in Tasmania. She recalled the time when Stan had taken her to Greenwich, and they had walked hand-in-hand to look at Tower Bridge. Then Cora was in the room she rented before her marriage and creating the cross-stitch under the weak light filtering through the front window. These unconnected thoughts flitted through her mind. Fragmented as the images which come in a dream. How long did she sit, hunched up in her private world, holding back the nausea?

"Hold tight!" a voice bellowed.

Cora tensed. Emily let out a whimper and pressed back in her mother's arms. And then it happened – a great wave hit the lifeboat from behind. It broke on the stern and drenched the occupants with icy water. Cora's thin woollen coat was soaked, and her back felt numb. Emily, mostly protected by her mother, screamed as a shower of seawater sprayed over her.

"It's all right, darling. We are safe," Cora murmured. The lifeboat settled and the sailors continued to pull at the oars.

Within the boat, the passengers fretted as they attempted to dry themselves and keep the worst of the wet clothes from their skin. A new fear came: that of freezing in the harsh conditions. It played on Cora's mind and she wondered how long her small daughter could endure the icy breeze. On the choppy waters, it was no surprise that seasickness came, and with little warning. Cora felt it rise and all she could do was push Emily to one side and lean forward. The vomit hit her bare toes, warming them for a moment.

Emily screamed; her mother had pressed her too close to the strange man seated beside them. "Where's my Pa?"

"Safe on another boat," Cora replied. She twisted in her seat, wanting to see the *Northfleet*. The sky was patchy with cloud, but the stars were bright, and the moon shone bravely. A path of light was cast across the turbulent sea, catching the tops of the waves. There were other lifeboats, but none near them. Cora could see the silvery trails of water falling from their oars. The *Northfleet* was listing badly, and most of it was submerged. If Cora had been closer, she would have seen the desperate men and women climbing the rigging, delaying death by a few minutes. What she did notice was the shapes of other nearby ships and pinpricks of light coming from them. *Of course, we saw other ships at anchor; they will have seen our distress signals.*

"We can't turn back..."

Cora's attention turned to raised voices within the lifeboat.

"There are ships back there; they'll be picking up survivors."

"If we return, we'll catch it when the clipper goes down," the sailor barked his reply.

"So, we'll just keep rowing?"

"I'll keep rowing and you'll keep your bloody mouth shut. We're not far off land. What do you think that lighthouse stands on?"

At that moment, the tip of a light-beam scanned the sea and touched on the lifeboat, adding a temporary touch of colour to the scene. There were navy sailors' jackets, coats and jumpers in all shades of brown and, still untouched by the water, there was the green felt hat perched on top of a neat coil of hair. Cora lowered her eyelashes; she had become accustomed to the dark and to see her world lit up made it seem more real. She preferred it not to be true, to be something she didn't need to cope with. Yet the green felt hat stayed etched in front of her eyes and Cora wondered how this woman had found the time to put on her coat and boots – she had seen the boots descend the ladder – and then to top it all off with a smart hat. None of the emigrants wore a hat like that, theirs were brown.

Cora closed her eyes and rubbed her feet against one another; they were sticky with vomit, but she knew the icy air must be kept from penetrating them to the bone. She nestled her face in Emily's hair; it was a little damp and smelt of salt.

The next time Cora gazed behind her there was no sign of the *Northfleet*. How was she to know if it was out of sight due to the distance they had travelled, or was it that the ship was now settling amongst the sea creatures and marine plants on the rocky floor of the Channel? Later, she would learn that the *Northfleet,* so laden with iron bars, had sunk within half an hour of being hit, and only her masts would stand proud of the water. She rubbed her eyes and looked again, but there was nothing to be seen from the stern of the lifeboat.

The light scanning the sea from its vantage point on the beach now exposed a stony promontory and white horses frothing as they charged at the shingle beach. Cora fixed her eyes on the shore. There was no joy; how could she feel such an emotion when rigid with both cold and fear for her husband? They would be saved, her and her daughter, but where was Stanley?

The mood in the lifeboat remained subdued. There were words of praise and thanks for the sailors who had chosen to row away from the *Northfleet* and the chance of them being picked up by nearby ships. But no one in the small wooden boat could be jubilant. Every one of them had left friends or family behind and they only knew the fate of the sixteen in the lifeboat.

Used to the sway of the boat on the sea, it was a shock for Cora to find her body jarred as the underside of the lifeboat beached on shingle. Without any words exchanged, the sailors and a couple of men clambered out, then jumped into the icy water. The boat was pulled onto the beach, and more men climbed out to help. Arms were extended and a wide-eyed Emily passed across before being held tight against the chest of an emigrant passenger. Cora felt someone's hand wrapped around her own and scrambled out of the boat, gasping as she stood in the seawater and a wave broke against her calves.

The light-beam once again opened the view to Cora, now ankle-deep in water and struggling against the stones giving way beneath her bare feet. She glanced upwards and noted the steep shingle bank before her. When the light passed over the scene again, a man had turned and was offering his hand. Cora moved forward, the man's strength easing her way. A minute later, and they were all standing on the beach, free of the water, but with an icy breeze biting at legs clad in sodden clothes. Cora noted that somehow the green felt hat remained intact on the other woman's head and she maintained a sense of dignity.

Chapter Three

Although the full moon shone steadily over the promontory, those who stumbled up the steep shingle bank were deluged by the light sweeping from the tower. When it passed, the land was nothing but blackness. The landscape appeared barren: flat and featureless, other than the lighthouse. But as they moved forward in one mass of sixteen, including Cora, little Emily and the other woman, one of the men shouted: "There's a building of sorts; do you see the lights at the windows?"

They all strained to see in the direction he was pointing, and sure enough the beam of light picked out a low building, with at least three squares of glowing yellow, which could only be windows. While they focused on the gables and tall chimney stacks, a door opened, and a figure appeared.

"Hey, hey! Over here," one of the sailors hollered.

"Our ship's gone down. Can you help?" an emigrant took up the plea.

Others were waving and calling out. Emily began to cry again and the woman in the green hat moved closer to Cora. She spoke for the first time, "Shush, shush. We'll soon be warm and dry beside a fire, and there is sure to be some warm milk." Reaching out, she rubbed the little girl's back, and the crying subsided as Emily gazed at the stranger.

Cora turned and smiled at the other woman, but it was lost in the darkness. "How am I meant to explain to her what's happened? I can't even understand it myself.

We were going to Tasmania and we've ended up God knows where."

The woman didn't answer at first; she was looking towards the open doorway, where a second man now stood. They continued to walk forward as best they could, then she replied, just when Cora thought her words had gone unheard. "Dungeness. I believe we are at a place called Dungeness."

The word rolled through Cora's befuddled brain. "Dungeness," she repeated. The name meant nothing to her. She had never heard of such a place.

Turning back to face the sea, Cora watched the light sweep over it. Steely grey with white horses frothing on their relentless approach to the beach, the waters gave away nothing of the tragedy that night. The ships at anchor and the last of the *Northfleet* – the tips of her masts, tightly furled sails and sodden ropes – could no longer be seen. Her gaze returned to the landscape before her: irregular low buildings, small boats pulled up at the top of the beach, clumps of sea kale and hardy plants. None of it came into focus properly before the light from the tower was gone and Cora was left with a mere hint of the place she had come to.

"Hey, over here," the call was repeated.

"Who's there?" a voice from the doorway questioned.

"We've come by lifeboat, from our ship," one of the sailors replied.

"We're soaked through and bloody cold," another added.

"How many of you?" came the response from the man at the doorway.

"Fourteen men, two women and a child."

Two more figures now stood within the light of the open doorway. Cora watched as they turned to one another and she knew they were exchanging the news. One raised an arm, as if to acknowledge the survivors, but ran to the east, closely followed by another who had now appeared. They merged into the inky darkness. "They are going for help," someone suggested. The hope could be heard in his voice. "Perhaps for a lifeboat?"

Cora's gaze returned to the two men nearing them. "There's a fire blazing in The Brit," the first announced.

"It's after hours," the other was cautious, perhaps wary of there being a licensing officer approaching. "Private gathering."

Within minutes all sixteen survivors from the lifeboat paused before a beerhouse named The British Inn. The emigrants stood in all they possessed: nightshirts and a jacket or cardigan. Most were barefoot. The sailors' feet were clad in strong boots; they had clearly not retired for the night and still wore their coarse trousers with shirts and jackets. And standing apart from the rest of them, in status rather than distance, was the woman in her green felt hat. The cut of her woollen coat confirmed its quality: it had sprung back into shape despite the earlier soaking.

"All we want is shelter and warmth," the sailor said.

"You'll have it here," a broad man of short stature replied. "I'm the landlord, Reuben Roberts. Ada, my wife, has tea in the pot and the men have gone to get blankets from the village hall." He stood back from the open doorway and the weary survivors filed in.

Cora found herself pressed against a table created from roughly-hewn planks on barrels. An ashtray was over-spilling and beer had slopped over the wood, soaking into the cracks. She felt an urge to wipe the table clean. The woman in the green felt hat stood beside Cora; their shoulders nearly touched, and they exchanged fearful looks. Emily was heavy in her mother's arms but clung on tightly.

"Will there be any others?" the landlord asked.

"Any others?" a sailor repeated.

"Any more boats?"

"I don't know," the sailor replied. "There were over three hundred of us, and plenty of lifeboats."

"But we are only sixteen," Cora found her voice; it was high and didn't sound like her. "Of course, there will be more of us."

"They may not land here, love," one of the emigrants said. His voice was low.

"But they'll be somewhere," Cora insisted.

"And we'll have men on the beach looking for them," the landlord asserted. "But we have no lifeboat here."

The landlady appeared with the first steaming mugs of tea. Scanning the room with dark eyes, her lips were pursed, and she shook her head a little. The tea was placed on the bar and she gestured to the women, "Come on through to the parlour. This is no place for you and I'm sure an armchair would be welcome."

"Thank you. How kind," the woman in the felt hat replied. She smiled at Cora and they both walked through the doorway near the bar.

At that moment two men arrived laden with blankets; they passed a couple to the women, who now found themselves in a narrow corridor, and then a small square room, clearly the domain of the landlady. An oil lamp burned on a lace-topped side table and a couple of armchairs sat either side of a burned-out fire. The floor was wooden, and a circular rag rug covered the central area.

"I'll bring your tea and some milk for the little one," the landlady said, through the open doorway.

Cora began to remove her coat. "You'll have to stand on the floor," she murmured to Emily. "Just while we take off our wet layers." But the child only clung on harder and Cora had to peel her off, then, kneeling beside Emily, she removed the child's cardigan and her own salt-encrusted coat. "Look at this lovely blanket," she whispered. "We'll wrap up together in it."

They settled in a chair, Emily's grey eyes were fixed on the other woman, watching as she removed the green hat, loosened her bun and pinned it back into place. Then she wrapped herself in a blanket, having placed her folded coat and the hat in a neat pile on the floor.

"I'm Harriet," the woman introduced herself.

"I'm Cora, and this is Emily." Cora ran her fingers through her daughter's knotted hair. "You weren't with the emigrants," she stated.

"No. I was the chief officer's wife."

"Was?" Cora repeated. "You can't say that. I was with my husband, Stanley, and I've got to believe he's safe somewhere."

"The captain always goes down with his ship, and the chief officer will be at his side," Harriet said. Her voice was calm as if recalling her husband's words.

Cora, rarely unable to share her thoughts, reached forward and placed her hand on Harriet's arm. For that moment they were equals; the felt hat and good woollen coat meant nothing.

"Here you are, ladies." Ada, the landlady, brought in a tray with two cups of tea and Emily's milk. There were thin slices of buttered malt loaf. She was a woman in her mid-forties, neither tall nor short, with chestnut-brown hair threaded with grey and coiled at the back of her head. Her face was kindly, and she appeared to be a woman who was rarely flustered. If her parlour was anything to go by, Ada was a tidy housekeeper who would be wiping the spilt beer off the tables in the bar before long.

The two women murmured their thanks and fell into an uneasy silence. Emily dozed and Cora took in the details of the room: a pair of china King Charles spaniels sat either side of the mantelpiece, with a carriage clock in the centre and a clutter of tiny frames containing small tapestries. On the walls there were countryside scenes, one with a thatched cottage and another with prancing horses. Although the fire had burned itself out in the grate and had not been replenished, not even for the chief officer's wife, the room still smelled of woodsmoke. Ada was busy in the kitchen and the slap of her slippers as she passed to and from the bar could be heard every few minutes. The sounds of activity in the bar area told of men coming in from the beach, perhaps with supplies or news, and plans were made to house the survivors overnight. Cora heard of a decision to send a man to a place called Lydd at first light, with news of the night's event. But in the parlour, the women sat sipping tea and exchanged no more words.

"There's women?" a man's voice questioned. "Can they stay here overnight?"

"I wouldn't mind, sir, but one of them's the chief officer's wife," Reuben, the landlord, replied.

"They must come back to the vicarage, then." The voice became louder as quick steps sounded in the corridor and a figure appeared in the doorway to the parlour.

A man of about forty years stood before them. He wore a vast thick cape of brown wool and a hat pulled low over his forehead. At his neck, a white band showed, revealing his place as vicar of this settlement on the beach. His eyes were lively, darting from Cora to Harriet.

"My dears, may the good Lord look down on the seas tonight and bring more survivors to our shores."

"Have you any news of any other boats coming in?" Cora asked.

"Not yet," the vicar admitted. "But we can hope. There is still hope. Our priority must be caring for you all overnight." He looked towards Cora, and said, "You and the child can have my bed in the vicarage. I'll be comfortable in my armchair. And the officer's wife..." He turned to Harriet, "You may have the bed in the small room. It is humble but has clean sheets and can soon be warmed with hot coals in a pan."

"Any bed is welcome although I fear sleep will not come easily." Harriet rose from the chair. "Thank you, Vicar."

Cora stood and placed Emily on her hip. The blanket fell to the ground. Stepping forward, Harriet reached down and folded the material, then placed it as a wide scarf around Cora's shoulders.

"Ta," the young woman gave a smile.

The vicar's pace was brisk as he led the way along a stony path, lit only by the moon and the passing beam from the lighthouse. Low buildings of irregular shapes were either side of the track, in a disorderly fashion, not in terraces, as in the streets where Cora lived, or behind privet hedges and set in their own parcel of land. These Dungeness homes were mainly in darkness; those inhabitants who had not been raised by the call for help were sleeping under layers of blankets, perhaps with a warmed brick at their toes.

Stumbling on the uneven stones beneath her bare feet, Cora was relieved when the vicar turned towards a single storey building with tarred plank walls. "Here we are. Not your usual vicarage," he announced, as he pressed the latch on the door.

Frowning, Cora wondered about the church. She couldn't see a solid brick or stone building rising in greater stature.

"There's no church here, my dear." The vicar seemed to have read her thoughts. "We make do with a small hall."

Cora didn't know quite how to respond to this. She frowned, knowing nothing of a hall being used as a church. It didn't seem right. Hitching Emily into a better position on her hip, she followed Harriet and the vicar.

It was nothing like the vicarage belonging to Cora's parish in Gravesend, or anything she would have ever imagined a vicarage to be. There was no hallway with neat square tiles, no front parlour or study for receiving parishioners. Here they were, straight into a living area which served several purposes. There was a range, a kitchen dresser, and a side table with a jug of fresh water. The dining table evidently served as a desk and was so laden with books and papers it seemed the vicar must eat his dinner from a tray on his knees. The two armchairs were layered with rugs and blankets, and it was obvious one had been abandoned in haste, as a blanket was trailing across the floor. Two doors led to further rooms, presumably the bedrooms previously mentioned. To the rear of the property, a narrow door was ajar and appeared to lead to a scullery.

"You're in there, with the child." The vicar pointed to a door, presumably leading to his bedroom. He continued to speak as he stepped towards the range and pushed a kettle onto the hotplate, "And I've a bed-warmer for the chief officer's wife. No one likes a damp bed and it's not been used in a while. Some hot coals in a pan and we'll soon take the chill off it."

"And the water closet?" Harriet asked.

"Outside and to the right," the vicar replied. "You won't find an inside WC here at Dungeness. I'll leave a lamp on this side table; take it with you when you feel the need."

Cora had never known a home where you didn't go outside to the privy and knew of some where several families shared just the one. *What will the officer's wife make of doing her business outside? It'll be new to her and I wouldn't mind betting there's no running water. Will she wear her hat if she goes out at night?* Cora pushed the irrelevant thought aside. "I'll take Emily out there now if you don't mind?"

Within the hour, Emily was fast asleep under the layers of blankets on the vicar's bed. Her head lay in the crook of her mother's arm. The vicar could be heard snoring from the comfort of his armchair, but Cora suspected that Harriet, like herself, lay awake dwelling on the fate of her husband. Tears rolled down Cora's cheeks until she finally fell into an uneasy sleep, waking just a few hours later as dawn broke over Dungeness, the rambling settlement on the shingle headland.

By ten o'clock the next morning, Cora was back in the parlour of The British Inn with Emily and Harriet. She still wore her nightgown and coat, but the kindly vicar had given her two pairs of thick socks as there were no shoes to fit her small feet. They had passed by the male surviving emigrants and sailors at the bar, all still in various forms of attire. Some were slumped, while others appeared agitated and eager to get away from this place, perhaps even anxious to join the next ship bound for Tasmania, land of sunshine and opportunity.

A policeman was standing in front of the bar and, while they settled in the parlour, his voice could be heard questioning each man and taking their details. Eventually he walked through to the parlour and drew up a dining chair to sit with the women and child.

"I've been called from Lydd," he said, rubbing his finger over the dark stubble on his gaunt face. "It's a sorry situation. Very sorry indeed."

"Have there been any more come in overnight?" Cora asked, and as she said those words the hope burned bright.

"Not here," he replied. "But if survivors were in lifeboats, like yourselves, then most likely they were picked up by other ships anchored offshore. As for the bodies, they'll wash up over the coming weeks, depending on the tides."

Pushing aside all thoughts of the bloated bodies of drowned men and women, Cora asked, "And what about the ones on the ships? Where will they go?"

"Most likely they'll be taken to a port to suit the vessel they are on. Rye... Dover... Newhaven – it will take a while to account for everyone."

"And some will never have a record of being found," Harriet added, her voice low and resigned.

The policeman turned. "And you're the chief officer's wife," he stated.

"Widow. I'm the chief officer's widow."

The policeman nodded, acknowledging the truth of it. "Can I take your name, please? For the records, and then I can plan the best way to get you home."

"Betteridge. Harriet Betteridge. I live in Rye. Church Square. I'd appreciate a pony and trap to take me there, and perhaps someone can go ahead with word of my arrival. The house has been shut up, you see. We were to be away for several months..." It was only those last words which trembled as the officer's wife thought of returning home without her husband.

"We're arranging transport to Lydd and on from there," the policeman informed. "People need clothes and shoes, so they are opening up a hall in order to take the men there and get them straight before they move on. But you, madam, you'll have a room at The George Hotel." He looked towards Cora, "And you..."

"I ain't got a home," Cora blurted out. "We were going to Tasmania to live. Stan said it would be a better life with our own house and fruit trees. I've got nowhere to go now." And without giving the matter any thought, she continued, "I'm going to stay here. Right here at Dungeness, and when my Stanley gets back to shore, he'll be able to find me. No point in going off here and there, and him not knowing where I am. Me and Emily, we'll stay right here."

Chapter Four

"Come on, Emily, we'll go out and draw some water for the vicar and then go down to the beach. Maybe Pa will arrive on a boat today and he'll be so pleased to see us waiting for him!" Cora took two enamel jugs from the shelf under the scullery sink and pulled at her young daughter's hand. Emily had been engrossed in a sketchpad of watercolours featuring the birds of the Dungeness headland. They had been painted by the vicar and several times a day the little girl sat on the rug, tracing a small finger over the lines, murmuring to herself in her own private language. She looked at her mother and pushed the book aside. Cora picked it up from the floor and placed it on a side table.

Emily stood but said nothing. It was like that every day: she chatted to the birds in the book but not to her mother or anyone else. When the gulls flew overhead, screeching and riding on the breeze, causing the little girl's eyes to light up, she would babble her pleasure, but the rest of the time Emily was silent. The child did everything her mother asked, but without attempting to communicate. She allowed herself to be buttoned up in a boy's tweed coat, which came past her knees and covered her hands. "At least it will help keep the chill out," her mother said every day, trying to fill the space with words. Pausing at the doorway, Emily remained unresponsive while allowing her feet to be pushed into an old pair of lace-up boots with worn soles. Then she had a woollen hat placed on her head and pulled down over her ears. "Aren't we lucky that kind people gave us these things and we don't need to wear our nightgowns?" Cora would say, knowing there would be no reply.

With the jugs in one hand, Cora lifted the latch on the door. "We mustn't let the heat out," she said, as they rushed outside. A comment repeated every day too.

It had been a week since the survivors were washed up at Dungeness. Cora and Emily had moved into the vicar's small bedroom not long after Harriet had left on the back of a cart bound for Lydd, before returning to Rye. On that same day, a package of clothes had been delivered, all kindly donated by the people of Lydd, the nearest small town.

"You can stay for a week, but it's not suitable. Not at all right," the vicar had said when he heard Cora was refusing to go with the other emigrants.

"We need to be here. To wait for Stan to come," Cora had insisted. Neither the vicar nor the policeman, nor Ada from the beerhouse, could persuade her to leave. And so, the vicar agreed to care for her and Emily until the young woman came to her senses and returned to Gravesend or wherever she could find family to take her in. Cora could see that they all believed she would leave within a week; it could be seen in their eyes and the set of their mouths when she declared Dungeness would be her home for however many days, weeks or months it took for her to be reunited with her Stanley.

The wind was sharp, piercing bare skin and penetrating the second-hand coats. It whipped at Emily's auburn curls, which flew out from under her hat, and teased the tendrils falling from Cora's bun at the nape of her neck. The clouds were high in the sky, racing from west to east, and the winter sun was low, a pale-yellow ball offering no warmth. Stones moved and crunched under the boots worn by mother and daughter, as they trudged towards a water-pump placed between the cottages.

The cast iron hand-pump was encrusted with icy crystals. Emily reached forward to touch those that had formed at the spout but stepped back as her mother pressed on the handle. One, two… and on the third time the water began to flow. The jugs were soon filled and placed by the door to the vicar's home. Cora rubbed her hands together; she had not been offered gloves by the people of Dungeness who had so little to share. However, under the light of an oil lamp, a pair were forming as she set about the task of knitting her own during the long evenings.

"Come on, Emily," Cora said, forcing a brightness into her voice. "Let's go down to the beach. You can throw some stones into the sea and maybe we'll find some to thread onto your piece of cord. They'll bring us luck, they will. Those stones with holes in them. Do you know what they call them?" She paused, giving her daughter the chance to speak, but Emily merely gazed at her boots as they pushed against the stones. "Hagstones," Cora continued.

The cottages formed a haphazard string along the top of the beach, with no paths leading to front doors, no boundary fences, nor a road. Cora had seen wide-wheeled carts moving along some form of track, a little way inland from the beach. This was merely an area where the stones had settled through being pressed down by the weight of them, not engineered by man to make it easier to pass along by pony and trap, or even on foot. Stepping away from the cottage, Cora prepared to follow a different form of path taking her from the top of the shingle ridge to the beach. An uneven trail of planks had been laid to ease the movement of a fishing boat on its journey to the water's edge, and now it served nicely as the easiest way of reaching the beach.

"The boats went out early," Cora informed Emily. "I saw them go from the window while you were still sleeping; it was before sunrise."

But the little girl merely watched the gulls wheeling and shrieking in the clear sky above, before a group of tiny wading birds caught her attention and she let go of her mother's hand in order to move closer to them. Cora stood on the very edge of the shingle bank and scanned the horizon. "How am I to tell if one of them is a lifeboat?" she murmured. "There's all those fishing boats, but one of them could be him, coming to me..." Taking tiny steps she began to descend the bank, moving from plank to plank and, as they walked, Cora scanned the ground for the lucky stones.

The pebbles with holes running through them had fascinated Cora since that day when she and Emily had first returned to the beach and gazed out to sea. It had been so calm, with the water a mere ripple as it lapped on the stony shore. They had stood there, hand in hand, still in nightgowns, for they had no clothes. Time had passed, perhaps half an hour or more, and the young woman had no sense of the chill pervading her body. Emily, still not understanding what brought them to this place, had moved away from her mother and had been examining the various colours and textures of the stones. The day may have been calm, but it was icy cold, and neither mother nor child were dressed for the beach. An old man had found them and led them back to the warmth of his one-room cottage. He had asked no questions nor made any observations but had placed them in front of the range and gone to fetch the vicar. When the vicar came, Emily was found to have three stones with holes in them secure in the pocket of her cardigan.

"Where did these come from?" Cora had asked. But as the words came, she immediately felt foolish for there was shingle as far as the eye could see.

"Them's special stones," the old fisherman had said. "Lucky ones. Hagstones."

After that Cora searched for them every day. She found a piece of string and believed that when the hagstones filled the string, then luck would come and with it the return of her husband.

"Cora." Ada Roberts from the pub was standing behind her. Cora hadn't heard her coming even though no footstep was silent on the shingle. Ada placed her hand on the younger woman's arm.

"Is there news? We're sure to hear any day..."

"The constable has been and he's with the vicar in his home, but your Stanley isn't on the list."

"He must be," Cora insisted. "He must look again. I know he'll find him."

"Go and see him, love. And afterwards pop along for a cup of tea; you know the kettle's always on the range. I've got an idea you may be interested in." Ada turned and began the laborious trudge up the steep bank. Wrapped in layers, topped with a shawl and woollen hat, she was a woman who was used to the harsh winds and open expanse of Dungeness, coping with it and accepting this unforgiving land. Although her husband, Reuben, was the figurehead behind the bar at The British Inn, everyone knew it was Ada who organised the running of the pub and she wasn't afraid to call out with a sharp word if there was any rowdiness beyond what she deemed acceptable. As a couple they were well-liked.

Cora watched her go. Already she felt an affection for the landlady who had checked on her and Emily several times a day since they had arrived, lost and bedraggled, at The British Inn just a week beforehand. It was Ada who had urged them both to eat, sat the silent Emily on her knee and combed out the tangles in her hair. She had placed a borrowed shawl around

Cora's shoulders when she found her wandering on the shingle ridges and listened to her reminisce about Stanley. Ada spoke the truth, giving comfort but never promising Stanley would be found alive. For now, Cora was not ready to face the fact that most likely her husband had perished within an hour of the *Northfleet* being rammed on that icy January night.

When Ada disappeared over the top of the bank, Cora called Emily, who was at the water's edge and, with her daughter's small hand in hers, they clambered up the steep shingle, then traipsed towards the vicarage. By the time she reached for the latch on the door, Cora's cheeks were rosy from the exertion and the skin on her slender limbs tingled from the chill of the frosty air. Once inside the cottage, the warmth from the range wrapped around her, and she unbuttoned her coat, discarding it on the old wooden coat-stand.

"Is there any news, Constable?"

"I'm sorry, Mrs Parkins, I've got the papers before me. As I told you before, only four lifeboats were released from the ship. A tragedy, that is, and there's no denying it. Despite the flares, only three ships in the vicinity of the *Northfleet* came to the aid of those onboard. They picked up survivors on the lifeboats and a few men were plucked from the rigging. The ship went down at such a pace and in those icy waters any man would have perished in minutes." The constable turned back to the papers and ran his forefinger over the list of names. "No Stanley Parkins was recovered."

"But there might have been other ships who collected men… and they might not have gone into port yet." Cora looked at the policeman and continued, "It was dark and stormy and so much going on. You don't know what it was like, sir, but there could have been another lifeboat or men rescued and we've not heard of them yet."

"I don't know what it was like," the policeman admitted. He was young and carried the burden of his duties, as he contacted the ports and tried to collate details of the men who had been recorded as survivors. "And if it helps you to hope of him being recovered... But I fear you and your daughter must leave here and return to Gravesend."

"Leave?" the word came out almost as a screech. "I can't do that and where on earth are we expected to go? We've got nothing, me and Emily. We'll stay here."

"We can only pray..." offered the vicar. "But you know you can't... well it's not the decent thing... a young woman living here."

"I know you don't want us, Vicar, and you've been good, letting us have a room and keeping us nice an' warm," Cora said, her determination still strong. "Me and Emily... we'll find somewhere else and I'll get a job to pay our way."

It had been a whole week since Cora had waded through the shallow waters and onto the beach at Dungeness. She had looked on as all the other survivors had taken the wide-wheeled cart to Lydd and then on to wherever they could find warmth and shelter, most likely with family members. She had watched the fishermen come and go in their boats, set up nets from the beach to snare fish, and dig in the sands for lugworms. Once, Cora and Emily had walked from the scattered collection of perhaps twenty humble cottages and two pubs, to the lighthouse on the point of this shingle headland, and then to gaze at the row of terraced cottages now standing within the ring of a Napoleonic fort. The wind had been strong that day, pressing on Cora's throat and making her feel sick. On a daily basis driftwood had been gathered for the vicar's fire, and water pumped from deep beneath the shingle they stood on. Cora had seen most of what Dungeness had to offer, yet absorbed none of it, if she believed a

53

life could be made for herself in this village. There was no boarding house for a young widow and her child, nor a factory, a shop or café to be worked in. But Cora was not willing to accept that returning to Gravesend, or to any place more substantial than this remote settlement, was an option. Something within her said that she must stay on at Dungeness and she wasn't inclined to question the sense in returning to her hometown. Not yet anyway.

The vicar and constable sat looking down at their cups of tea, digesting the latest outburst.

"Perhaps the vicar in Lydd..." The Dungeness vicar tried to pass the awkward package of mother and young child onto a larger community.

"I ain't going to the workhouse, you know," Cora declared, snatching at her coat and the boy's coat given to Emily. "We're going along to The Brit; Ada wanted to see me. She's been bleedin' good to us, if you'll excuse my language, Vicar. I'll see you tomorrow or the next day, Constable, when you've got good news and can tell me where to meet my Stan."

Neither vicar nor policeman knew how to respond before the young woman and her daughter had left, with a flurry of red hair and long slender limbs.

Stomping on the stones, dragging Emily along beside her, Cora felt the tears begin to well up. She turned to the south, facing the lighthouse, and passed several fishermen's cottages before reaching The British Inn. Rather than go through the bar, the domain of the men, they walked past ramshackle outhouses to the kitchen door. Cora wiped her tears with the sleeve of her coat, and knocked as she opened it, calling for the landlady.

Ada was swathed in an apron, and the salty-sweetness of raw fish was strong in the air. "Sometimes the boats can't go out at this time of year," she told Cora. "You can imagine what it's like when the winds get up, and I've known the sea to freeze, so we're thankful when the boats return with a fresh haul even if it's not a big one." She had several silvery fish on the table and was gutting them with a confidence Cora admired.

"I've seen the constable," Cora offered.

"And he had no news for you," Ada stated.

"No news, but perhaps tomorrow..."

"It's brought a tear to your eye though and there's no shame in that," Ada observed. She nodded towards a pile of starched white bedlinen and clothes piled up in a basket on the floor. "And I suspect no one has thought to give you and the little girl a hanky to use. Have a look through my laundry and take some to keep for yourselves. I hemmed a dozen from old sheets just last week, so they're nice and new."

Cora turned to the folded linen in the basket, while Emily pulled herself up onto the chair beside Ada and watched in silent wonder. "There's tea in the pot and I hope you're getting used to the goats' milk because it's all I have. Emily doesn't seem to mind, do you sweetheart? If you pour us both a cup, then I'll be done with the fish in a minute. I've got some for you and the vicar, which will please him, no doubt."

"It will," Cora said, stuffing the handkerchiefs into her pocket. She looked around the kitchen. It was a good-sized space, square, with shelves and cupboards either side of the range. The sink was huge, with a wooden draining board sloping towards it. There was a drying rack on the ceiling and the central table was surrounded by four chairs, although it could have easily fitted six or eight. There were boots by the back door and pegs for coats. This kitchen served both the home and the bar area, as could be seen by the basket of clean tankards on a side table.

"Why can't you go back to Gravesend?" Ada asked, once they were seated with cups of steaming tea before them and Emily was occupied with a chalk and slate.

"I've got to wait for Stan..."

"But he's not going to wash up here, is he?" Ada reasoned.

"The constable knows where I am."

"Tell me what it's like in Gravesend?" Ada tried a different approach.

"It's by the river, and that's wide, wider than you'd think, an' it don't sparkle. It's like some great grey-brown slug," Cora began. She spoke of the *Earl of Essex*, the steamer that journeyed to Tilbury and back every day, and of the tiny home they once lived in.

In her mind's eye, Ada saw the pawn shop, the factories and the grey streets lined with brick terraces. She could almost smell the mud as it oozed when the tide fell, and the riverbanks were laid bare on the lower reaches of the Thames. The landlady could almost taste the mists laden with the smoke emitted from belching chimneys, whereas now she savoured the salt-laden air of Dungeness.

Ada had been to Rye where the ships came up to the Strand, but there the air was clear and ancient buildings remained free from the grime of modern times. She had also been to Ashford, where Romney Marsh sheep went to market and great steam engines clanked, but she had never ventured further than these towns. The world Cora spoke of was both new and fascinating to her.

"It's not the sort of place I'd want to live," Ada admitted. "I'm settled here in The Brit, by the sea, and it will do for me and Reuben. I'm thinking of your family though, and your friends. They'd welcome you back, wouldn't they?"

"My ma's dead, and my pa, he's not a well man. It's his lungs," Cora explained. "Pa lives with my sister and she's got four young ones. My other sister is in service, and my brother is courting but he lives in lodgings. And I can't go to Stan's family. His pa, he's too fond of the drink, if you know what I mean."

"It's not sounding good, love."

"It's the workhouse for us," Cora declared. "That's why I want to stay here."

"I needed to hear about it before we spoke anymore," Ada paused, and took a long sip of tea. "I can see you don't want to move on from here and I've got an idea..."

Chapter Five

Ada's bread pudding lay heavy in Cora's stomach, as the landlady led her along the top of the beach and towards the lighthouse. Emily had been left with a young woman who had three little ones of her own, "...and one more won't make any difference," she had said. "Not when she's as quiet as your Emily." Cora had leaned down to kiss the top of her daughter's head and left her for the first time since they had arrived at Dungeness together.

How foolish I am, Cora thought. *What would Stan say? First, I want to stay here in Dungeness and when there may be a chance of work, then I'm so bleedin' scared I want to get on a train back home.* She glanced towards Ada, who was striding out, and tried to match her pace, not wanting to show any sign that her heart was pounding, and her head felt giddy with nerves. Cora took a deep breath through her nose and felt the cold air flow deep into her lungs. She licked her lips and tasted the salt on them; it distracted her, and she felt a little calmer.

The two pairs of feet slapped down on the shingle. A few days beforehand, amongst the bundle of clothes provided for her and Emily, Cora had been given a pair of curious wooden boards with leather straps running across them. "They're called backstays," the vicar had told her. "You slip your boots in and then you won't sink into the stones." Having eyed them with distaste, Cora had tried them and immediately cast them aside, feeling foolish in her attempts to walk across the shingle with the boards slipping, and stones becoming caught up with them. But Ada, who could see this incomer needed a firm hand at times, had insisted she persevere. Cora had found a way to tighten the straps; her boots were secure and she was able to move, albeit awkwardly, across the shingle.

Fixing her eyes on the lighthouse, Cora wondered about the type of men who worked there. *It must be cold and lonely. And miserable having to stay up all night, keeping watch on a light.* The tower stood proud, with four sturdy buttresses at its base and tapering slightly as it soared high. Rows of small windows, one above the other, reached upwards and Cora imagined the men pausing to gather their breath as they ascended a staircase, or perhaps ladders, and took the opportunity to gaze out over land or sea. The lighthouse was topped with some bands of brickwork, supporting rings of square windows from where the guiding light would blaze. On the summit, the roof was like a little cap, proudly displaying a beaten weathervane. It was an impressive upright building, painted in traditional white with red stripes, although even from a distance it was clear the paintwork had taken a battering over the past few years. At the base, there were various brick buildings both attached to the tower and set on the land nearby.

"What's he like, this Mister Rose?" Cora asked.

"Well…" Ada considered her answer. "He's not a drinker, at least he has a couple and then he's done. Not much of a talker either. He comes in The Brit and sits himself down with his pipe and I'd say he's happy enough with his own company."

"Serious then?"

"That's not to say he's a moody type, just because he's not getting rowdy," Ada continued. "He's decent enough. Of course, you'd expect him to be a bit serious, wouldn't you? With his wife barely cold and three boys to take care of."

"I'm not used to boys," Cora pointed out.

"That's nothing to worry about. They're just children and most likely missing their mother badly. You'll have your hands full with little Emily as well, I won't deny it." Ada gave a smile and said, "It might do her the world of good. Perhaps the poor lamb will find her tongue with three boys around her."

"I don't want you to think I'm not grateful..." Cora began.

"It's just all a bit scary, isn't it?" Ada slowed down and gestured towards the scattering of small homes. "You can see what it's like here. You're not going to pick up a job in a corner shop or a tearoom. Reuben says he'll clear out the storeroom for you and the child, but the pub's no place for her to be running about and I'm too busy to be looking out for her. If Jacob Rose takes a liking to you, then it will all be for the good. I'm sure of it."

They moved on in silence, other than the scrunch of the backstays underfoot. The lighthouse loomed before them and Cora could see that a couple of the brick buildings were accommodation for the keepers. Chimneys rose from the slate roofs and smoke curled out in grey streams. Ada turned towards one of the cottages and they paused on reaching it, kicking off the backstays, then propping them up against the wall. The front door was sturdy and painted black; Ada reached up and rapped on it with a brass knocker.

The first thing that struck Cora when the door was opened by the lighthouse keeper was that his hair was an even brighter shade of orange than her own. Whereas she and Emily shared glossy auburn curls, this man had a crop of glowing ginger, and neat sideburns. The smile he forced on his lips did not reach his pale blue eyes. He was tired. Cora could see that in the lines around his eyes and the way his body slumped a little. Perhaps, like her, he was wary of meeting someone new.

"Jacob, this is Cora Parkins." Ada did the introductions. "She's been here a week and has a fancy to stay. As you know, I was thinking you could do with some help, and Cora needs to earn a few shillings."

"Pleased to meet you," he said. Then he paused, looking into her face, and Cora waited, knowing he had something more to say. "I'm sorry to hear of the tragedy that brought you here, and if we can help each other..." He held out his hand and Cora took it. They shook hands briefly. Hers felt tiny within his.

"You've had your own loss too..." Cora replied. "And I hear you've got three boys."

They moved into the room and Ada followed. The space was square with a range sitting within a brick fireplace. An open door led to a small scullery. Jacob looked towards it and spoke to one of the boys who had all turned to stare at Cora and Ada, "William, close the door. It's letting the cold in." The oldest boy, who was perhaps eight years old, stood and did as he was told.

The other two remained seated at the plain wooden table placed in the centre of the room. There was a game with counters set up, and it seemed as if the visitors had interrupted the youngsters as they played. Now all their attention was on the two women in their midst, and the game forgotten. The room was tidy, and this came as a surprise to Cora who was brought up to believe that men were not capable of fending for themselves. There was washing hanging on an airer, but not so much that it would lead her to believe that Jacob Rose left it there once it had dried and hadn't bothered to put it away. The two armchairs had neatly folded blankets hanging over the back of them, and the plumped cushions were laid square on the seats. The shelving on either side of the chimney breast was stacked with tins, crockery and baskets, each one seeming to have its place, and none of them jostling for position. Cora wondered if the cupboards below were as orderly, and did they contain packets, jars and tins of food?

"Here they are." Jacob waved his hand in the direction of his sons. His shirt fell back a little at the wrist, revealing a forest of red hairs running up his arm.

Cora smiled at the boys, "Hello, I'm Cora. Cora Parkins. Aren't you lucky living next to a lighthouse? Have you climbed to the top?"

For a moment, they all stared back at her, their faces serious. They were all so alike, each one with a mop of orange curls, and pale skin. Then the middle one smiled and Cora noticed his eyes were brown, while the others had pale blue like their father. *He must take after his mother,* she realised. And he, the middle one, had a bold smattering of freckles across his nose and cheeks, whereas his brothers had just a few.

"We have been to the top, but we must be very careful and always listen to Pa," the brown-eyed boy informed her. "We go one at a time, while our Ma looks after the others."

"But we don't go now, because there's no one to watch us," William continued.

The middle child looked down at the table, perhaps embarrassed. The younger one pushed at the counters on the playing board, unsure of how to react.

"Perhaps one day I could come and look after you, while your Pa goes to work?" Cora suggested. The words were bold for she had no idea how she could manage the three boys and Emily, although they seemed to be well-behaved.

"William's been looking after us," the smallest one piped up. "And sometimes Mrs Jefferies comes in. She cooks us our dinner. William can't do cooking."

Cora studied Jacob Rose. Was this correct that the young boy was left to care for his brothers? Her thoughts were left unsaid, but her eyes questioned their father.

"It's not all the time," Jacob explained. "William and Johnny take their lessons in the mornings and the wife of one of my colleagues keeps an eye on young Frank. But the rest of the time… It's not right, they are far too young... but I've got to work, and the house comes with the job."

"Of course you have," Cora agreed; it wasn't her place to judge him. "You've moved away from your family to work here and it's not easy now with three children to care for."

Walking towards the stove, Jacob said to the boys, "I'm going to make Mrs Roberts and Mrs Parkins a cup of tea. You carry on with your game and do as William says. Make yourselves comfortable in the chairs, ladies." He lifted the kettle and poured water into a brown teapot, then popped a knitted cosy over it.

Cora and Ada seated themselves and the landlady spoke, "You've got three lovely boys there. Very well behaved."

"They've been a bit quiet since..." Jacob looked towards his sons. "Well, you know what happened. It was a bit of a shock to all of us."

Cora thought of her daughter, who was now so withdrawn and spoke none of the words which had come so readily just weeks beforehand. "You keep a tidy home, Mr Rose," she said, changing the subject. "And I'm sure you're doing a good job looking after your boys."

"Call me Jacob," he said, placing the cups of tea on a small table between the armchairs. He pulled one of the chairs from the table and sat opposite the women, holding his cup in a large hand. The china was delicate, and a matching set. It was clear Mrs Rose had taken care of the home and collected lovely items for it. Ada had said that Jacob Rose didn't waste his money in the pub, and so it seemed likely that all his wages went towards caring for his home and family.

The boys moved from the table and began setting up wooden blocks in towers. They fetched a bag of marbles and shared them, clearly preparing to play a game of knocking down the newly-created structures.

"Would you be able to help me?" Jacob asked Cora. "I know you've got your little girl and that would be four of them, but William and Johnny go to their lessons in the mornings, which makes it easier. The boys will need their breakfast, and they'll take themselves off to do their schooling. Frank is only three; he'll have a nap later in the morning. Then it's dinner time when the older boys are home again. You know how it is… the chores that need doing while the children play or sleep. I work all hours, so it won't be regular. There's a girl who has been sleeping here when I'm away all night, but she is only twelve and I don't want to ask her to look after them all the time. She's too young but could carry on overnight when needed."

Cora picked up the cup and saucer, studying the delicate band of roses encircling the rims. Then she tried to imagine herself looking after the boys: washing their clothes, making their meals, playing games and reading books. She would wrap the boys up and take them exploring the shingle ridges, and in time her daughter would learn to play alongside them. But then a conflicting picture came into her mind: Stanley picking his daughter up and kissing her soundly on the cheek and all of them leaving Dungeness for a new life together. Cora opened her mouth to speak, but no words came. She frowned a little and bit her lip, trying to hold back the tears. Looking towards Ada, the older woman gave a knowing smile.

"It's all a bit unexpected, isn't it?" Ada showed her understanding. "You're thinking of Stanley, but if you want to stay here in Dungeness then you won't get a better offer." She turned towards Jacob and said, "Cora is hoping her husband will be found."

"Of course, you are," was his response. "I'd be the same, if I had any hope at all..."

They understood each other and, although he most likely believed Stanley had drowned in the icy waters, Jacob Rose had the compassion to let her come to that conclusion in her own time.

Cora forced the image of her life at Dungeness to the forefront of her mind. "If you're happy for me to bring my daughter, then I'd like to look after your boys. I'll have a lot to learn and be run off my feet with four of them, but there's no harm in keeping busy."

"There's one thing worrying me," Jacob admitted. "It's not a live-in job. That wouldn't be right, and I've not got the space. Where will you stay?"

"Reuben's clearing out the storeroom," Ada announced. "It's not perfect, living at The Brit, but it's not too far for them to walk and the room is sound enough. We're going back now to give it a good scrub and see what we can do to make it homely."

They spoke for a while longer and, as they talked, the three boys finished their game, then moved closer, hearing their names spoken and curious about the plans. Between themselves, it was decided that Cora would come every morning, regardless of whether Jacob was at work or not. There were meals to prepare, washing to do, and a home to keep clean. If Jacob were there, he would be free to collect wood for the fire, do any repairs needed and help with the boys. They agreed that the girl would still come to sleep at the lighthouse keeper's cottage when he worked overnight.

"You'll have your meals when you're with us and I can give you three shillings and sixpence a week," Jacob offered. "Is that fair enough?"

Cora glanced at Ada, who smiled her agreement. "That will be fine, thank you," Cora said. "As long as you understand if my husband is found then we'd have to go elsewhere, and I'd be sorry to let you down."

"That's understood," Jacob smiled. "And I'd be the first to be happy for you. Now, I'm not at work tomorrow morning so come at nine o'clock. And on the days I'm working then it will be just before eight o'clock."

"Shall I stay and read them a story before I go?" Cora asked. She knew that whatever she did to make the children feel comfortable with her would make the next few days easier for them all.

Not long afterwards, Cora and Ada left the three Rose boys and their father. They moved away from the house and walked to the very point of Dungeness. In the time they had been inside, the skies had darkened and to the west, over the hills at Fairlight, it was taking on a purplish hue. The tide was rising and with it came the return of the fishing boats. In those few seconds Cora paused to scan the west bay, the distant hills became obscured as the low rain clouds wrapped around them. The past week spent at Dungeness had been one of blue skies, thin clouds, and a sharp breeze, but those dark grey nimbostrati told of different weather to come.

Cora thought of Emily, who had been left with a stranger for some time. Mrs Barton, who lived in a cottage to the north of The British Inn, was friendly enough, but her husband would be home with the fish soon and it wasn't fair to leave the little girl with her any longer. Cora wrapped her shawl tighter around her shoulders and set off on her backstays, trying to catch up with Ada who had taken the lead.

"When you first spoke to Jacob, it seemed as if you were admitting your own loss," Ada mentioned, as they moved along, side by side. "I think if Stan had been saved, we'd have heard by now, don't you?"

"I was just being polite. I've still had a loss, all my belongings for a start, and my dreams of a new life. My Stan will come back, I'm sure of it, and that makes me worry about taking on this job. I don't want to let Jacob down, not when he needs someone to care for those poor boys."

"Let's take one day at a time," Ada suggested. "And for now, I suggest you get along to collect Emily before the heavens open, and I'll make a start on preparing some vegetables and fried fish. Then we'll start clearing out that storeroom and you can tell the vicar you'll be able to move out next week."

Chapter Six

Another week passed, and the locals of Dungeness found themselves entering the coldest time of the year. Icy rain had fallen over the headland for days, and those blue skies of the week before were almost forgotten. People moved about under the cover of oilskins, hats and coats, their heads lowered and shoulders hunched. They passed each other without recognition, their only focus being on travelling safely from one place to another on the cumbersome shingle. In the homes, fires barely smouldered, stifled by the damp wood and rain that seeped down chimneys.

The storeroom of The British Inn would have been as miserable a place as anyone could imagine, had it not been for the small stove installed by Reuben. Often it was obscured by a wooden rack Ada had supplied for Cora to dry her clothes on, layered with their coats and shawls. Sometimes a small kettle sat on the hotplate and Cora was able to make a cup of tea in the privacy of her own space. The stove, rack and pile of logs took up a fair-sized area, but without them the damp would have penetrated the plank walls, bedding and their clothes stored there. At least the radiated heat made it a cosy place to come home to, and Cora was grateful.

As she stood at the doorway to the storeroom, the stove and all its trappings were placed in the corner to Cora's right, and at the back there was the bed she shared with Emily. The iron bedframe was a little rickety, and the mattress thin but not too lumpy. Between the bed and stove there was an armchair, and a small table just large enough to take an oil lamp and a few books. The room was not much wider than the length of the bed, and Reuben had fixed hooks on the walls for their clothes. To the left, there was a pine chest of drawers not in the best condition, but there was so little on offer for someone making a room out of an old store. The people of Dungeness held onto their possessions and repaired them when necessary. They were practical and couldn't afford the time nor the money to be choosing new furniture from the local towns.

There was no window and although there were plenty of gaps in the plank walls, Cora would often leave the door ajar in order to let fresh air flow through and to sweep away the damp created by the clothes as they dried. "If you plan on staying here for a while," Reuben had said when they surveyed the completed room, "...then we'll fix you up with a window and repair that old bed and chest of drawers. But it's not something we want to do in the rain, nor when the snows come. And we can put some boards inside the walls to keep the wind out."

"Maybe there'll be news of Stan..." Cora said. "I wouldn't want to put you to too much work." But the words were uttered with less conviction. It was almost as if they came out of habit. Reuben had nodded, as was his way. He had learned it was best not to contradict a young woman.

When Cora woke in the morning, it was still dark, and the only glow came from the embers of the last log she had put on the stove the evening before. If it had been summertime then the sun's rays would have penetrated the gaps between the planks, but in early February only the damp air seeped through. It was snug in the bed, but Emily was stirring beside her and Cora knew the little girl must crouch over the chamber pot before it was too late.

As she swung her legs out of bed, the skirt of her nightgown fell to the floor. Cora slipped her feet into some slippers and reached for her shawl hanging over the bedstead, quickly wrapping it around her. At this early hour it was bitterly cold, but to put a log on the fire would be wasteful. They would be walking over to look after the three Rose boys and would be gone as soon as they had dressed, given their faces a lick with a flannel, and cleaned their teeth and brushed their hair. "Come on, Em," she said, "we need to go to see the boys." As the little girl was waking, Cora was already lifting her from the bed and pushing her arms into a cardigan.

Their routine was for Emily to use the chamber pot and then sit back in the warmth of the bed. Cora would then get herself dressed: first putting her corset on, then pulling up thick woollen stockings, before slipping a petticoat over her body, followed by a plain dress. She brushed through her thick hair and coiled it at the back of her head before securing it in a bun with several hairpins.

"Thank the Lord you don't need a corset yet," Cora muttered, as she started to pull on Emily's clothes. "Lift your arms up, there's a darling. The boys will be waiting for us."

The last thing Cora did before they left for the lighthouse was to race to the privy with the chamber pot and rinse it out with water from her wash bowl. But on leaving the storeroom-cum-bedroom that morning, she walked through the covered way with a frown on her face. There was a strange light about the place and, as they stepped outside, the reason was clear. Snow had fallen overnight. "Well, it's got to be better than rain," was all the young woman muttered. She just had to get on with whatever life threw at her, and if she ever thought her days living in Gravesend were hard, then it was only because nothing had been known of Dungeness life.

It was a silent eerie world Cora and Emily moved through on their way to the Roses' home. The snow lay several inches thick on the ground and the backstays made a comforting scrunch as they pressed into its softness. Sometimes Emily walked, and other times she travelled by a wooden sledge built especially for pulling a young child about on the stones. At two years old, it was a struggle to move in backstays, and they didn't have a pair small enough for her. Today she was in the sledge, her eyes wide and her mouth opening and closing, as if wanting to share her wonder but unable to express the words. For Cora, pulling on the rope, it took less effort to drag the little girl over the snow and she liked the soft swish of the runners gliding along.

The sky was dark, but not the inky blackness of a clear night; it was more like the colour of dying ashes lying in a grate. The sun should be just rising over the sea, but there was no hint of its early morning arrival. Boats lay, slightly lopsided, on the shingle ridge by the beach, their individual personalities lost under snowy icing. The gulls were, for once, silent. The air was fresh, with the occasional hint of woodsmoke. Cora found a peace settling on her, and a childish enthusiasm for the day ahead.

There was one constant feature in this changed landscape. The beam from the lighthouse swept over, and for a few seconds the land was a pure glistening white. The tower on the point was Cora's guide, as it often was in the mornings when she left her home to be with the three boys, and their father left for his early shift at the lighthouse.

Having given a short rap on the door, Cora opened it and walked in. Jacob was kneeling before the range, with the ash bucket nearby and shovel in his hand. He turned and gave a smile. "I'm glad I saw this snow coming and brought the wood in last night, and I've found one of those sledges we used for the boys when they were smaller. I hope you can cope with them and this weather!"

For the hundredth time, Cora thanked her blessings that she came every day to a well-ordered home. The boys were nicely behaved and Jacob Rose, although he was a serious man, was a good father and hard-working. She watched as he cut a thick slice of bread and spread some dripping over it, then wrapped it in greaseproof paper. Next Jacob was pulling on his jacket and fingerless gloves. As always, the boys came to him and he ruffled each one on the head, starting with the youngest, Frank, then Johnny, then William. "Be good for Cora," he told them.

Then he gave Emily a pat on her shoulder, and said, "Have fun." He had done this every day for a week, and she had given no response. This time the little girl looked up at him and although she said nothing, there was a small smile. Cora noticed it and her heart felt lighter.

"Now come on, boys, it's time to get dressed." Cora knelt beside Frank and asked, "Would you like any help?"

"No, William help me," the youngest boy said, his expression serious.

"That's good of him," Cora replied. "Look, your pa has made the porridge. I'll brew the tea and we'll all get some warm food in our bellies. Emily will be sitting up at the table waiting for you."

"She'll need a cushion; she's so small," Johnny said. At six years old, he already had a soft spot for the little girl and liked to take care of her." He placed it on the chair and lifted her, albeit in an awkward manner, onto it.

"Ta," Emily said, wriggling to get comfortable.

"I didn't know she could speak!" Johnny said, a smile spreading across his face.

"She had a lot of words, but just got a bit shy," Cora explained. Her spirits lifted as she looked at her daughter, "Good girl, Emily. I bet you're hungry. The porridge won't be long." Johnny ran after his brothers into their shared room.

The children ate well, even Emily, who admired the boys and followed their lead. The breakfast was soon spooned into their mouths and milky tea followed. Once they were finished, Cora went around them all, starting with William, and wiped their mouths. She paid more attention to Frank and Emily, who often had sticky hands as well. Then, one by one, they slipped down from their chairs and sat on the thick rag rug covering the wooden plank floor between the armchairs.

Emily, at first sitting on the very edge of the rug, was slowly moving closer to the boys. There was a basket of books and they leafed through them, sometimes sharing. The little girl had discovered a picture book of birds on her first day with the young Rose boys and had become quite attached to it. As Cora cleared the table, carrying dishes to the sink in the scullery, she watched Emily sidling closer to Johnny, her auburn curls almost touching his fiery waves. Her daughter was pressing the book on his arm, silently asking him to look at it with her. "What's this?" Johnny said, as he took it. "You like the birds, don't you? Shall we talk about the pictures?"

Cora saw her daughter's lips move a little as she whispered her thanks. With a smile on her face, the young woman plunged her hands into the sink and began to wash the bowls.

When Jacob had mentioned his sons doing their lessons, Cora hadn't thought about there being no school at Dungeness. In her mind, she pictured them setting off to a small red brick or a stone building with a bell in a cupola perched on top. She envisaged a school mistress in a long black dress, with her hair pulled back severely, and rows of children at desks diligently copying what the teacher had written on the blackboard or repeating important facts in sing-song voices. So, on her first day looking after the children, it came as a surprise that schooling for those living in this remote settlement was a casual arrangement. In the case of the Rose boys, it was a local woman giving them an informal education.

Now, after a week, Cora was becoming used to her routines. "Come along, boys," she called when their beds had been made, the stove replenished with logs, chamber pots emptied, and the condensation wiped from the windowpanes. "We'll all walk together to see Mrs Jamieson and you must try to stay dry, but after your lessons I promise we'll go out to play in the snow."

"Aw, we can throw a few snowballs, can't we?" William asked. "It's not fair if they go out playing and we're doing arithmetic and all that other dull stuff." He scowled in the direction of the younger children, Emily and Frank.

"You're right, it wouldn't be fair," Cora agreed, keeping her voice firm. "I'll have to take them to get the milk and fish, but there will be no playing. I've got the ironing to do and dinner to prepare. There's no time for having fun in the snow till later."

"All right. Thanks." William gave a shrug and reached for his coat.

A few minutes later and they were all stepping out onto a thin layer of snow. "Someone has brushed the snow away," Johnny remarked. "I thought we'd get a bit snowy." He nudged the thicker layer at the side of the path with his boot.

"You will," Cora reassured him. "It's landing on you now!"

The air was filled with thick flakes drifting, settling on the swept shingle path and their coats and hats. The boys, who usually ran ahead, stood and gazed at the scene with awe. Emily, in her mother's arms, fidgeted and said, "Down! Get down, Ma."

"Go on then, but be careful," Cora replied.

"She's talking again," Johnny observed.

"She is! I bet the words won't stop now!" Cora held her daughter's hand to help keep her steady. "I think we're going to have a good day, boys. It's snowing and Emily has found her voice! Come on, Mrs Jamieson will be waiting with her fire going and some nice buns for your morning snack."

The boys picked up their pace, chatting and pointing as they walked the short distance to another of the brick-built homes close to the lighthouse. Mrs Jamieson, wife of a keeper, gave up two hours of her time from Monday to Friday in order to teach the older Rose boys, along with another three siblings. Her own children were now grown up, and Mrs Jamieson had taught them successfully with one of them going on to be a teacher herself. There was no other regular schooling on offer, and it suited the small community of lighthouse keepers who, in many ways, kept themselves apart from the fishing families.

They rapped on the door, and Mrs Jamieson was waiting to usher them in. She waved one hand in Cora's direction, the other was on William's shoulder as he squeezed past her. "I walked them over, to make sure they stayed dry," Cora called. "But I'm happy for them to make their way home."

Now the morning routine began with Cora pouring flour into a large bowl and preparing to make bread. She always made two loaves and one would be taken over to Ada and Reuben at The British Inn. The younger children played at her feet, and sometimes they would have their hands washed and be given their own piece of dough to knead. They enjoyed this part of the day, singing as the chores were completed. As Cora moved from the kitchen table to the scullery and the range, three-year-old Frank would join in, while Emily watched, her grey eyes serious.

Once the bread dough had been left to rise, Cora turned her attention to the salted fish which had been soaking overnight. She tipped the briny water into the scullery sink and poured some fresh over them to wash the remains of the salt away. "We'll have to go to the pump soon," she said, partly to herself, as she filled the kettle with the last of the water.

When the older children came home from their schooling, their faces were flushed and eyes bright. "Can we play in the snow?" William asked, before it had melted from the toes of their boots.

"Of course you can, but please be sensible," Cora replied. She was already kneeling before Frank and Emily, stretching mittens over their small hands and securing their scarves. "Go back outside before you get the floor all mucky. Your pa has left your old sledge behind the scullery; bring it around to the front, and don't play silly buggers with it."

With hats pulled low over their brows and scarves across their chins, Cora ushered the younger children outside. "Now we'll all have to take it in turns," she ordered. "William, you can pull Frank, and Johnny can take Emily's sledge." She tucked the loaf of bread in with Emily. "Hold onto this, Em. We'll take it along to Ada."

They took a few steps away from the lighthouse and surrounding buildings. The sun was now almost at its highest point in the sky and attempting to make itself seen through the soft grey clouds. The snowflakes were sparse and fell slowly; there was no wind and the sky no longer threatened with purple-grey clouds. The headland was uniquely beautiful and even now, in the late morning, the landscape appeared to be barely touched by man. Although paths had been swept in the area around the lighthouse, no one had ventured towards Dungeness village. The snow-topped cottages lay squat in the distance and, like up-turned beetles frosted with snow, the boats sat atop the shingle ridge.

Cora tried to pick out the paths she usually ventured upon, but it wasn't long before the dips within the shingle had claimed her and the snow was tickling against her woollen stockings. She held up the skirt of her dress and shrugged her shoulders, knowing that fresh stockings could be fetched from her room at The British Inn. There was no point in cautioning the children to be careful; their clothes would soon dry on the rack in front of the fire and, as the snow was light, it was easily brushed off before it soaked into their clothing.

"Come on, Cora," Johnny called. "This is fun, isn't it?"

"I'm not even cold!" William was saying.

"That's because there's no wind," Cora replied, picking up her pace. "Who wants me to have a go at pulling a sledge?"

Johnny handed over the rope and ran alongside Emily who had a huge grin peeping out from above her scarf. "Look at the mess we're making!" he shouted.

Behind them, the ragged trail of footprints and sledge runners left scars on the landscape. "Oh, it will snow more, and be beautiful again tomorrow," Cora said, thinking nothing of the trouble caused by the snow and only of the respite it gave herself and the children. It seemed that for this moment they were free to enjoy themselves and were released from the grief they suffered.

The walk to deliver bread to The British Inn was no easier for those who had to trudge through the snow, but the screams of delight coming from the two on the sledges brought joy to everyone. "Come on, swap over," Cora called out after a while. "I'll have to pull the bigger boys, so one of you will need to wait for your turn." It was cold sitting in the sledge and Cora made sure each child kept warm by walking, even though it was a struggle for the two younger ones, and she kept them at her side.

"It's hard work!" Cora admitted to Ada, as they handed the bread over at the kitchen door. "Just me with four children and two sledges."

"You're making it hard for yourself," Ada said. "There'll be children sliding down the shingle banks until dusk. Send William and Johnny out and they'll soon see the best places to go, then you can take Frank and Emily for a nice little ride."

"Ta, I'll do that." Cora looked at her gloves which were now soaked through. "I'll get them home now though, or we'll all be frozen. Once there's food in their bellies, and I've done my other jobs, hopefully the gloves and the boys' trousers will be dry."

Before Cora had turned away from the doorway of the inn, Reuben had come through from the bar area. "Cora... I thought I heard you," he said. "I knew you'd be along with the bread. There's someone at the bar wanting to have a word with you..."

Chapter Seven

"Someone wanting to see me?" Cora repeated. Her heart began to race uncomfortably; was there some news? She glanced at her wet gloves, then back at the children, each one of them had snowy boots and they were encrusted with snow up to their knees.

Ada followed her gaze. "They'd better come in then. I'll pop all the mittens next to the range." She leaned past Cora and spoke to the children, "There's some bread and butter pudding for every one of you who can shake the snow off your boots, and hand me their mittens."

"Ta, Ada," Cora felt the urge to give the landlady a hug, but it wasn't Ada's way of doing things. So, she kicked the snow off her boots and stepped into the kitchen.

"It's that policeman from Lydd," Reuben informed her, as he walked back to the bar. "I'll tell him to go into the parlour."

How foolish I am, Cora thought. *For a moment, just a moment, I thought it was Stanley come for me. But he wouldn't wait in the bar, would he? He'd be in the kitchen with Ada or coming to find me.* She moved through to the parlour, her throat tight and body tense.

Constable Wilde followed Cora into the room. His cape was slung over his arm, so his belted jacket was on full display, with silver buttons running down the centre and on epaulettes at his shoulders. He carried a leather satchel, clasped before his stomach, along with his helmet. The policeman brought with him the smells of the bar, tobacco smoke and ale, and his cheeks above his shapely whiskers were a little flushed.

"Mrs Parkins." The constable gave a nod.

"Constable Wilde." Cora forced a smile. "What brings you here in the snow?"

"There's been a body washed up at Sandgate," he began. "A young man, dark haired, and wearing a nightshirt."

"A body?" Cora repeated. Her heart began to thud violently against her ribs.

"It's not the first," the constable informed her. "There has been two dozen or more. Some of them clearly crewmen, women, children, and men who don't match your husband's description. But if this one was your husband, then it may set your mind at peace to have him laid to rest."

"I'd be happier to find him alive," Cora pointed out.

"There have been three ships into port at Dover, carrying survivors from the *Northfleet*, all of them on the day after the incident," the constable told her. "Your husband was not among them. Those men who came ashore were rescued from the rigging as she went down or from the lifeboats in the sea. They tell of it being impossible for a small ship to approach the sinking vessel; she would have sucked them with her. Only a steamer could have stayed stable in the sea near a sinking ship, but none went to the rescue, and witnesses say a steamer's paddles would have caused terror and great danger to anyone in the water."

"But you said they rescued men from the rigging?" Cora questioned.

"They did, but by then the main body of the ship had gone and it was safe to approach."

"I see." Cora fell silent, and the policeman allowed her the time to digest this information. He placed his satchel and helmet on one of the armchairs and turned to examine an oil painting on the wall; he didn't recognise the rural scene.

When Cora stepped towards the fire to warm herself, Constable Wilde spoke again: "This man who was found. He had a scar, a deep one, on his thigh. Did your husband...?"

"No," Cora replied. The tension eased from her limbs and her heart began to calm.

"It wasn't Stanley then," he stated.

"No."

"We don't like to show a photo," the policeman began to explain. "It's not nice, not after days or weeks..." his voice trailed off. There was no need to share what condition the bodies were in. For the first few days they had shown photographs to the people they believed to be family of those washed up. But not now; the images were unrecognisable. Instead they had to look for a feature to distinguish the body. Many of these men, women and children would be buried as 'unknown'.

"Ta for coming to see me," Cora said. "I've got to go back to the children. I'm staying here, you know, looking after three boys."

"Good to keep busy," Constable Wilde said. His tankard of ale on the bar beckoned.

Cora backed away.

The novelty of the changed landscape was beginning to wear off as they turned towards the lighthouse on the headland. After the warmth of Ada's kitchen, the children fretted over their damp clothes and bickered over which one of them would pull the sledges. They were all hungry and thinking of filling their stomachs. "I'll have the fish poached in no time," Cora told them. "And there's some kale to boil, and our warm bread."

"Aww, not salted fish again," Johnny whined.

"Aww, yes, fish, and we'll be glad of it," Cora said, with a grin on her face. "But I'll tell you what I've forgotten, the goats' milk, so no moaning about your dinner or I'll be sending you out to fetch it."

"I don't want to do that," Johnny replied. "Fish will be lovely. Ta, Cora."

"After we've eaten, you and William can watch the young ones and I'll fetch the milk," Cora told him. "When your clothes are dry, there will be time to go out to play again. Ada says there will be plenty of children playing out on the slopes; you can go as long as you're back before dusk."

Cora returned home to the pub before the sun set that afternoon. The air had become frostier and she hugged Emily close rather than use the sledge. The rest of the day was spent in Ada's parlour. The two women were making repairs to clothes, while Emily played at their feet. Darkness fell early and the dense snow clouds closed in on them, waiting to release their load over the desolate peninsula.

"I've had a good time," Cora admitted, as they packed away the needles and threads. "I never thought I'd be able to manage four children, not with them all suffering the loss of a parent, but they're good boys and keep me busy."

"You've not got much time to be dwelling on your husband," Ada observed, while she folded Reuben's jacket.

"He's never far from my thoughts." Cora felt her spirits sink, recalling how carefree she had been at times during that snowy day. She had seen her daughter smile again and the words begin to flow from her lips; these small things had brought so much pleasure.

"Of course he's on your mind," Ada soothed. "It's only been two weeks, but you're making a life for yourself here, and not many people would want to do that."

"I love it here," Cora declared. "I love it away from the smog and that stinking river. It's not what we were planning though, is it?"

"It's not Tasmania!" Ada agreed. "I can promise you that there will never be an orange tree growing here!"

"And I've still got hope," Cora persisted. "Like you said, it's only been two weeks. But I'd miss those boys if we had to leave."

The women moved through to the kitchen and Cora washed glasses and clay tankards brought on a tray from the bar, while Ada cooked bacon and eggs for them all. She left hers to keep warm and took her place behind the bar while Cora ate with Emily and Reuben.

Cora was already becoming fond of the landlord. He was a man of few words and they often sat in silence, but when he spoke, she found him to be a person who believed in treating people fairly and he was always kind to her and Emily. But it was Reuben's actions that led to Cora's good opinion of him. He had offered the storeroom to them and worked hard to make it a decent, warm space to spend time in. And it was Reuben who had appeared one day, when they had only been there a week, and presented Emily with a wooden box filled with bricks, books, a puzzle and a ball, along with the rag doll she now took to bed with her. "I had this old box and made it good for you," he told Cora. "And I've been all over the village collecting toys she might like."

So, although they spoke little at the table or in passing, Cora felt welcomed by the landlord in his home. "I'm sorry the policeman had no news," Reuben said, as he wiped the egg from his plate with the last of his bread.

"It was good of him to come," Cora said.

"We're pleased to have you here." Reuben paused and considered his words, "At least we would be if it wasn't for your loss."

Cora stood and began to gather their plates. "I know... I quite like it here myself."

That night, as Cora slept deeply, she dreamed of Stanley coming to claim her and Emily. The heavily-laden clouds thickened over Dungeness and began to cast their flakes upon the land; wind built up force and blew from the east, causing snow to drift against the cottages and beached boats. And through the wintry night, the foghorn belted out its warning. The blast filtered through her dreams and took up a rhythm with Stanley's footsteps as he neared her. He was wearing backstays and they slapped down upon the snow. She lingered in the covered way between her room and the kitchen; the plank building housing the privy blocked her view of the outside world. But Cora heard his steps, and the foghorn heralded his arrival. Waiting for him to come closer, her body became stiff; unable to go to meet him, she opened her mouth, but no sound came.

Then a great thud rocked the thin wall of Cora's room, and as she woke the foghorn sounded. Someone called out; at least it seemed they did. "Stan?" she screamed, thinking only of her husband and not her young daughter lying there beside her. "Stan, is that you?"

Still in a state of being half-asleep, Cora was jumping from the bed, where Emily still slept despite the racket. Her feet found their way into boots, and she reached for her coat, hanging on the drying rack in front of the stove. "Stan?" she whispered, as consciousness came, and she grasped that it was still night-time. "Was that you? Did you call?"

As she opened her door, footsteps came from the house, and Cora stepped out to find Ada and Reuben running towards her from the main part of the building.

"What was that?" Ada put her arm around Cora's shoulder. "I thought for a moment that we hadn't made the old store safe enough."

"I'm sorry, I screamed... I was sleeping and..." The freezing night air and the snow drifting into the covered area had forced Cora from her sleepy state. The foghorn blasted again, and a low thud came from somewhere nearby.

"It's the woodshed," Reuben said. "I'll take a look; I reckon the snow was too heavy for it." He carried a lantern and Cora realised that, unlike herself, neither Ada nor Reuben were in their nightclothes. She frowned, unclear as to why they were still dressed, "Were you not in bed?"

"We were about to turn in," Ada said. "We had a brandy by the fire in the bar after the men had gone home. They left early on account of the snow. It's a wonder they come out at all in this weather."

Cora was about to respond when raised voices were heard and, as two figures came into view, she heard a man saying, "I'm sorry, Pa, I had no idea it would be so rough here. I should never have come at night."

"Oh Lord, it's James!" Ada shrieked.

"And he's knocked the bloody woodshed down," Reuben called out. "Almost took out Cora's room too!"

"I've come all the way from Lydd an' I got myself lost on my own doorstep," came the second voice. "I was trying to find the kitchen but found myself at the old shed. I told you to fix it, Pa. Didn't I tell you last time I was here?"

"You never said a word about it," Reuben declared with humour in his voice. "It seemed good enough, but the snow must have been too heavy for the old beams."

So, this must be their James they've told me about, Cora realised. *I hope he's not funny about a stranger being here with his family.* She retreated to the doorway of her room.

Ada stepped forward with no thought to the deep snow and flung herself at the young man. "James, what brings you here at night?"

"There wasn't much snow in Lydd. I never thought it would be worse here on the coast..." his tone was apologetic, and he shrugged his shoulders, "or I'd have stayed in The George Hotel for the night. There's been times I wished I'd gone back, I'm telling you."

"Come through to the bar." Reuben had his arm on his son's shoulder.

"A brandy would do me the world of good," James replied.

Cora shrank back further into her bedroom, as parents and son turned to the back door leading to the kitchen. For a moment she felt lost, no longer seeing her place within The British Inn and the people who lived there. Chilled through, she knew it would take some time before sleep came to her. The kitchen door closed, and their voices could still be heard vying with each other – there was so much to be told. James would be taking his coat off and his mother would be placing it near the fire to dry. Perhaps Reuben would be fetching dry socks and a pair of slippers from his son's room. Cora had never been in James' room, but she knew it was left ready for him whenever he returned home.

"We'll have to air his bed." Ada's voice rang out, and then the back door opened again. "Where's Cora? I thought she came in with us. Cora..."

"I'm here," Cora replied, clutching at the neckline of her coat.

"Come and meet James. He's home!" Ada enthused.

Cora looked back at Emily and felt a responsibility to stay close to her daughter. She didn't know this man; he was just a name heard in passing conversation. Suddenly it seemed that this storeroom was the only safe place in the world for her and Emily; she didn't want to be meeting strangers in her nightgown and felt an unreasonable fear of his presence. "I'll see him tomorrow," Cora suggested. "You'll want to spend time with him, and look at me not properly dressed... it's not decent, is it?"

"All right then, but he'll be glad to see you..." Ada's voice trailed off as she closed the kitchen door.

The last Cora heard of them was James's voice enquiring, "Who's that you're talking to, Ma? Not taken in a lodger, have you?"

The bed was chilled now. Cora felt for the warm brick wrapped in cloth and pushed it so she could place her feet either side of it. She lay there listening to Emily's breathing and the occasional soft thud of snow sliding off the roof, before finally falling into an uneasy sleep.

It was still early when Cora woke, too early to stir Emily and walk to the Roses' home. She pulled on her corset the best she could with a blanket around her shoulders, then her woollen stockings and petticoat. Her dress had been hanging before the fire and brought some comfort as she slipped into it. Grabbing her shawl, she moved from her room to the covered way. The snow had drifted in the night and was several inches deeper than the previous day; it came into the passage between the old store and the kitchen. Footprints told the tale of last night's visitor. She pressed on the latch, but stalled in the doorway, not expecting to see James Roberts sitting at the kitchen table. It was too late to retreat to the security of her room, so Cora stepped in and closed the door behind her.

"I didn't expect..." she began. "Sorry, I thought you were all in bed. It's so early."

He sat there, the son of Ada and Reuben, with the light from the one oil lamp casting shadows on his face. Cora judged him to be of medium height and his hair was mid-brown. As he looked up at her and grinned, she noted James' blue eyes and bushy eyebrows.

"You're Cora then, who came off the lifeboat and ended up here at Dungeness. I didn't get to see you last night."

"No. You were here to see your parents, not me." Cora's words sounded sharp and she didn't like it. She was usually pleased to meet new people, but this man made her doubt her place here in the home of his parents.

"And you were in your nightgown..." He smiled, or perhaps smirked. That's how Cora saw it.

"It was late." Her tone was defensive as she turned to the kettle, moving it onto the hot plate. It would have been easier to return to her room, but then he would have known she didn't like him. She tried again, trying to lighten her voice, "Did you sleep well? You're up early."

"I slept well enough," he replied. "But I'm used to the sounds of the city. It's too damned quiet here."

She wanted to know why he was here. If he planned to stay? But Cora asked, "Would you like some tea?"

"I was thinking of making some," he replied. "Thank you."

Cora sensed him watching her as she reached for the cups on the dresser and scooped tea from the caddy. "Where have you come from?" she asked, hoping the water would come to the boil soon.

"London," he said, as if there were no other place. He rubbed at the stubble on his chin, and Cora wondered if he were one of those men who would grease his shapely moustache.

"Of course." She recalled Ada speaking of her son who lived in Camberwell and ran his own shop. Cora wondered if he would need to return soon, but instinct told her that James Roberts had left London for a reason as yet unknown to her.

"Ma says you like it here at Dungeness," James commented. "I don't know why. It's a strange old place."

"People have been good to me." Cora felt her body tense again and she was relieved to see the kettle was boiling. "And I've got myself a nice job. It keeps me busy and means I can look after my daughter."

"A pretty young woman like you could get a job anywhere," he said. "I'll find you work if you get fed up with the wind and the mists."

"I don't think I will," Cora replied. She poured the water into the teapot and reflected on his words, then replied with a smile fixed on her face, "Ta very much. That's good of you. I'll just pour the tea and then I'd better get back to Emily."

Chapter Eight

"Pa's got a plan!" William announced as soon as Cora walked into the Roses' home that morning.

"A plan?" she repeated, looking towards Jacob. "Have you seen out there? The snow's deeper than ever." He was already in his coat and boots.

"I know," Jacob replied. "I've been out for the water. But you won't have to go any distance at all. How about you bring the little ones over to the lighthouse and we'll go to the top and look at the view. We can carry Frank and Emily if the stairs get too much for them."

"And after lessons," William interrupted, "Pa says he'll take me and Johnny up!"

"That would be wonderful," Cora said, as she unbuttoned her coat and turned to help Emily with hers. The restless night was forgotten and once again, in the company of this family, Cora felt an interest in life. "Imagine being able to see beyond all these stones, and you could show me the places people talk about, like Lydd and New Romney."

"I'm glad you like the idea," Jacob said. He gave a rare smile, and continued, "I'm off to work now. Come after the boys have gone to Mrs Jamieson."

An hour passed and Cora was walking to meet Jacob. The sky was blue, with all trace of snow clouds gone, but a sharp breeze brought a chill to the air. The snow lay in drifts against the buttresses at the base of the lighthouse and again paths had been swept between the tower, outbuildings and homes. Emily and Frank walked at her skirts; the little girl was uncertain and pulled back, but Frank understood what was to come and chattered away. Cora knocked and pushed on the door leading into the base of the tower.

The ground floor area was dark and smelt damp. They stood for a moment, allowing their eyes to adjust, having been amongst the snow which sparkled white in the winter sun. Cora became aware of different smells, which were particularly strong after being out in the fresh air. She tried to place them: there was the scent of old wood… coal… and something else she couldn't be sure of. Screwing up her nose, she sniffed again… oil? The items stored on the ground floor came into focus, lit by the winter light coming in through small windows and the open doorway. There were crates of tools and piles of coal, a box of rags and a couple of buckets.

Cora was alerted to a movement in the shadows, and Jacob stepped out from amongst some barrels. "I hope you don't mind a few steps," he said. "There are over 100, so we'll take it slowly."

Cora gazed upwards, following the path of the wooden stairway before it disappeared through a gap in the ceiling. She assessed the handrails and saw the children would have to be closely watched. "We must be careful," she said.

"Of course," Jacob replied. "I wouldn't have all three boys here at once; we'll take a child each."

"What were you doing, Pa?" Frank asked. "Were you hiding from us?" He looked towards the area from where his father had emerged.

"Hiding!" Jacob gave a short laugh. "No, I was looking to see if we had a decent cup so I could offer Cora a cup of tea. I was sure we had a few with no cracks. We put them away for special visitors!" He reached out to Frank. "Let's show Cora and Emily the next floor."

Interested to see where the stairs would lead them, Cora followed. "Come on, Em, we've got a lot of climbing to do."

With Jacob taking the lead, they made their way up the first flight of stairs at a good pace. "It's best not to look down," he advised. The staircase was against the outer wall of the lighthouse, with the only bannister rail being attached here. It ascended far higher than a flight of stairs in a house.

They reached the first floor, a cave-like space, again with a staircase snaking its way up to the next level. This appeared to be an area to either rest or work. A large table was set under a window, and within the shaft of light there was an open logbook with a pen, ink and blotter. The stove, with a couple of chairs either side of it, warmed the room. "Our place to sit and relax, or fill in the paperwork," Jacob explained. "It gets quite cosy." Then he picked Frank up, and carried him halfway up the next staircase, before the little boy struggled to be free. Cora followed with Emily.

At only twenty-three years of age, Cora was still young, and fitter than ever from battling the shingle ridges daily, but by the time she faced the third staircase, she was beginning to tire. It was more of a ladder now, rising steeply through the centre of the room. The fourth flight of steps was the same, steep and rickety, leading to the last and smallest habitable space in the tower. This circular room couldn't have been more than ten feet in diameter, with the low ceiling making it feel smaller. A narrow bed filled almost half the area, awkwardly spanning the room, and a small unlit stove offered some hope of comfort in this spartan space.

Cora's legs were aching, and she was fed up with catching the toes of her boots on the hem of her dress and petticoat. She placed her boot on the first rung and moved upwards.

Having pulled themselves through the trapdoor leading to the lamp room, all the effort was proved worthwhile, to stand and be drenched by sunlight from all sides. Cora was drawn to the windows which, in their wooden frames, reached from floor to ceiling and were about eight feet in height. She stood, at first looking inland, with Emily held at her side, ensuring that the child was unable to reach out and touch the glass; fearful that, should she lean on it, the window could break.

The landscape was sheeted in white as far as Cora could see. It glistened in the sunshine and, at this height, there was no sign of the snow being disturbed. A fleeting image of the blackened snow and melting drifts in the streets of Gravesend crossed her mind. Here it brought images of fairy tales and new beginnings. Trees were sparse and there were no buildings to break up the rolling snow-topped shingle ridges. Cora knew whichever way she had ventured during her time at Dungeness, there had been no end to the stony landscape. Now she saw it in its entirety, yet the snow concealed the line where the soil began to blend with the beach and grass was able to take hold, until finally the land was fertile enough to be farmed.

"Is that Lydd?" Cora asked, pointing to the north-west. "It looks like a town, but I'm not sure. I think there's a church."

"It's All Saints," Jacob said, coming to stand beside her. "Big church for a small place."

"And that's the nearest town to Dungeness," Cora stated. "Where's New Romney?"

"Along the coast, this way..."

Now Cora followed the line of the east bay, as it arched towards the distant hills. She saw The British Inn and the fishermen's cottages, the boats laid up on the bank, and the indistinct forms of winches, carts, tanning coppers and piles of crates. As the coast continued, there was the occasional building, but all definition was lost to her. "I can't see it," she said.

"It's further away, and a mile inland from the sea," Jacob told her. "We don't leave Dungeness often, but if we do then we generally go to Lydd."

It was inevitable that Cora's gaze would then turn towards the sea and the remains of the *Northfleet*. Sixteen days after the tragedy, the ship still hadn't slumped into her final resting place. The masts could not be seen from the beach, but from this vantage point they seemed all the more poignant, reminding her of the reason she was there in the lighthouse at that moment. With the sunshine and the views, Cora had been fully absorbed, but now a chill came over her and she felt all her energy drain away.

Standing beside her, Jacob must have sensed her distress and he reached, placing his hand on her arm. "I didn't think," he said. "Sorry."

"I know..." Cora forced the words out. "It was a lovely idea. I didn't think either..."

"Shall we go down?" he asked.

She looked at the trap door. He had pulled the cover across the hole. Then she turned to the lamp. "No. No, tell me about the light. Tell me what you have to do up here."

He reached and picked up some rags from a box. "I can do better than that. You can all help me clean the lens."

With her back to the sea, Cora picked up the cloth Jacob offered her. "I hope I don't make it worse," she said.

"It's just a case of wiping the dirt off," Jacob replied. "We used oil here until ten years ago; before my time that was. Now it's electric and not much muck at all. Just a case of brushing away the cobwebs and a bit of dust."

"But I can smell oil downstairs." Cora was puzzled.

"We use it to grease the mechanisms, here and on the fog trumpet, as well as on the generator," Jacob explained. "And all that coke you may have seen, it's to fuel the generator which is needed to make the electricity. It's still a mucky business to make an electric light – which isn't as reliable as the oil lamps!"

"That sounds complicated!" Cora grinned.

"This modern lamp is a damned sight easier to look after in some ways. No wicks to trim and the glass is easy to wipe clean." He gestured towards the lenses, "You can imagine the dirt that gets on them with an oil lamp. But the oil gave a more reliable light."

"That's what is most important," Cora reflected.

"It is, and so there is often talk about us changing back."

"I never thought what it was like, looking after a lighthouse," Cora said. "I mean they're not always near a town and it's not easy to get supplies to a place like this." She had wiped a pane of glass clean, while Emily was absorbed with trailing her finger through a cobweb.

"The coke comes out like the beer!" Jacob told her. "By cart."

Cora had a vision of the wide-rimmed carts that moved across the shingle, not with ease, but it seemed as if the barrel-like wheels effectively spread the weight over the stones. Would they venture out in the snow? Probably not. It was likely to thaw in a day or two. She found a clean area of cloth and gave her second section of glass a final wipe. Aware the children had lost interest, Cora knew it was time to leave the lamp room.

Jacob opened the hatch and the ladder was revealed. "I'll go first and carry the children, one at a time," he said, lowering himself through the void.

Cora placed first Frank, then a moment later Emily, into Jacob's arms. She gave the masts of the *Northfleet* a brief glance. "Sleep peacefully, my love," she whispered. In that moment Cora accepted Stan's

95

passing and readied herself for a time of mourning. She placed her boots on the rungs of the ladder, gazed across the snow-covered wastelands and a new feeling washed over her: she no longer wanted to rail against those who said her husband was gone.

That afternoon, with Frank and Emily in one sledge and the older boys running about, Cora ventured out to buy milk. She had been told the goats roamed freely over the headland, nibbling on whatever greenery they could find, hardier than cattle and providing the settlement with much needed nutrition. But in January the weather kept the animals close to their shelters. Cora had no choice, the family needed milk, so she trudged back towards The British Inn and then on to one of the cottages where it was usually possible have her jug filled. The sun was strong in the sky, and the snow glistening. She could see the frosty covering was melting and that any extra layers formed overnight would be short-lived.

Cora stepped onto the veranda and knocked on the cottage door. "Hello, do you have any milk for us?" she asked, as a woman opened the door.

"Hello Cora. Yes, they're good milkers, my goats are. Is that William with the jug? I can hardly see him, all bundled up like that." The woman, named Sarah, was equally wrapped up with a crocheted shawl of all colours tight against her shoulders. She didn't wait for an answer but took the jug offered by William and closed the door.

"She won't be long," Cora said to the children. Emily and Frank tipped themselves out of the sledge and pressed the snow on the veranda into balls.

The door opened and Sarah stepped out with the near-full pitcher. "I hear James Roberts is back," she said. "And I can't help wondering what he's after. He doesn't come to Dungeness often. I'd say he likes the city better."

"He must have wanted to see his parents," Cora offered.

"I'd wait till the spring if I was him," Sarah said. "I'm thankful my Gracie has moved to Rye and married well."

"Your Gracie?" Cora questioned, uncertain of the connection.

"She had a fancy for him and I'm telling you, he led her a merry dance," the woman revealed. "I'm glad he went."

"He only came last night." Cora took the milk. "I don't know what his plans are. If he likes the city, and that's the impression I got, then most likely he'll be gone in a day or two."

Although disinclined to speak of the son of Ada and Reuben with one of the village women, it eased Cora's mind to know her discomfort was not unfounded. This confused her. Already so fond of the couple from The British Inn, she expected to feel warmth towards James. Instead, in those first moments of his arrival, Cora feared her place in the pub was no longer secure. She had tried to shake off the concerns, but those few words from Sarah gave fuel to her doubts.

"I'm sure he'll be gone in a day or two," she said, with exaggerated brightness. "The snow will pass, and we'll be back to normal."

"I hope so dear. This weather is no good to anyone."

It was mid-afternoon when Cora returned to The British Inn. The sounds from the bar were lively and she felt sure James Roberts was at the heart of it. Laughter rang out and a harmonica regularly broke into a disjointed tune. The door between bar and home was closed, but tobacco smoke snaked its way through to the kitchen and parlour, then lingered amongst the saltiness of the smoked fish from lunchtime and the wood burning in the grate.

Cora sat with Emily on her lap, looking through picture books, still thankful that her daughter had found her voice and new words were flowing every day. Ada joined them and brought cups of tea. In the beerhouse, this was a quiet time for the women. Emily would often doze on Cora's lap or wrapped up in a blanket. Ada would sew or write letters at the gateleg table.

The door to the bar opened and James' voice rang out. "He'll be telling them all about life in the city," Ada commented. "He's always full of stories."

"Is James back for long?" Cora asked.

"He's keeping that close to his chest," Ada admitted. "But I'm certain he has plans. Why else turn up here in the snow?"

Cora didn't respond to this. There did seem to be a mystery surrounding the appearance of their son on that snowy night. Was he running away from something, or had he left another heartbroken woman in his wake? No doubt his plans would be revealed within the next day or two and, as she stroked Emily's curls, the young mother hoped there would be no disruption to the fragile pieces of her life. An hour passed, and the women stirred. There were chores to be done and together they moved into the kitchen.

The next morning, Cora wasn't needed to help with the Rose boys, as their father would be at home until he went to work a night shift. When she ventured out of her room to use the privy, the landscape had changed again. Melting snow dripped from every surface – rooftops, windowsills, discarded barrels and the old cart resting by the storerooms. It no longer lay smoothly on the shingle ridges but was slipping away, cleansing the stony promontory.

The stove was stirred into life and Cora made a pot of tea. "Sit in the chair and I'll pass you the beaker," she said to Emily, while adding a generous amount of milk to cool the drink.

They dressed and walked through the covered way to the kitchen, planning to join the Roberts family for breakfast. As she went to place her hand on the latch, the door opened and Cora stepped back. James came out, wearing a long black overcoat. *He looks like a city gent,* she thought. *I ain't seen no one dress like that at Dungeness.*

"Good morning!" James said, raising his hand to the brim of his hat, almost as if he were going to doff it in her direction. But he merely tapped it before raising his face to the sky. "We have a thaw, thank God. I'll be in Lydd in no time." Reaching down, he took a pair of backstays from their place propped against the wall and slipped his polished boots into them.

"You're going to Lydd?" Cora asked, and then felt foolish. He had already said where he was heading. So, she added, "Safe journey. Take care out there." But the last of her words were lost to him, as he had turned his back and set off, albeit a little cautiously as the snow still lay in the dips.

In the kitchen, the porridge was already thickening on the stove. "Who knows what his plans are?" Ada was saying from her place at the range. "Sit yourselves down. It's ready to dish up." With that Emily began to clamber up into her usual place.

"He'll tell us soon enough," Reuben advised. "No point in asking any questions, he'll only say less, and you know it."

"A mother worries..."

"Perhaps I'll go to Lydd myself one day soon," Cora suggested. She was just as curious to learn of his plans, but it was clear James held them close to his chest.

"We'll go there when the spring comes," Ada told her. "It's quite a trip for the little one, but she can ride on the shingle sledge for part of the way. And the promise of a bun in the tearooms will put a smile on her little face."

And so, the subject of that day's outing to Lydd was deferred. When Cora went to work at lunchtime in order to cook for Jacob and his sons, James had not returned. It wasn't until the evening when she was to learn the reason for his trip, and some news about her own situation.

Chapter Nine

The bar was quieter when Cora returned from the Roses' home that evening. She had settled the boys in their beds and then carried Emily back; the little girl was sleepy and ready for her bed. Jacob would work, tending the lighthouse for the whole night, while a local girl stayed with his sons.

"The fishing boats haven't been out for days," came Ada's reply when questioned as to why the pub wasn't as lively as usual. "And if there's no fish, they've no coins in their pockets."

"I see," Cora said, reflecting on the fragile income of the fishermen.

They were sitting in the parlour, sharing a pot of tea. Emily was already asleep, and Cora would join her before long. Just as the night before, there was one voice ringing out above the others, that of James Roberts. They couldn't catch his words, but he sounded jubilant.

"James came back from Lydd full of his news," Ada offered. "We were surprised, Reuben and I were, but he's always been a one to catch us out."

Cora looked towards Ada, waiting for her next words, but at that moment the door to the bar opened and James walked through, laughing and shouting out a retort to the men who sat with their tankards of beer. A cloud of tobacco smoke, laced with beer fumes, followed him and he paused at the doorway to the parlour.

"It seems as if our... our visitor will be all right..." James began. He was flushed and his words slurred. "No... no need to live in a storeroom for much longer!"

Not understanding, Cora frowned and said nothing. It was Ada who replied, "She's very welcome. It's lovely to have a woman and child about the place and don't you say otherwise, James Roberts."

"I wasn't saying she wasn't welcome; a pretty young woman is always nice to have about the place," he continued. "I'm saying, Ma, that she'll be able to find herself and the girl a nice cottage or something. No need for them to be in the old store."

Cora felt a chill settle on her, despite the fact the fire was burning well, and there was a blanket over her knees. She lifted her chin a little and asked, "Where is it I'm going to be living then? I've got no home back in Gravesend and if you heard different then you were misinformed."

"But it was the talk of The Dolphin," he began, a knowing smirk on his face. "You'll do well from the compensation."

"Compensation? What compensation? I've not heard nothing about that," Cora declared, the colour now rising in her cheeks.

"There's to be money sent from the shipping company to replace what you lost on the boat, and more to set you up in a home somewhere."

"Well, if that's so, then it's no more than we're due," Cora replied. "We've suffered badly, us and all those who survived."

"That's wonderful news, isn't it?" Ada stood to refill their teacups. "Perhaps the vicar will know and if he doesn't, then Constable Wilde will be able to tell you about it." She paused and reflected on the news, then spoke again, "It's not right though, gossip spreading through the town; Cora should have been told first."

"I'll go and see the vicar in the morning," Cora said. She thought of the snow and wintry weather and rebuked herself for being foolish: "But the news won't have reached him yet; it would be wrong to think he would know and not tell us."

"Whereas Lydd will know it all." James sat himself down at the small table where the tea tray was placed. His cheeks were reddened from the drink and warmth in the bar. "There's shops and tearooms for the women to spread the news, and bars for the men to escape their gossip. Perhaps our Cora would like a little cottage in Lydd when she gets bored with the stones and the wind. There's a fine green for the girl to run about on, and houses built of brick." He waved his hand in the direction of the walls, and continued, "Don't stay here for so long that you forget what a brick house looks like."

Cora turned to Ada, uncertain of how to respond, and knowing this talk was fuelled by the ale or brandy. When the landlady spoke, her tone was sharp: "We'll take no notice of this talk, James. Lydd or New Romney would be fine places for young Emily to grow up, but here she has the company of the three boys and can go to work with her mother. They'll stay as long as it suits them."

"Of course, she will," James agreed. "She's doing a great job helping out the family and no doubt Mr Rose is incredibly pleased with the arrangement." He moved away from the doorway and ambled along to the kitchen. They heard the back door open and close as he went to use the privy.

"He's full of talk when he's had a drink or two..." Ada commented. There was affection in her voice. "It's no wonder if he's a bit excitable this evening and no doubt he was celebrating in Lydd beforehand."

"Celebrating?" Cora queried. Of course, Ada had been about to share news of the trip to Lydd before James came through from the bar.

"I was about to say, wasn't I?" Ada continued, and now she couldn't hide the pleasure felt. "We are so pleased, Reuben and I; we could hardly believe it when he said..."

He's going to be staying. Right here in Dungeness. What else could bring such pleasure to his parents?

"He's buying The Dolphin!" Ada announced.

"The Dolphin?"

"It's a public house in Lydd," Ada elaborated. "We thought he was gone off to the city for good, but he's back and he'll be just a few miles away. Isn't that fine news?"

"It is." Cora gave a huge smile and found herself relaxing. James would be keeping himself busy and it may only be a few miles away, but there was no decent road to Lydd, just swathes of shingle. He would soon be moving on and her life would continue as it was.

The next morning, when Cora and Emily ventured from The British Inn, there was a misty rain enveloping Dungeness Point. The foghorn blasted its warning – a doleful sound penetrating every building and shingle bank as it signalled its presence to passing vessels. The snow was almost gone. Only the deepest of drifts remained, sorry reminders of their former sparkling beauty. Together, mother and daughter walked to the vicar's home and rapped on his door.

"I was wondering..." Cora began, once she was standing in the familiar living area, with its piles of paperwork and books, the teapot in the centre of the table and a rack of damp clothes before the fire, "I mean to say, I've heard there is a fund to help the survivors."

"I thought you'd come about the funeral," the vicar replied.

"Funeral?"

"Of course – news travels slowly through the snow. It's a wonder we hear much at all here at Dungeness."

It seemed as if the vicar's attention had wandered. Emily pulled her hand out of Cora's and moved towards a pile of books on a side table. She recalled the book of seabirds which had enthralled her over the week following their first coming to stay with the vicar.

"Funeral?" Cora repeated.

"Ah yes." His attention returned to the moment. "There is to be a funeral."

"Someone from the *Northfleet*?" Cora felt her throat tighten. It wasn't Stan, of course; she would have been told. But it was one of them – an emigrant or a sailor who had perished on that icy night.

"It's to be held in New Romney," the vicar said. "The gentleman must have some connection with the town."

"And where was he found?" Cora was compelled to ask.

"At St Margaret's Bay," the vicar replied. "A small place beyond Dover."

"Are they still finding bodies?"

"They are," the vicar said. "They've all washed up to the east; it's the way of the tides."

Cora understood about tides: she had seen the Thames flow past Gravesend, and then the waters being pushed back by the tidal wash. "Have there been any more survivors?" she asked.

"No, only the ones taken to Dover on the morning after the incident."

"But there could be… there could be men picked up on a ship which was going to foreign lands and it didn't care to turn back."

"It seems unlikely, after three weeks," the vicar replied. "But these things are in the hands of our Lord."

Cora no longer railed against those who suggested Stanley would not return, but the hope remained within her. It was a small flicker of hope. Now she considered that if he had perished and his body was not recovered then there would be no grave to visit, nor a proper period of mourning. "This might be my only chance," she began. "If my Stanley isn't recovered, I won't be able to say goodbye."

"You'd like to attend the funeral," the vicar stated. "It is to be Friday at noon."

"There's going to be a burial," Cora told Jacob when she joined the family in their home not long before midday. The older boys had come home from their lessons and were playing outside. Jacob was filling the teapot with boiling water and, as she chatted, Cora reached for the sack of potatoes and tipped some into the scullery sink.

"A burial?" he repeated.

"It's one of the bodies that was washed up somewhere beyond Dover. He's to be buried at New Romney. Would it be hard to get there?"

Jacob didn't reply. He tended not to waste words if there was nothing to say, or until he was sure of his answer. But Cora could see he was thinking the matter through. She started peeling the potatoes and dropping them in a pan of salted water.

Before long, he asked, "When is the funeral? You'll need to get to Lydd. Walk or hitch a lift with one of the carts, then the horse-drawn bus to New Romney. I'd say it would take half an hour or more from Lydd to New Romney. It would be a long day and the nights are still drawing in early."

"It's Friday," Cora said. "I'm being foolish though. I didn't know the man."

Jacob took a sip of the scalding tea. Cora went to the front window and wiped away the condensation so as to watch the children playing. Emily was laughing as Johnny swung her around in circles. Cora smiled to herself; she had thought her family would grow by her and Stanley having more children, but instead Emily had become the youngest of four, not the oldest. She moved from the window to the scullery and started to rinse the salted fish.

"It's been four weeks now," Jacob said. He stood at the doorway between the living room and scullery. "Perhaps you're coming to terms with your loss? Perhaps Stan has survived and news of him will be with you any day now?"

"I'm beginning to think that's unlikely," Cora admitted.

"So, going to this funeral may bring you some peace?"

"I think I'm finding my peace here at Dungeness," Cora suggested. "It's been a fresh start and a challenge every day."

"It's certainly that." Jacob opened the range and threw a log in it.

An hour later, he said goodbye to his sons, and then to Emily who now stood at his legs with the boys when their father left for work. Then, as he was poised at the door with his hand on the latch, Jacob said to Cora, "I've not forgotten what we spoke of earlier and I'm giving it some thought. But it's no place for the children, so we'll have to arrange something." She said nothing in reply but smiled and nodded. It wasn't the time to discuss it any further.

It seemed strange to be leaving the shingle peninsula without Emily at her side. Cora glanced up at Jacob, curious as to if he ever left his three boys other than to go to work. He was looking ahead, his attention on the stony path. They were taking the route created over time by the brewer's dray, the coal wagon and the grocer's cart. It was well-used, and already a wide-wheeled cart, loaded with crates of root vegetables, and sacks of flour, oats and dried beans, had passed them. Cora had wondered if it also contained some packets of luxury foods amongst the daily staples. Perhaps some dried fruit, treacle or spices.

"If we walk at a fair pace, we'll be in Lydd in an hour or so," Jacob had advised when they arranged the day ahead. "We'll leave at nine and then we can be certain of catching the horse-bus to New Romney. And you never know, there may be a cart going our way which offers us a lift."

At times it seemed as if the shingle ridges stretching from Dungeness Point would go on forever and even if they trekked all day no sign of civilisation would appear closer. However, the faint outline of the church tower in Lydd did offer some relief that they would eventually reach their destination. They spoke little, conserving their energy for the walk, for although the path was well-trodden, it was uneven. An hour passed, and finally the rooftops and cottages of Lydd became distinct. Above them all was a slender church tower, topped with spindly pinnacles, extending towards a clear blue sky, with a few scattered clouds.

Beneath their feet, soil melded with shingle until the roots of grasses and weeds were able to thrive and their backstays were no longer needed. Sturdy boots were now the best footwear for the walk. The track crossed a waterway and became more established after they had passed a farmhouse. Jacob suggested that they leave their backstays by the roadside. "We don't want to be carrying them all the way to New Romney," he said, and Cora was grateful not to be burdened by the pieces of flat wood.

They entered the outskirts of Lydd, passing by cottages of brick, stone and rubble, with roofs of slate, tile or thatch. At first, the homes were surrounded by plots of land and, eager to peek into the lives of these townsfolk, Cora looked through hedges and over fences. She saw pig shelters of corrugated iron, chicken coops and rows of weather-worn leaves in vegetable plots. There were outside privies, water pumps and washing lines. The grass was sparse, and Cora saw that although Dungeness was behind them, Lydd was not blessed with the most fertile of soil.

A road junction offered a choice of direction. To the left, a lane appeared to lead back towards the stony peninsula and, to the right, a magnificent smock mill stood, its sails turning slowly in the breeze. Ahead, there was a barn-like grain store, and the road was flanked by cottages. They took none of these, instead following a track between the lane to the left and the granary, walking past a red-brick building. A sign indicated this was the First and Last public house. The track widened, and the scene before Cora was unexpected as a vast green, intersected with pathways and dotted with stunted trees, was revealed. Sheep grazed and children played with carts, balls and hoops. To the left, at the far end of the green, there was a windmill, and the sails of the other could still be seen above the cottage rooftops. Here and there, terraced houses, cottages and a huge barn looked over the green.

"It's called The Rype," Jacob informed her. "I always think this was one of the first areas of Romney Marsh to become dry land amongst the marsh when the sea receded."

"When was that?" Cora asked.

"They say the Romans came here," he told her, as they began to skirt the edge of the green. "I'm thinking of two thousand years ago."

"The Romans?" Cora queried. "I wonder why? I mean, what would bring them here?"

"I can't think of any good reason!" Jacob gave a rare grin. "You would think they would want pasture and woodland, but I believe they came to fish. The shingle ridges sheltered a waterway passing behind Dungeness."

"But how do we know?" Cora couldn't imagine it. She knew Lydd to be a lone settlement, surrounded by low-lying land and the shingle peninsula. There was no woodland or river, or rich pasture. What would tempt the Romans here, when they could take their pick of the more tempting areas of the island they had conquered?

"There are Roman remains in the church wall." Jacob looked towards the ancient building. "That's how we know."

"I'd like to see them," Cora said. Unanswered questions formed in her mind: Where did they bring their stone from? Did they keep their animals here on the Rype, and did they farm the land with crops? She left these questions unasked, guessing that Jacob wouldn't have the answers.

"You'd like to see the Roman remains," he repeated. "Perhaps we'll all come over for the Mayday celebrations and look then."

"That would be wonderful," Cora replied. Once more she found herself accepting that nothing would change when the spring came, and then the summer after that. At the funeral today she would say a silent farewell to her husband.

Jacob and Cora changed direction and walked across the Rype. They passed a pub – The Dolphin – and Cora realised this was the one James Roberts spoke of with such pleasure. *He'll be settled there soon enough, and I'll be glad of it.* The road led to a small square, fronted with houses and cottages dating from Tudor and medieval times. Some were converted to typical little village stores selling a variety of goods and produce. The women of Lydd scurried to and fro with shopping baskets. Delivery boys pushed carts, and a postman passed by carrying a fully-laden leather satchel. Small children ran about at their mother's skirts and babies travelled in cumbersome prams. It was a busy time of the day. The square, named Wheeler's

Green, led to the High Street, another road lined with buildings of all ages, their doors opening directly onto the pavement. One of these was The George Hotel, a building of fine proportions, standing beside the equally impressive Town Hall, outside of which there was a pair of horses and a covered cart awaiting those who were journeying to New Romney.

Having paid the fares and boarded, they seated themselves on the well-worn oak seats. "I didn't promise you a comfortable ride, did I?" Jacob asked, as he flashed a grin in her direction after paying their fares.

His smiles reach his eyes now, Cora noticed. *We are both suffering but finding pleasure in life again.* "I was hoping for cushions," she retorted, tapping the bench seats. Then she looked away, remembering a time when she and Stan were courting, and he had used his jacket as a cushion for her. *No need for Jacob to have any thoughts along those lines. Not that he would. He's much older than me and I know he misses his wife terribly.* They sat down, side by side, each of them careful not to be touching each other as the horse-bus filled.

Chapter Ten

The journey to New Romney was tiresome. At times Cora thought it would be preferable to walk, rather than be jostled about as the wheels of the horse-bus lurched through ruts on the road. She fixed her eyes on a sturdy church tower and in time they neared the town of New Romney. The road turned a corner and the wide High Street opened up before them, fronted with buildings dating back several centuries. Cora noted how they had been altered over the years, as fashions and the use of the properties changed: facades had enhanced the appearance, windows enlarged, and extensions added. There were windows displaying goods for sale and tables on the pavements where potential customers could browse the items on offer. Pulling up outside The New Inn, Cora saw a public house with similar proportions to The George Hotel – an imposing structure in the centre of the town.

They alighted with caution. Jacob stood close to Cora and his hand rested on her upper arm. The pavement was crowded, and they jostled to find their place amongst the townspeople going about their shopping or other business. A flock of sheep being herded through the streets made it unwise for them to step into the road, and they watched as the animals poured around the horse-bus with a dog at their heels, which obeyed the commands of the shepherd's whistle. As well as the sheep, horses and carts vied for space with delivery boys pushing barrows, and a young couple with a smart pony and trap.

"We could have a sherry or a light ale?" Jacob suggested, looking in the direction of the inn.

"That would be nice," she said. "We've got nearly an hour before the funeral, so there would be time to do a bit of shopping too."

The coffin came by open cart along the centre of the street, bedecked with flowers. Two fine black horses pulled it with ease. On the roadside, people turned and bowed their heads as a sign of respect. Men removed their hats. "Those flowers must have come from hothouses," Cora whispered to Jacob. "Who would have thought it?"

He gave no reply, but there was a hint of a smile. *I wonder where his wife is buried,* Cora thought. *Lydd, most likely. I don't think they bury bodies at Dungeness, but I've not seen it all. There's no church and no soil to lie them in.* She pondered the matter while the coffin passed by.

Jacob and Cora followed at a distance, walking down a side road and towards St Nicholas Church. A short flight of stone steps led to an archway and they entered at the base of a Norman tower. The building was vast, with long aisles reaching the full length of the nave, and they paused for a moment, both taking in the splendour of the building. Then Jacob placed his hand on Cora's back and guided her along the aisle. In silent agreement, they seated themselves in a box pew midway along the nave, judging it the proper place to be. The church was full, not with people who knew the dead man, but with locals who felt the need to show their support. Some of them were lifeboat men, or fishermen, who appreciated the dangers of the sea. Three hundred people had been lost that fateful night, just a month beforehand, and several of them had washed up on the beach near the town of New Romney. It was a funeral of a stranger, but it touched their hearts.

Cora found the utterings flowing from the priest were strangely soothing; she didn't listen to his every word, but the rise and fall of his voice gave her a sense of peace. She inhaled the familiar aroma of ancient stone and wisps of smoke emitted from the wicks of many candles. With Jacob at her side, Cora was one of about two hundred people who adjusted their coats and shuffled their shoes as the service progressed. She sang, prayed and gave the correct responses, while reflecting on other times and places. Occasionally her thoughts strayed all the way to that far-off land where the sun still shone and the oranges grew, and then she was back in the terraces of Gravesend, caring for her husband and child.

When the priest prayed for the soul of the man who lay in the coffin, Cora's own prayers were for Stanley: *It was a good plan, and you were a good husband to think of giving us a better life. I don't know where you are now, Stan, but I hope with all my heart that you rest in peace and know Emily and I are safe and well-cared for. God bless you, my love.*

Then they were turning their backs on the altar and filing outside. Cora held her shawl more tightly around her upper body and Jacob adjusted his hat. It had been cold inside the church, but at least the stone walls had given protection from the chill breeze.

The drowned man was laid to rest in the western edge of the graveyard, an area shared with other shipwrecked mariners. Many of them were not native to Romney Marsh, and some were nameless. After the body was lowered into the ground, the mourners dispersed. Drawn to explore the churchyard a little, Cora moved away from Jacob. Before long she was standing at the stone wall, with her back to the church, looking across the fields of pastureland. A path passed through the rough grass in the direction of the sea. The landscape was ragged after weeks of rain and snow; it

114

longed for the spring sunshine and for fresh growth when the greenery was once more regenerated by warmth and light.

New Romney was a mile inland, and Cora never considered that the remains of the *Northfleet* would be seen in the distance. Beyond the fields, the sea was a thin grey band, and from this the masts of the stricken ship reached upwards. Transfixed by the unexpected sight, for the first time Cora wondered if she had made the right choice to stay in this place where the visible reminders of the tragedy remained. She stood, allowing the chill to seep into her bones, knowing she should seek out Jacob and take comfort from his company.

Cora didn't hear a man approach; his footsteps were soft on the grass. "Mrs Parkins, I believe?"

Turning to look at him, her grey eyes met his blue. She didn't respond, but in that moment, Cora knew this man meant her no good.

"Reginald Street," he announced with relish. His dark hair was parted at the side and lay in gentle waves across his head. Generous sideburns and a moustache were styled to show this man as someone who paid great attention to proving himself to be a gentleman. He looked out to sea and Cora noted a straight nose and firm jaw. "You can see the ship from here," he said. "My condolences to you and your daughter."

Sensing his words were spoken with no feeling, Cora asked, "What do you know of us?" She realised her tone was rude but her distaste for this man was strong.

"I'm a reporter. A journalist for a London paper," Mr Street stated. Then he smiled, and continued with, "But I would hope you will see me as a friend."

"What do you want with me?" Cora replied, taking a step away from him.

"Your story."

"I have no story." Her tone was sharp, and she flashed a scowl at him.

"No story?" he repeated, offering the warmest in his repertoire of smiles. "Mrs Parkins, the nation needs to hear the tales of the survivors. They will open their hearts to you and your beautiful daughter."

"We've suffered enough; I don't want to talk about it." Cora glanced towards the people still gathered around the grave and the lines of mourners leaving the churchyard. She was not alone, but it felt as if it were that way. The people who had attended the funeral were unknown, apart from Constable Wilde, who had journeyed from Lydd that morning and was now leaving through a gate in the low wall. Jacob was not in sight, despite his distinctive red hair. Cora recalled that he had wanted to look at a monument inside the church and must have returned there.

"People want the full story behind the *Northfleet* disaster and I'm the one to write it. I'd prefer to speak to you, but I'll write your story regardless," the reporter persisted.

"I've got nothing to say," Cora insisted. "And you don't know about my life."

"It will be much the same as that of any young woman from the terraces of Gravesend," Reginald Street stated. "Your husband worked on the ferry, didn't he? And you stayed at home caring for the house and your daughter. You made the best out of a low wage, struggling to keep yourselves warm and enough food in your stomachs. Then he told you about a new life in Tasmania – a place where the sun shone, and you could provide a better home for your daughter."

Cora felt her skin pale. "How do you know all that?"

The man standing before her gave a self-satisfied smile and replied, "Just as I said, it doesn't take much imagination to conjure up the story of your life, but I would rather hear it from you. Otherwise I may well get it wrong, or feel the need to embellish..."

"Embellish?" Cora knew she should walk away, but stayed, fearful of his next words.

"Embellish," he repeated. "Make it a little more interesting for the readers. Spice it up, as they say."

Cora looked back towards the fields and the coast; she wondered if Stanley lay entwined with the wreckage or if his body were journeying towards land and one day word would come to say he had been recovered. Then, turning back towards Mr Street, Cora saw Jacob approaching and relief eased the tension from her limbs.

"We need to return to the High Street, Cora." Jacob gave a brief nod in the direction of the reporter. "The horse-bus is due."

"You must think carefully, Mrs Parkins," Reginald Street said, knowing his time was running out. "If we can work together, then everything will be so much more pleasant."

Jacob frowned. "Work together? Is this gentleman bothering you?"

"He's from a paper," Cora said, her words coming out in a rush. "A London paper and he wants my story, mine and Emily's."

"And you've told him you're not interested?" Jacob confirmed.

"I've told him, but he doesn't want to listen."

"I think Mrs Parkins has made it clear her story is her own business," Jacob said, looking the reporter straight in the eye. He placed his hand on Cora's shoulder, as if to protect her. "Good afternoon, sir. I suggest you look elsewhere for your news stories."

Reginald Street, used to nosing out a piece of gossip, was not about to let Cora go. He pushed a piece of paper towards her. "Perhaps you and your gentleman friend can discuss this and, when you are ready, send me a line."

She shoved it in her pocket without looking. Cora could feel her cheeks beginning to blaze as they turned their backs on the reporter and walked away. She averted her face from Jacob's view, pretending an interest in the Norman church. *Gentleman friend*, the phrase rolled over in her mind. *What a thing to say about Mr Rose; he must be ten years older than me. Well, he's older than thirty anyway, and both of us newly widowed. The poor man must be so embarrassed too.* Cora took a quick look at Jacob; his face was serious, and he was gazing straight ahead. He had removed his hand from her shoulder before they had taken less than half a dozen steps.

It wasn't until they got off the horse-bus in Lydd that Jacob spoke to Cora again. "I'm sorry that man upset you. He wasn't the sort of person anyone would want to talk to."

"I'll be putting his details on the fire," Cora replied.

They walked back to Dungeness almost in silence. Cora needed to collect Emily from Ada and then she would be returning to the Rose home to make supper for the family. They parted at The British Inn. "I'll see you shortly," Cora said, forcing herself to look up at him. "Thanks for taking me. I appreciate it. I really do."

"You're welcome. If it helped in some way then I'm glad," Jacob replied. He moved away and it seemed as if the easy friendship, slowly forming over the past weeks, had been lost in the churchyard of St Nicholas.

Cora walked into the kitchen of the pub and swept Emily into her arms, burying her face in auburn curls. *I need to be careful with him,* the words screamed out in Cora's mind. *I need to be careful in case people think... in case they think that me and him...*

The skies over Dungeness cleared and the foghorn no longer belted out its mournful siren. It was mid-February now, almost four weeks since Cora and Emily had landed on the beach and stepped out of the lifeboat. "I can't imagine it ever being summertime here," Cora said to Ada, as she delivered the bread freshly baked that morning.

"It will come," Ada said. "But we've many more weeks of hardship to suffer. Then one day you'll see fresh growth on the sea kale over there on the bank, and the goats will be seeking out the tender new shoots of grass. A few weeks later, you'll spot tiny flowers growing amongst the stones, and see spring really does come to Dungeness. It won't be spring like you know it, but there will be changes nonetheless."

"I can't imagine Emily in a summer dress and sandals," Cora smiled.

"She'll still be in stout boots." Ada was forever practical. "And there won't be many days when the pair of you would want to go without a cardie. I didn't say the wind would stop blowing, did I!"

"You didn't!" Cora gave a grin. She looked towards Frank and Emily, who each had a piece of crust to chew on. "I'd better get back to the house; William and Johnny will be back from their lessons, and when their pa wakes from his sleep it will be time for a meal." She knelt before the children and buttoned up their coats, helped with mittens and retied their scarves.

Four days had passed since the funeral. Cora and Jacob continued their pattern of caring for the children and his home together. A local girl still stayed with the children when Jacob worked overnight, tending both the lighthouse and foghorn. There was an unspoken agreement that if Cora were to spend nights at the Rose home, it might be seen as if she were almost living there. When she returned to the cottage with Frank and Emily, the older boys were leaving their lessons and running along the path between the homes. They kicked at stones with the toes of their boots, enjoying the noise and destruction.

"Your pa will be sleeping," Cora warned them. "I don't want him being disturbed, not when he has to work all night again. Imagine that – not being able to sleep in your bed at night."

"I'd like it," Johnny declared, screwing up his freckled nose. "It wouldn't bother me to stay up all night and all day."

"Well, you can find out what it's like when you're a man," Cora retorted. "But your pa needs to sleep, so you big boys can look after the little ones and play out here while I start on the dinner."

"What are we having, Cora?" William asked.

"I've minced up the leftover mutton and there's mash to go on top," Cora told him, knowing the boys would be glad to be spared salted or smoked fish.

"Ta ever-so," William ran up and wrapped his arms around Cora. She smiled, and returned the hug, feeling a warmth for all three of the boys. "I'll call you in a while; it's too cold to stay out here for long."

"Did you sleep well, Mr Rose?" Cora asked when Jacob walked through to the living area an hour later.

He rubbed his eyes and gave a smile. "I did, and all the better for the foghorn not being needed at the moment." Jacob walked through the scullery, grabbing a coat as he passed, and went out to the shared privy. When he came back, Cora had poured a cup of tea for him. "Thanks, Cora," he said, seating himself at the table.

She had been calling him Mr Rose since the funeral, but Cora felt comfortable with him using her first name. He was her employer and so different rules applied. But by calling him Mr Rose, it put their arrangement on a formal footing. It had been good of Jacob to take her to the funeral and, while she cared for his sons, there would be many occasions when it seemed almost as if they were one big family. *But we are not family,* Cora said to herself, *even though I'm beginning to love those boys as if they were my own. I know there's not much chance of my Stanley coming back to me, but it's only been four weeks and he – Mr Rose – has been a widower just a month or so more than me. And even if it had been longer, that's not to say I'd be wanting to go courting with him. Of course, I wouldn't.* And so, Cora told herself the same thing time after time, and insisted on no longer calling her employer by his Christian name. He had said nothing about it, but she had a feeling he understood why and accepted her decision, despite preferring them to go back to their previous ways.

Cora took the pan of potatoes from the hotplate and tipped the boiling water down the scullery sink, then carried it to the living area and placed the pan on the table. She took a fork and started breaking them up. "William, can you fetch me the jug of milk and some butter from the larder?" she asked. The children were now playing on the rug while waiting for the call to say their dinner was ready. "I hate mashing spuds. It takes an age for it to go right."

"I'll take a turn," Jacob offered.

Cora sighed. *It might be a bit easier if he wasn't so darned nice and helpful. If he were to spend more time at the pub and less time helping around the house and playing with the children.* "No, ta," she replied. Her tone was curt, she could hear it and did not like it. "I can manage, or I won't be earning my way."

"You're here for the boys seven days a week," Jacob replied. "You certainly earn the few shillings I can afford to pay you. Please say if you need a hand, or if you want some time off. I can manage, can't I boys?"

"Aww, but we like Cora here," Johnny complained at the thought of doing without her.

"I'll be here," Cora said, her voice now softer as she spoke to the child. "Perhaps I'll take a day or two off in the spring and summer and take Emily on a nice trip out. But for now, I'll be here with you."

Chapter Eleven

It was on the month's anniversary of the *Northfleet's* demise at sea, when a young man from London braved the long trek across the shingle ridges to Dungeness. He had stayed overnight at The George Hotel, Lydd, and the following lunchtime he was at The British Inn shortly after Reuben Roberts opened the doors for trade. The only two customers at the time were a couple of elderly fishermen who eyed the newcomer with distaste. The landlord shared their feelings and forced a cheery smile when the gentleman approached the bar.

"A glass of red wine, please landlord." The stranger spoke with confidence and placed a smart leather bag on the bar, having already assessed the surface was free from beer slops.

"Wine?" Reuben repeated, with a hint of surprise in his voice. "Very well." The usual drink at The Brit was ale, sometimes a brandy or rum. He kept a few bottles of sherry for when Ada sat with her friends in the parlour.

At that moment, Cora opened the door between the home and bar with a basket of clean glasses in her arms. Her body stiffened when she saw Reginald Street standing there. A smile of recognition spread over his face. She placed the basket on the bar, and it pressed against his leather bag.

"Thanks, Cora," Reuben said.

She was about to retreat when the reporter spoke, "What luck to come across you straight away, Mrs

Parkins. I felt sure you would get in touch with me, so have saved you the effort of putting a stamp on a letter and decided to come and see you in person!"

"I wasn't planning to write." Her voice was curt, and Reuben took a step closer, ready to defend the young woman who had become like a daughter to him and Ada.

"But now I'm here, it wouldn't hurt to have a nice talk," Reginald Street suggested.

"There's nothing to talk about," Cora replied. "There was a terrible accident and hundreds of people died. I've lost my husband, at least I think I have. That's all there is to tell."

"Oh, Mrs Parkins, you are wrong." The reporter's voice was smooth, as if tempting her to confide. "There is so much to tell. The people of Great Britain are curious to know about the survivors. They have taken you and your little girl to their hearts. Did you know there were only two women who survived the disaster? We know all about the chief officer's wife. But you, Mrs Parkins – may I call you Cora? – you are the one who interests them."

"Me?" Cora frowned, not understanding. She glanced towards Reuben.

"You go through to the kitchen, and I'll speak with Mr Street," Reuben suggested. "Go to Emily."

Cora gave him a grateful smile and backed towards the doorway. There was a movement from the old men who had been sitting with their pipes and tankards. She saw they were now standing, as if forming a further line of defence against the incomer. Cora's heart swelled with appreciation for this strange place now called home; she didn't know the names of those old fishermen, but they had accepted her as one of their own.

"I think Mrs Parkins has made it clear she has nothing to share with you," Reuben said.

Cora closed the door between the bar and home. She paused, waiting to hear what was to come next.

"A red wine, you said?" Reuben queried.

"A red wine would be splendid," the other man replied, his voice still full of bravado. "But you are mistaken, landlord. Mrs Parkins has told me that she *believes* she has lost her husband, to quote her very words: 'I've lost my husband, at least I think I have'. She is a lost soul, as she still holds onto the hope Mr Parkins will return. The readers will be so taken with her story: they will feel the desperation to be reunited with Stanley. Yet, when all hope is lost, as surely it will be, then we have something else to bring fresh joy to the audience..."

"I think I've heard enough," the landlord replied. "I suggest you leave now and don't bother finishing your drink."

"I'll be back," the reporter replied. "I hear wedding bells for Mrs Parkins. Her potential second husband is already showing a protectiveness for the young widow, and she would do well to nurture the love of a good man such as our lighthouse keeper."

"Enough!" Reuben barked.

Cora heard a scuffle and could picture the landlord moving from his place behind the bar, and the elderly fishermen closing in on Reginald Street. She opened the door a crack and saw Mr Street was being ousted from The British Inn. She heard his feet on the shingle and saw the beerhouse door slam behind him. Cora, overcome with emotion, fled to the comfort of Ada, and the warmth of the kitchen, tears falling down her pale cheeks.

"Wrap yourself up nice and warm, and go out for a walk," Ada suggested, once she had listened to the whole story. "It will help you get your thoughts in order. Don't let that reporter spoil the friendship you have with

Jacob. How must that poor man feel to hear you calling him Mr Rose, and being all formal?"

"I think he knows why," Cora attempted to defend herself.

"That doesn't excuse it," Ada pointed out. "He's given you a job and welcomed you into his home. Jacob is a good man and has his own grief to cope with."

"I know..."

"And this Reginald Street, he won't come here bothering you again. It's a long way from London and he needs to be back in Fleet Street, or wherever he comes from, writing his news stories."

"But he's going to write about me and Emily!" Cora tried to defend herself.

"He is. It sounds like people are interested in you," Ada agreed. "But the people down here are not interested in that sort of gossip. They know the truth of what happened and they are getting used to you and Emily living here with us. It will be in the paper one day and the next day it will be cut up in squares to use in the privy. Try and think of it like that, love. News one day and forgotten the next."

"I suppose so," Cora replied, but it didn't make her feel any better. Her body felt heavy as she thought of those words printed in newspapers and distributed throughout the land.

"Emily is asleep and, when she wakes, she can sit in here with me. I'll warm her some milk and cut her a slice of bread. She'll be perfectly happy, so you can take yourself off for a walk and let the wind blow those worries away."

"Ta." Cora gave Ada a brief hug. "You're so good to me."

The sky over Dungeness was a stunning bright blue that day. Had it been summertime then the day would have been glorious, but in mid-February there was an icy chill to the air. Clear skies meant heavy frosts in the mornings, but they lifted Cora's spirits as the day progressed. Turning away from the usual path she trod between the lighthouse and The British Inn, she walked towards the north. Before long, Cora was amongst the fishermen's cottages but wasn't feeling a need for company so continued towards the beach. She passed between the fishing boats on the bank, the winches, the sheds and the piles of oak skids used to ease the boats' path across the shingle. In a sideways crab-like motion she moved down the shingle bank and onto the slope of the beach. The tide was going out, leaving a strip of damp sand to walk along. With her head bowed, Cora was able to avoid looking at the masts of the *Northfleet* and concentrated only on the beat of her boots on the rough stony-sand, and the surge of the waves. After a while, she began to feel calmer and scrambled up the bank a little, then sat looking out to sea.

Now Cora faced the *Northfleet* and all her thoughts were with her husband. She recalled the happy times, and tears rolled down her cheeks. As they fell, and were brushed away, her heart felt soothed. Focussing on the waves, she allowed them to take over her whole being as they tumbled forward, frothing and spitting in the breeze, then pulling back, dragging the stones with them. There was no end to the rhythm of the tide, and in time it was all Cora became aware of. Her mind was no longer crowded with images from the past or the fear of what could be reported in the London paper. There was only herself and the turbulent water before her.

Over time, Cora's limbs became stiff with the cold. The coat and shawl could not prevent the chill from invading her body. She became aware of footsteps on the shingle bank behind her, but it seemed like too much effort to move. Cora waited for the person to pass by. Instead, a hand was placed on her shoulder and someone was crouching beside her. Turning to the side, she looked straight into Jacob Rose's blue eyes. She saw his pale eyelashes and fine lines in the thin skin. Tiredness was etched in the deeper lines around his mouth and, across the lower part of his face, his stubble hinted at the flame colour it would be if allowed to flourish. He wore a thick woollen hat and his overcoat was pulled up at the collar.

"Jacob?" Cora began to pull herself up, knowing it would be foolish to sit there any longer.

"Am I to be Jacob again?" he asked.

"I'm sorry. I was being foolish. Making sure we were proper."

"We are proper. We've done nothing wrong," Jacob reminded her. They began to walk up the bank.

"I know."

They took a few more steps in silence and turned towards the south. Cora could see three small figures running along the top of the shingle ridge; they darted between the fishing boats. "The boys?" she questioned. "Why aren't they with you?"

"I told William to take the others home," Jacob replied. "I thought we should have a talk on our own."

"Have you changed your mind about me looking after the boys?" There was panic in Cora's voice. She'd been lucky to find this job, and with such a lovely family. Looking at Jacob, she said, "I'd understand if you didn't want me anymore, but I love caring for them. And Emily is so much happier."

"Now you're being foolish," he said; his voice was gentle. "I just want you to stop worrying about what that man said, and to call me by my Christian name again."

"You're my employer." Cora tried to justify her behaviour. "I thought it was the right way to be."

"I'm not Lord Smeaton of the lighthouse," he said. "And you're not my maid. You're looking after my boys and, while you're with us, you and Emily are part of the family, like a favourite aunt and cousin. I think that's fair enough, don't you?"

They had reached the path to The British Inn now, and Cora's body felt lighter than it had done since the funeral in New Romney. She gave Jacob a big smile, "Ta, you've been really kind, and I've made things difficult for you. I'm sorry and tomorrow we'll go back to as it was before."

"Now, you had better get back to your lovely daughter and I could do with twenty minutes sitting in front of my fire," Jacob said. "I'll see you tomorrow morning, Mrs Parkins!"

"None of that from you!" Cora said. She had a grin on her face and spun away, then ran the last few steps to the pub.

A further week passed, and with it came news of another funeral. This time it was in Lydd.

"Do you want to go?" Ada asked.

"No, I can't go to them all, and there will be plenty," Cora replied. "I said goodbye to Stan when we went to New Romney, and I pray for his soul every night."

"You're making your peace with it then," Ada said. She was rolling pastry on the kitchen table, while Cora fried the onions to go in a pie.

Sometimes Cora was amazed by how swiftly the news, local and national, reached the ears of those living at Dungeness. There was no road, and no railway line, although it was rumoured that the trains may one day come to the shingle peninsula. The fishermen and their families, the coastguards and the lighthouse keepers, and those who ran the two beerhouses, relied on the delivery men and boys, or family members, to bring the news.

It was now five weeks since Cora and Emily had come to live at Dungeness. The first day of March had brought with it a light misty rain, and yet again the foghorn blasted its message across the headland. "It won't seem like spring without the daffodils and

129

crocuses," Cora observed. "And the cherry trees; don't you miss the spring blossom?"

"I've lived here all my life," Ada reminded her. "I'll get my pleasure from other things. You wait and see, there will be poppies and viper's bugloss, and pretty little grass-heads."

"And perhaps in a few weeks it will become warmer," Cora suggested. She tipped potatoes and turnips into the pan, before adding water to make a thick gravy.

"Then we'll take our trip to Lydd," Ada said. "I'll treat you to a dinner at The George Hotel, and we can do a bit of shopping."

"I'd love to buy some material and patterns to make Emily a couple of summer dresses." Cora's face lit up at the thought of her daughter in a cotton dress and light cardigan.

When the women shared their plans with Reuben that suppertime, he suggested Cora make the trip to Lydd long before the weather warmed, and they could think of summer dresses. "You should go as soon as the rain clears," he suggested to Cora. "Do you remember what James said about you being entitled to some money? He mentioned it to me again earlier." Reuben took a forkful of pie and chewed slowly before continuing, "James says you'll be entitled to compensation. It's your right as Stan's widow; there's money there waiting for you and Emily and it's time to find out about it."

"How will I do that?" Cora asked.

"There's a solicitor, Charles Scott, who has an office in the High Street. He's the one to see," Reuben told her. "And if he's not the right person then he'll be able to tell you where to go."

"It's a wonder where James hears these things." Ada's voice was full of love and admiration for her son. "After all, he's only been back five minutes."

"He's buying a pub and he's up there doing all the paperwork," Reuben reasoned. "And the rest of the time he's sitting at the bar learning about all the local news. He's been away nearly five years and he'll be wanting to make sure that people see him as one of them when he takes over the pub."

"And when will that be?" Cora asked. After three weeks she still didn't feel comfortable with James Roberts and felt sure she would never see him as a friend. Thankfully, as his father had said, James was spending a lot of his time in Lydd.

"He says it will all be legal in another week," Reuben said.

"That's wonderful news!" Cora gave a huge smile. She needn't see much of him once he was running The Dolphin.

It was another week before the fine rain lifted and Cora was able to walk to Lydd. She chose a day when Jacob was at home to look after his sons and decided to take Emily with her. Having packed a bottle of water, sandwiches and a slab of bread pudding, Cora was ready to leave not long after breakfast. At first she carried Emily on her hip, then her back, but whichever way she tried it was difficult to make any progress with the shingle underfoot. She still hadn't mastered the backstays and to carry the small child unbalanced her, making it awkward to move onwards with a rhythmic step. Eventually, it was easier to allow Emily to walk and they took their time, looking at the birds and playing 'I-spy'.

On reaching Boulderwall Farm, there was now a rough track underfoot. Cora left her backstays on the verge and scooped Emily into her arms. They set off at a brisk pace, slowing every so often to allow the little girl to walk. Now there were sheep, cattle and horses in the fields and plenty to occupy a child who had lived at first in a town, and later in a place with stones rather than soil underfoot. Emily chattered all the way to Lydd and was keen to be up high in her mother's arms, so as to have the best view of the animals nibbling on the fresh spring growth.

Cora's mind was filled with the new experiences she was giving her daughter, and it was only as they crossed the green, known as The Rype, that any concerns began to press on her otherwise happy thoughts. *It don't seem right going and asking for money,* Cora pondered. *To think I was worried we would end up in the workhouse and here we are going to ask about money for doing nothing. I'll carry on working though and there's nothing much to spend it on so perhaps this man, Mr Scott, can tell me where to go to get a savings account. Fancy that – me with money in the bank! But would they let someone like me have a bank account? What if I don't understand all those forms, or my writing isn't good enough?*

With Emily holding her hand, Cora wandered through Wheeler's Green, resisting the temptation to look in the shop windows. Then she was on the High Street, with The George Hotel, Town Hall, and numerous homes and shops fronting the pavements. She walked slowly, trying to recall the directions given to her by Reuben, and then crossed the road before turning her back to the church. The solicitors' office was identified by their names painted on a board above the doorway: Scott and Browning. It was just as Reuben had said it would be. Cora raised her hand and knocked on the black painted door, then twisted the handle and stepped inside.

Chapter Twelve

Cora walked straight into a room not much larger than Ada's parlour. The paintwork on the doors, chair rail, and window frame was a mid-brown colour, and below the rail the wallpaper was a burgundy flock, its pattern seeming almost too flamboyant for the space. Above the rail, in contrast, the pattern was smaller and more subdued although rich burgundy reigned supreme. The spring sunlight cast square patterns through the sash window, falling across the corner of a heavy oak desk and onto the polished floorboards. Opposite the doorway, a fire burned in a small grate, adding warmth and a feeling of homeliness to the space.

Behind the desk a young woman sat and looked expectantly at Cora, before saying, "Can I help you?"

"I… Yes, I came to see Mr Scott."

"Do you have an appointment?" She cast her eyes towards the ledger on the desk and flicked the pages to and fro.

"I've come from Dungeness and had no way of getting in touch, other than sending a letter. And I could only come if the weather were fair." Cora stopped, aware she was waffling.

"Oh." The young woman made another show of looking through the pages before her, even pausing to run her finger over one of the entries.

"Can I make an appointment?" Cora asked. "I was hoping to see Mr Scott today."

"Well… you can." The young woman glanced at the clock, back at the ledger, and then at Cora. "Mr Scott is free until half-past eleven, so I expect he'll be happy to see you now."

The time was almost ten o'clock. "If Mr Scott could see me then I'd appreciate it," Cora said.

"Take a seat." The young woman nodded in the direction of a row of three chairs. "What's your name, please?"

"Mrs Parkins. Mrs Cora Parkins." Cora lifted Emily onto a chair and seated herself beside her daughter. "It's about the *Northfleet;* the ship that sank."

There was a door leading from the reception to the rear of the building. The woman knocked and entered the next room, leaving the door ajar, and Cora could hear her words. "There is a woman and a little girl here to see you, Mr Scott. Mrs Parkins she is and it's about the *Northfleet*."

"Thank you, Annie," the solicitor replied. He sounded cheery and Cora's spirits rose a little. "If you could show Mrs Parkins through, then perhaps you could make us both a cup of tea?"

Annie, as Cora now knew her to be called, walked through the doorway. "You can go through," she said, giving the door a slight push so it remained open.

"Charles Scott," the solicitor announced. He was standing as Cora and Emily entered, and extended his arm across the desk.

Cora found that she liked him immediately. He was tall, with dark curly hair not yet greying, despite him being about forty years of age. Mr Scott's smile was friendly, while his eyes seemed to tell her that he already knew the reason for her being there. She reached out and took his hand; his handshake was neither weak nor too strong.

"Cora Parkins," she said. "And this is my daughter, Emily."

"Good to meet you," the solicitor replied. "Please take a seat and tell me what I can do to help you, although I have a feeling I already know your story." He sat in his chair and Cora noted that when his suit jacket opened an ample stomach was displayed. *Too many pies and a liking for the ale,* Cora heard her mother's voice in her mind, and smiled a little.

"I was on the *Northfleet*," she began. "We came on a lifeboat and ended up at Dungeness. The others went back to their homes and families. But me and Emily, we stayed and we've made our home at Dungeness."

"I heard there was a young woman who remained," he said. Then he paused and studied her as if thinking about the situation. His eyes were hazel, she noticed, or maybe green. It didn't really matter, but they were kind, nonetheless. "And you have found a job?"

"I have," Cora smiled, and she thought of the red-headed Rose boys. "I'm looking after three little boys."

"I have my own son," Charles Scott told her. "Quite a handful!"

"I heard..." Cora tried to explain the reason for her being there. "...I heard there was money, like a charity. Money to help us out if we need it."

"There certainly is, and each case is assessed on its own merit."

"On its own merit?" She didn't understand the term.

"I mean you would have to say why you needed the money. They are giving it to help the survivors rent and furnish a new home, or to buy mourning clothes, or to replace things lost in the ship."

"Oh." Cora's face fell. "I've got a home. A room at The British Inn, and I don't need mourning clothes. At least I didn't because I thought Stanley would be found alive, but he won't now. It's been six weeks."

Mr Scott gave a small smile and shook his head a little. "It seems unlikely," he agreed. "But you must try to claim some money and do not feel that you are being greedy or don't deserve it." He seemed to understand Cora very well, despite them having only just met. "You are staying in a beerhouse and, if your job were to end, or it became difficult to remain at The British Inn, then you would probably have to leave Dungeness."

"I should ask for some money because I might need it later?"

"You should," Mr Scott agreed. "And perhaps you'd like me to help you write a letter? I have been following the case with interest and it seems the widows are being offered about six pounds. I see no reason why we shouldn't expect the same. I suggest we ask for it so you and Emily can rent a home of your own and buy the furniture you need. Also, your little girl could do with a better coat and some decent boots. I suspect you could do with a few more outfits as well."

"I… Yes, that would be nice, but I have the few shillings Mr Rose gives me," Cora offered.

"Like I said, one day you might need more, and you can keep the money in the bank until that time." Charles Scott lifted the top on his inkwell and picked up his pen. "There will be no charge for writing the letter. In fact, you have saved me the walk out to Dungeness as I wanted to help you with this anyway."

When Cora left Charles Scott's office, her back was straighter, and she gave a bright smile to anyone passing by on the street. Women gave her curious looks, not recognising the pretty young woman with her glossy auburn hair. Men glanced at her shining eyes, pert nose, and imagined a firm young bosom with a trim waist under the layers of coat and shawl.

They reached The Rype and Cora sat on a bench, before unwrapping the small parcel containing the bread pudding. The little girl climbed up beside her, and soon her cheeks were bulging with the treat baked by Ada. After a few minutes, Emily slipped off the bench and took a few tentative footsteps towards a group of children playing with hoops. They seemed familiar, reminding her of the streets of Gravesend and the children she used to see playing there. Memories of those times were fading fast in the mind of the two-year-old. After a while, a little girl spotted the newcomer and walked up to Emily, offered her hand, and included her in her game.

Cora gazed across the green, at the thatched cottages and the tithe barn with its vast cloak of thatch almost reaching the ground. She looked behind her at the brick and stone houses. They had narrow strips of garden behind low walls and wrought-iron gates. She smiled to see the bold daffodils and clusters of dainty crocuses. There were fruit trees with blossom about to burst free from the buds, a contrast to the weathered Scots Pine trees growing alone or in short rows on The Rype.

After a while, Cora began to feel chilly and stood up, calling to her daughter, "Come on Emily, time to go now."

They turned to the centre of the small town. Two buildings were prominent amongst the low roofs of the houses: the church and the windmill. Recalling the burial in All Saints Church just the week beforehand, Cora felt an urge to give her respects to the dead man. And so, with Emily skipping along beside her, they veerd again into Wheeler's Green and entered the churchyard near the tall tower.

Cora chose to take the path running near the southern side of the church. It was peaceful amongst the ancient stone walls and the listing headstones. She spotted a pile of new earth and stepped on the grass to take a closer look. On nearing the fresh grave, a woman approached from the opposite direction. They met at the same point, beside the pile of stony earth.

"There's only one here with a name to go on the memorial." The woman waved her arm in the direction of the disturbed soil.

"Only one?" Cora asked, not understanding.

"There's been six buried, but only a sailor was identified."

"I only knew of the one," Cora replied. Her body went cold; it could be Stanley under there and she wouldn't even know. "I heard there was a burial last week."

"There was. But since the shipwreck there have been five burials, and then this is the last. I walk this way into the town, and I always stop to pay my respects." She clasped her hands together and lowered her head. For a moment it seemed as if the older woman was deep in thought, or prayer.

There's only one here with a name to go on the memorial. The words rattled about in Cora's head. *Five men unknown.* "It's good of you to do that," she said, as the woman raised her head and took a step away from the grave. "These men, they have no family to pray for them, but they have you."

The woman frowned a little. "You're not from around here, are you?"

"I'm just visiting," Cora replied.

"Have a nice day then." She walked away, a shopping basket under her arm and a shawl wrapped tight around her shoulders.

On leaving the churchyard, the lure of a sweet shop was too much for Cora. She pushed open the door and stood for a moment, breathing in the sugary sweetness. It was dark inside, with a wooden counter and shelves rising to the ceiling on three of the walls. A girl appeared through a door to the rear of the shop.

"Hello, Missus." Her voice was friendly. "Can I help you?"

Cora peered towards the glass jars. "Two ounces of jelly babies and two of coconut ice," she said, before noticing a slab of fudge; it would make a wonderful treat for Ada. "And this fudge, please."

"You're treating yourself," the girl said, making conversation.

"I know!" Cora gave a grin. She spotted a pile of newspapers on the counter and added one to her collection of purchases; it would make a change to have something to read in the afternoon before the light dimmed. "I'll have this as well."

"There's something about Lydd in there," the girl offered. "Fancy that, Lydd in a London paper. They'll all be sold by noon!"

"Oh? About Lydd?" Cora repeated.

"It's telling the story of the burial in the churchyard," she informed, as the sweets were weighed and placed in twists of brown paper. "We had five buried and then another one. From that ship, you know."

"I know," Cora replied. At least if it was reporting the latest burial, then there would be no mention of her and Emily.

They arrived back at Dungeness in the early afternoon, having stopped once to eat their sandwiches and drink water, and then again later to eat the coconut ice. The jelly babies had been nibbled on throughout the trek home. Both mother and daughter were exhausted, and Cora immediately placed Emily on the bed for an afternoon nap. Ada had made a pot of tea, and the two women flopped in the armchairs beside the fire.

"I picked up a newspaper," Cora said, reaching into the bag containing the paper and fudge. "And a treat for you."

Ada thanked Cora for the fudge and asked, "What's the news? I wonder if there is anything on the royal family."

"I haven't opened it." Cora reached for the paper, unfolded it, and started flicking through the thin pages.

"I was told there's a story about last week's burial in Lydd. Here it is." She began to read, her finger following the lines and a frown of concentration on her brow.

The nation has taken to their hearts those few who survived the tragic sinking of the Northfleet. The good people of Great Britain have fund-raised and sent all they can spare in order to clothe those who were left in only their night-clothes. Every day, we feature the story of one of those who lived through that terrifying night on 22nd January of this year.

Cora's body tensed, and she looked up at Ada, "Oh Lord. It's not about the funeral; it's the stories of the survivors and he's written about *me*! It was that Reginald Street – the one who came here."

I was fortunate enough to meet Mrs Cora Parkins when she attended a funeral in New Romney last month. She was standing in the churchyard where, even though its resting place was a couple of miles offshore, the masts of the Northfleet could be seen. Young and vulnerable, I found her at first reluctant to speak of her loss, and who can blame her when the memories are still so raw? But as we stood there, Mrs Parkins shared her story with me: She and her husband, Stanley, both from Gravesend, North Kent, met when she was 18 years of age and he just 22. He worked in the engine room of the Earl of Essex ferry, and she worked in a bakery. Her world was just the few streets between home and bakers; his was the grey stretch of the lower Thames and the filth of the coal-fired boiler. They courted, as young couples do, walking hand-in-hand through the town's parks, and spending time in the tearooms or dance halls. Cora and Stanley married a year after they met, and eighteen months passed before they were blessed with a baby daughter.

Emily Parkins is now two years old and one of only two children to survive the disaster.

Mr Parkins had a dream of a better life for his wife and child. In a place where the sun shone, and he could earn better wages. The young couple decided to leave their families and friends in order to emigrate to Tasmania. They boarded the Northfleet, knowing they would endure up to 100 days at sea, but with excitement and hope in their hearts.

"He's done it, Ada. He's done just what he said he would, and he's written about me, even though I wouldn't tell him a thing."

Dear Readers, you know by now the circumstances of that night when the Murillo ploughed into the Northfleet while she rested at anchor. You have read of the crew and emigrants who were picked up by other ships and taken to Dover. But our young woman and her daughter were placed on a lifeboat which found its own way to land – the stony shore of Dungeness, home to a community of hardy fishermen, coastguards and lighthouse keepers. While her fellow passengers were soon moved on to the town of Lydd and then to their homes, Mrs Parkins chose to stay in Dungeness.

"I had nowhere else to go," she told me. "Our home had gone, and furniture sold. My family couldn't offer us a place to live."

The good people of The British Inn, Mr Reuben Roberts and his wife, took in the young widow and child. Their beerhouse is like none you would see on the streets of our towns, or villages. Dungeness is a strange place, windswept and lonely. The homes are made of tarred planks and sit with no foundations on the ground, which is entirely beach pebbles. The Brit, as local people call the beerhouse, is much the same: a

141

ramshackle building with plank walls and a corrugated iron roof.

"Oh, he's writing about you and Reuben and The Brit now. He's saying how you took us in."

Sadly, the body of Stanley Parkins has not yet been washed up by the tide and it seems likely he will remain entombed within the wreckage or lie in an unmarked grave. As I write this, six bodies are at rest together in Lydd churchyard, but only one of the six has been named. When I met with Mrs Parkins, at St Nicholas Church, New Romney, she was in the company of a gentleman friend. My sources reveal him to be Mr Jacob Rose, lighthouse keeper from Dungeness. He is said to be the employer of Mrs Parkins, but I would suggest that his defensive manner towards me and his care of Mrs Parkins may lead to happier days ahead for our young widow and her daughter.

Cora stood, her face pale and tears already shining in her eyes. The newspaper fell to the ground, and she did nothing to stop it. "I thought it was over; I thought he would leave me alone," she said, her voice high. "Will you watch Emily?" And without waiting for an answer, she was flying out of the parlour, only pausing to snatch her shawl, before leaving by the kitchen door.

Chapter Thirteen

With no thought to where she was going, Cora stumbled over the shingle ridges, tripping over ragged broom, brambles and grasses. Every so often she brought the back of her hand to her eyes and dashed away tears. Sometimes she paused to pull her handkerchief from the pocket of her dress and blow her nose. The British Inn and the trail of cottages along the coast were behind her, and the town of Lydd in the far distance ahead. Although there was no plan in her mind, she had no intention of going to the town. All Cora knew was that she felt utterly wretched and could not be amongst people who would think, if only for a day, that she would cast aside the memories of her husband in order to set up home with another man. And what of Jacob, who had been so kind to her? She had brought trouble to his door, and he too would feel the pain caused by these words set out in print.

Cora turned and looked back at the lighthouse and with her next step floundered. She was a young woman and able to right herself, but in a fit of frustration, not unlike the anger displayed by a young child, Cora threw herself onto the stones, then sat looking at the toes of her boots and the laces, which were becoming loose. She wore no backstays, but that didn't matter. However, the sky was clouding over, the sun offered little warmth, and Cora had only her shawl over her brown checked dress. Both her woollen coat and hat were in her room at the beerhouse. She pulled the shawl up, so it covered her head, and held it tight around her upper body.

143

Lost in self-pity, and fear for her future, Cora huddled up and stared ahead, seeing nothing. She had little awareness of time passing and no thought of her daughter who would soon wake and need her mother to care for her. "What shall I do, Stan?" she whispered to her dead husband. "I thought you would come back to us, and now we're all alone. What will people think? They'll say I have improper thoughts about Mr Rose, even though he's a widower and perhaps nearly forty years of age. He'll want nothing to do with me now, and I can't stay here without a job, even if that Mr Scott manages to get me the six pounds. It sounds like a fortune, but it won't buy much when we have nothing at all."

When she stood up, perhaps thirty minutes later, Cora's whole body was chilled through. She looked around, almost as if seeing the area for the first time. There was a rise in the shingle, not far to her left; it was an area she knew once held a Napoleonic fort. For the first time since reading the words in the newspaper, her mind was receptive to something other than her own misfortune and she had an urge to explore.

Strange as it may seem, in this place of wooden single-storey homes, there was a row of brick-built terraced houses sheltering within the protection of the ring of shingle. Cora had seen their slate roofs and dormer windows, but never walked that way to explore the whole building. Now with a purpose, she strode out and reached the bottom of the slope. Having spotted a break in the bank, Cora turned to her left and walked until she came to the gap in the shingle circle and had a full view of the terrace.

There it was: an elegant row, encased in a concrete render, with lines of matching sash windows, tall chimneys, and a more substantial house to one end, with its own bay window and porch. *I'd have thought myself in heaven to live in a house like that.* Cora recalled her cramped home in Gravesend. She stood there, drinking in the details and wondering about the people who worked for the Royal Navy and were homed within a Napoleonic fort.

After a while, perhaps five minutes or so, Cora crossed the wide pathway leading into the ring and continued to walk around its circumference. Her steps slowed. Unsure of what to do next, Cora was ashamed of herself and embarrassed to return to The Brit. A few minutes later, she slumped on the ground, her back to the fort, and stared out into the nothingness. There were no cottages, or tracks. No boys out fetching their goats, or men looking to snare rabbits. *This must be the bleakest of all views of Dungeness,* Cora thought. *There's just stones and ragged weeds. It's the best place for me. I've made such an awful mess of everything.*

Cora wrapped her arms around her knees and bowed her head, so she no longer took in the view. Her shawl remained around her shoulders, leaving the lower part of her body vulnerable to the chill from the stones. She allowed her head to empty itself of thoughts; any awareness of time passing was lost to her. Closing her eyes, the young woman allowed the heavy woollen blanket of depression to settle upon her.

An hour later, Cora felt a hand on her shoulder. The weight of it gave comfort and she sensed no danger to herself. There was the sound of stones being displaced, and someone seated themselves beside her.

"I saw you from the lighthouse," Jacob said. "You were standing looking at the houses here in the old fort."

Cora opened her eyes and twisted towards him; her whole body was stiff. "I went for a walk," she said, then looked away into the nothingness.

"Reuben came," Jacob told her. "He said you were upset by what was written in the newspaper.

Tomorrow's chip paper that is. Not worth getting upset about."

"But I am upset," Cora reasoned. "Me and Emily need to be left alone to mourn and make a new life."

"I know," Jacob replied. "And you will be. He won't be bothering about you anymore." The stones shifted and scattered as he stood up. "I can't sit around here, and you shouldn't either. It'll be dark in an hour and you could get lost as well as ending up with a chill. Come on, I want to show you something, and I'll make you a cup of tea."

"But Emily..."

"She's fine with Ada and they know I was coming to get you. You can't hide from a lighthouse keeper. We see a lot from up there." He nodded towards the lighthouse and Cora, while struggling to her feet, gazed in the direction of the tower on the Dungeness Point.

"Tea would be nice, ta." Cora scurried alongside Jacob. His strides were longer than hers and he faced ahead. He didn't turn to check if she was all right, perhaps sensing how uncomfortable she felt. Cora appreciated his thoughtful manner. Thinking of his kindness encouraged her eyes to fill with tears again and, frustrated with herself, she wiped them away with the back of her hand.

Walking the shingle ridges every day had made Cora strong. She began to warm through; the numbness caused by the cold eased and her muscles relaxed. It didn't take long before they were nearing the base of the lighthouse. For the first time, Cora considered someone other than herself and she asked: "What were you doing up there? I thought you were at home with the boys."

"I was, but Reuben came knocking and said you were upset. I left William in charge and thought the best way to find you was to go up high." He looked at Cora and continued, his voice a little sterner, "It would be a different matter once it got dark, you know. It's not safe to go wandering off."

A dart of guilt ran through Cora's body. "I know," she said. "I'm sorry."

Jacob pushed open the door and they stepped into the base of the lighthouse. The windows were small and much of the area was in shadows; Cora found the darkness strangely comforting.

"We need to go to the next floor." Jacob reminded her, and Cora scrambled up the wooden staircase to the second level. The small stove was alight, and she walked towards it, stretching her hands out to the warmth. They exchanged no words and, having put a kettle on the hotplate, Jacob busied himself with preparing the teapot and mugs.

"Why didn't we go back to the house?" Cora asked, when they were sitting either side of the stove with mugs of tea in their hands.

"Because the boys would want all your attention and I think we should have a talk," Jacob replied. "But not yet. Let's drink our tea and then we'll take a climb up all these steps and I'll show you what Dungeness looks like without the snow."

"It's getting dark," Cora reminded him.

"The lights at the cottage windows make it magical," he told her.

They didn't speak much while they sipped at the tea and Cora's body warmed through. *He must know what upset me so much,* Cora reasoned. *There is no need to go through it again. Did Reuben show him the newspaper though? And how did it make him feel, for it to be there in printed words... the suggestion that me and him might... I've brought so much trouble to this place.* Had she voiced her thoughts, Jacob would have insisted that she brought nothing but joy and comfort to the lives of his three sons, and eased his mind of the burdens of caring for young children without the support of family members nearby. Cora didn't give him the opportunity.

"Come on then," Jacob took her mug, and turned to the steps ascending to the next floor of the lighthouse. "Up we go, and then you can return to your daughter."

Cora attempted a smile and gathered the folds of her skirt, holding it free from her black boots. As they paused at each level, she went to the windows and gazed out. Every time she glimpsed a view of the headland, her spirits lifted a little, and the next set of stairs seemed easier to climb. Soon she was standing at the base of the wooden ladder and placing her boot on the first rung, then rising through the trapdoor and the view was no longer restricted by the small rectangular windows.

The sun was setting behind the hills at Fairlight. "They call those the fire hills," Jacob told her. Streaks of orange and rich yellow filled the sky to the west, while behind her it was a dark blue velvet. The colours changed by the second, turning to red and then losing their intensity. Cora walked slowly around the circumference of the light room, her gaze roaming across the dark sea and the shingle ridges. She paused to pick out The British Inn, and then other cottages such as the Bartons' and the Webbs', where she regularly bought fish, and Sarah's home, where goats' milk could be bought. The view soothed her and, as Cora looked at The British Inn again, she recalled the newspaper article and it no longer seemed to matter as much.

When Cora looked towards the fire hills again, Jacob came and stood beside her. "I think it's too soon for either of us to be falling in love, not when we were blessed with good marriages," he began. "Cora, I don't want to go upsetting you again, but I want you to listen to me."

She turned her attention from the cottages and the boats on the beach bank and looked at him. Jacob's woollen hat was pulled low on his forehead, and his scarf wrapped up to his chin, but between those layers there was a face that was perhaps weary, perhaps a little serious, but it was the face of a good and kind man. She saw the fine lines around his eyes and mouth, and the curl of his hair as its fiery waves licked around his ears.

"Falling in love?" she repeated, with a slight frown. "That's just words written by that man..."

"It's not just words, and I know it's too soon, but I'm very fond of you."

"Don't go saying that." Cora's voice was low, and she glanced towards the trapdoor.

"Cora, I will say it," Jacob replied. "I've seen Reginald Street upset you twice, and I know how it makes me want to take you in my arms and protect you. I can take care of you and Emily, and we can make a happy home together, the five of us. I'll treat you well, you know that, and perhaps your feelings for me would grow."

"I think we'd better not talk like this." Cora took a step back. "It's time for me to get back to Emily, and you have your boys."

But Jacob was not to be stopped. "I'm asking you to marry me," he said. "Marry me, Cora, and make your home with me and the boys. Not yet, but one day."

Her body froze and Cora stood there, gazing at the light emitted from the windows of the distant fishermen's houses. She allowed the yellow slants and spots to dance before her eyes, and then to blur when she refused to blink. Her mouth was dry, and mind blank.

"It's too soon," Jacob began to defend himself. "I know it is, but if you could consider that perhaps... in perhaps six or nine months, we could make a new family from ours which have special ones gone from them. If you'd let me hold you, just put my arm around you, then I could offer you comfort. And love."

Turning again to look at him, Cora saw kindness in his eyes and for a moment she wanted nothing more than his arms around her. And maybe she had been a little harsh in thinking him to be as old as forty. Jacob was probably just six or eight years older than herself. He would have experience of life and could offer a nice home for her and Emily. Better than a storeroom in a pub. If she were to lay her head on his chest and be held in his arms, then Cora knew there would be a feeling of safety. It was too soon though. He had said it himself.

"I wasn't expecting..." Cora heard those well-worn words uttered by young women in novels. She had only known what it was like to be held by Stan, and now yearned for that comfort. A vision of Reginald Street came to her, and then James Roberts, both men she felt a distaste for. Tears welled in her eyes and she stepped forward, allowing him to wrap his arms around her, and for her cheek to lie on the rough wool of his jacket.

Jacob's chin was nestled in Cora's hair, his fingers entwined in the thick wool of her shawl. His frame was sturdier than Stanley's and she liked the strength of his arms around her. "You're beautiful, and it wouldn't be hard to fall in love," he murmured. "I'd be good to you, I promise." He moved back a little, and with his forefinger Jacob brushed a strand of hair from Cora's forehead, then kissed her pale brow. She wrapped her arms around him and pulled him back, so he was once again holding her tight against him. Standing there, her eyes closed, Cora felt safer than she had done in the past six weeks and felt the tension flood from her body.

I can't let this happen, the voice in her head insisted, although she longed to stay just as they were. She had no urge to kiss him; Cora had never considered Jacob

150

in that way. But to be held, if only for a moment, brought a comfort she hadn't realised was lacking.

When Jacob loosened his hold, Cora stepped back and she knew what needed to be said: "I know you'd be good to me, and I understand we must think of our children. But if I married you, then it would be for the wrong reason and besides, I have to be sure my Stan has gone."

"Of course, you do," Jacob replied. "I need you to know that you don't have to face these worries alone. You have Ada and Reuben, and Emily, but if you want someone to hold you and to share your thoughts with, then I was hoping you would consider me."

Stepping towards the trapdoor, then leaning to pull it open, Cora turned towards him and said, "You've been very good to me, Jacob, and I won't start calling you Mr Rose again, but I don't want to speak any more of this." She tilted her chin upwards a little, and continued, "I'm flattered, but this has come all of a sudden and we had better get back to our children now."

They went down the ladder and then the stairs, exchanging no words, other than Jacob reminding her to be careful. "Ta for coming to find me," Cora said. "It was good of you."

"I'd do it again," Jacob replied, a reminder of his growing feelings for her.

Chapter Fourteen

Winter came to an end, and new life began to emerge on the desolate headland. It wasn't obvious, not a show of daffodils or the glorious blossoming of cherry trees, but it came, nonetheless. Tender new shoots sprouted amongst the stems of woody broom, succulent leaves began to unfurl from the midst of the sea-kale plants, and grass-heads stretched towards the sun. The wind was still brisk and brought with it an all-pervading chill, leading Cora to believe that the summer days existing elsewhere would never bless Dungeness.

The newspaper which brought such upset to Cora had been burned the next day, its sheets twisted into suitable firelighters for the kitchen, parlour and bar. But the words were not so easily blotted out; they stayed in Cora's mind, repeating over and over. And the masts of the ship remained out at sea, although it appeared they were gradually sinking from sight.

Watching Jacob as he played games with his sons, brought coal in for the stove, or appeared bleary-eyed after working all night, Cora noted a softening in his manner. He seemed to smile more often, joke with the children, and encourage light-hearted banter. Her employer was coming to life again, and the worst of his mourning had passed. Cora's mind was jumbled, partly thriving on the new challenges she faced, yet still suffering from the suggestions made by Reginald Street. She missed her husband and the love they had shared.

There was no more mention of marriage from Jacob, and Cora tried hard to put his words behind her. That evening when she had returned to The British Inn, her first reaction was to pack a couple of bags and flee the headland. Sitting by the fire in the parlour, Cora had confided in Ada and sought her advice. "Of course it's too soon to think of Jacob in that way," Ada had agreed. "But he's not going to make a fuss over it. Go to work tomorrow and he'll act as if nothing ever happened. Think of Emily and those little boys and don't go rushing into any foolish decisions."

Despite there being no more intrusion from the newspaper reporter, and the pattern of her life remaining the same within the Rose household, Cora couldn't help thinking it was time to abandon Dungeness. A picture of her and Emily leaving and making themselves a home elsewhere, perhaps in a local town, played in Cora's mind. Not Lydd or New Romney, she told herself. They were too close, but there was no need to return to North Kent when there were numerous market towns within the area to choose from. She scolded herself daily, berating her ingratitude to those who had offered her a home, work and, more importantly, friendship over the past months.

Two weeks after her last trip to Lydd and the upset caused from her buying the newspaper, a letter came for Cora. She opened it in the kitchen, while Ada poured the tea and Emily chewed on a piece of bread and dripping.

"It's from that Mr Scott," Cora said. "Look at the fancy lettering at the top of the paper, 'Scott and Browning', it says and there's the address set out all proper." She waved it in Ada's direction.

"It must be about your money," Ada said.

Cora read slowly, a finger running under the words, sometimes pausing to sound out the letters or to consider the meaning of a word. "He's got the money," she announced. "Seven pounds! And he says when I have time to go to Lydd, he'll help me with the forms so I can have a bank account."

"That's wonderful news," Ada replied. "It will be a comfort to know it's there for you. Not that you need it now, but you never know what's around the corner. This will bring a bit of security for you and Emily."

Ada was right, Cora didn't need the money now. She was already saving a shilling a week in the tin placed under her bed. However, the seed of an idea, previously ignored, began to germinate in her mind. Over the next few days, she nurtured this seed, rather than allow it to die. By the end of the week, new plans had been made and the young widow prepared to cast aside everything that had become dear to her and Emily over the past months.

"I can't stay here anymore, Vicar." Cora didn't pause to exchange polite words when she entered the warmth of the vicar's living room. "Me and Emily are packed up to go, and I wanted to say thank you for taking us in that night when we arrived."

"To go?" the vicar repeated, gazing at her over the top of his glasses. "You mean to say…?"

"We've said our goodbyes to Ada and Reuben, and the Rose family, and are about to walk to Lydd. Then I'm hoping to find someone to take us to a town," Cora explained. "I was thinking of going along the coast to Hastings; there will be plenty of rooms there until I can find a job and a proper home."

"I said enough times that this was no place for a young woman and child, but you seemed happy enough."

"You were right," Cora declared. "I need to be in a place where no one knows me, and I can find a proper home. I'll leave after breakfast in the morning and go to see Mr Scott. He's sorting out my money, you know. But I've got a few shillings and that will see us through the next couple of weeks."

"And you are looking for a job?" The vicar seemed distracted; he was rifling through papers on the low table beside his armchair. His mind was clearly elsewhere, and Cora felt no need to respond.

"Goodbye then." She moved away and reached for the latch on the door.

"But you said you needed a job," the vicar said, raising his voice and brandishing a letter. "My dear girl, you must take this."

"Take it?" Cora stepped towards him. "The letter?"

"From a friend; he and his wife need a young woman to care for their daughter. Would you consider going to Ashford rather than Hastings?"

"I don't mind where I go!" Cora replied, and she flashed a grin at him. "A job? In Ashford! Do you think… do you think I should go?"

"Of course. This only arrived yesterday and if you take it… Wait a moment. I'll add a note of recommendation and you can read it on your own in a moment. Take time to consider it."

Cora watched while the vicar scrawled a few words on the letter, then refolded it and slipped it back in its envelope. Desperate to know more, she gave her thanks and rushed off as soon as the letter was in her hand.

Once outside, Cora sheltered from the wind by the back wall of the vicar's home and slid the letter from its envelope. She scanned the words coming from the reverend in Ashford to his friend, until she came across the relevant lines. They told of his wife who was ailing since the birth of their daughter six months beforehand, and the decision to find a suitable woman to assist with the care of the baby. There was no more to be learned, as this was women's business and merely a passing reference to the writer's family life amongst talk of politics and news from the town. The date on the letter was only three days beforehand. With stones scattering beneath her boots, Cora raced back to The British Inn, certain she had made the right decision and now set on travelling to Ashford the following day.

Cora and Emily left Dungeness not long after daybreak the next morning. They took just two bags with clothes, and a small package with sandwiches, fruit and biscuits. For the first part of the journey, neither Emily nor the bags travelled by the shingle sleigh. The little girl was silent, knowing her mother was taking her away from all she had grown to love over the past months. Remembering the man called Papa, she wondered if they were returning to him, but Mama was crying and that was confusing. Watching the gulls swooping in the sky above, Emily retreated into her own private world.

The sleigh was left near Boulderwall Farm, where a track would take them directly to Lydd. "Use the sleigh and leave it. Someone will pick it up and bring it back," Ada had suggested the evening before. Now Cora struggled with both the child and their bags, and was determined that once in Lydd, she would pay someone to take them either to a train station or to Ashford itself.

By the time they reached the outskirts of the town, Emily was unresponsive to her mother's chatter about all the new flowers and wildlife to be seen. She walked without faltering, her expression serious and face seeming paler than ever. When they reached The Rype, Cora lifted her daughter onto a bench and unwrapped a sandwich for them to share. "It's not time for midday dinner, but I'm hungry and I bet you are too," she said. Emily took one bite and declined any more. "It's probably still breakfast time," Cora commented. She wondered if the Rose boys had managed to eat a decent meal; she pushed the thought of their faces from her mind.

They were at the door of Scott and Browning, solicitors, before nine o'clock and it was Charles Scott himself who strode along the street to open the door that morning.

"Mrs Parkins!" His voice was loud; it sounded as if he enjoyed life. But the smile on the solicitor's face faded, to be replaced with a frown when he saw the bags at Cora's feet. "You're not leaving us, are you?"

"I'm finding it's not suiting me, living at Dungeness," Cora offered. "There's a chance of a job in Ashford and that's where me and Emily are heading, but I came to see you about the money first."

"Come in." Charles Scott slotted a key into the lock and opened the door. "I'm sorry to hear that, I thought you rather liked it. Now I'll get the paperwork and we can walk along to the bank together. I'll help you with the forms."

"Ta ever-so," Cora said. She fell silent as he searched for the letter regarding her compensation.

A moment later and they were heading for the local branch of the Rye bank named Curteis, Pomfret & Co. The solicitor took both Cora's bags and walked quickly, nodding and calling out greetings to anyone they passed. *He ain't a bit posh,* Cora thought. *He treats everyone the same from the man on the brewer's dray to that woman in a posh coat and hat.* She scurried along as best she could, with Emily in her arms.

They were soon all ushered into a private room where the solicitor showed the letter stating Cora had been awarded seven pounds compensation. He handed the bank manager the cheque and proceeded to explain that she needed to deposit the money and would need a bank book but had no formal identification. "Everything was lost when the ship went down," he explained. "Her husband's body has not been recovered so we don't have a death certificate."

"And her address?" the bank manager spoke directly to Charles Scott, and Cora was glad.

"Her address will be my office until further notice," the solicitor stated with confidence.

They left the bank with a slim book, encased in leather and embossed with the bank's emblem. Feeling rather overawed, Cora stammered her thanks.

"When you need some money, you must go to the Ashford branch named Pomfret, Burra and Simonds," Charles Scott informed her. "You show your book and sign for the money you take out. Keep it safe."

"Ta," Cora said, putting the book deep in her handbag.

They stood on the pavement. It was time for Cora to leave and she suddenly felt very lost. "You need to get to Appledore station," Charles Scott said. It was as if he saw she needed further guidance.

"Is it far?" Cora asked.

"You certainly can't walk there with a young child and these bags," he replied. "It must be ten miles." He saw Cora glance towards the horse-bus, now drawn up alongside The George Hotel. "I'm sorry, that one doesn't go there, but I'll have a word."

The solicitor dashed across the road, narrowly avoiding a pony and trap; he still had Cora's bags in his arms. She watched him pointing and nodding, then extracting some coins from his pocket and offering them to the man standing beside the heavy horse. It seemed as if an arrangement had been made and the next minute Cora was being ushered towards the church and turning down the lane opposite. To her right there was a substantial house, perhaps dating from the last century, with rows of sash windows and an elegant surround to the panelled front door. Opposite, there was a yard with stables, carts and a small trap.

"Percy! Where are you?" Charles Scott bellowed, causing Emily to clutch at her mother. "You're needed to take a young woman and her child to the railway station."

A lad of around fourteen years of age appeared from a barn, with a broom in his hand. He acknowledged the newcomers with a nod but said nothing.

"I've paid your pa," Charles Scott said. "This young lady is Mrs Parkins. She and her daughter need a nice steady ride over to Appledore station where they are catching the train to Ashford."

"I'll get the trap ready," Percy replied.

"Good chap." The solicitor, who was a head taller than Cora, leaned towards Emily, who took a further step back into the folds of her mother's skirt. "Now you and your ma are going on a special ride. Look at that, he's bringing the horse out to pull the trap. And later you'll be on a steam train!" He straightened himself and said to Cora, "I don't know why you're leaving but something tells me you are not too happy about it. It's not my business but someone needs to look after you, and so if you find Ashford isn't where you want to be, then write to me and I'll have a word with my wife and we'll see if we can find you some work and a cottage here in Lydd."

Cora nodded, her eyes began to brim with tears, and she couldn't find the words to reply. He stood close to her, not fully understanding all her fears and regrets but said no more about it. Instead the solicitor reached out and rested his hand on her arm for a moment, then ruffled Emily's curls before turning away.

It wasn't long before Lydd was behind them and, sitting up high on the two-wheeled trap, Cora was able to see the countryside stretching inland to a ridge of distant hills. This was Walland Marsh beyond the shingle ridges of Dungeness: arable fields were dotted with sheep, intersected with winding drainage ditches and earth banks. Cora knew nothing of the history of the area and could only look on with a mild curiosity. Her companion, Percy, had not spoken, other than when he helped them climb into the cart. Emily had closed her eyes, although she did not appear to be sleeping. There were occasional farmhouses, barns and cottages, and the end wall of what appeared to be an abandoned church. They came across a village: it was small with an inn, a church and a couple of small shops. Cora would have liked to have known the name of the settlement, but Percy had his back to her, and she wasn't inclined to bother him.

The road straightened out and became wider, with more traffic on it, and two more villages were passed, the second being no more than a beerhouse, a row of cottages and a church large enough to seat a thousand people. Cora frowned and looked into the distance, wondering where the people came from to fill the church. Not long after, she saw the railway track and soon a well-proportioned red-brick station building came into view.

Percy steered the horse and trap to the side of the road and jumped down. He held the horse steady and left Cora to clamber out and drop to the ground. She held her arms out for Emily, and then pulled their bags from the trap. "Ta," she said to Percy, who gave a nod. *It's easier this way. I don't want no one being too friendly or I'll start crying, I know I will.*

The tender engine, emblazoned with the emblem for the South Eastern Railway Company, eased to a halt beside the platform. Cora lugged the bags and Emily through the ticket office and seated them on a bench outside the waiting room. Emily froze when the pipes beneath the boiler let out a long hiss and emitted a jet

160

of steam, but not a sound came from her lips. A couple of doors opened, and porters stepped forward ready to assist with bags where needed. Grateful for some help, Cora gave a smile to a young man dressed in a smart jacket and hat; he took her bags and passed them into the carriage once she had lifted Emily up and stepped in to join her daughter. It was wonderful to sink into a padded seat after the discomfort of the trap.

"Look at us on a steam train!" Cora said to Emily. The little girl gazed out of the window but said nothing. The whistle blew and the carriage jolted, then they began to move forward slowly as the engine belched great puffs of smoke from her chimney.

Chapter Fifteen

Mother and daughter journeyed across fields scattered with sheep before the tracks took them away from the low-lying land and through ancient woodland. Before long, the trees were in turn replaced with open fields, again intersected with streams and areas of marshland, although Cora knew they had put Romney Marsh behind them and had risen beyond sea-level. They crossed a shallow river, and occasional cottages now mingled with short rows of terraces and detached houses in their own plots. Then the housing became denser with brown-brick homes, and beyond these a cluster of chimneys and industrial buildings began to take shape.

"My daughter lives there," her only companion in the carriage informed Cora. "She married a fitter at the Works and got herself a house. She did well for herself, Mary did."

"The Works?" Cora queried.

"Where they build the steam engines." The older woman frowned a little. "Don't you know Ashford?"

"No."

"It's a fine place to be, with all sorts of shops in the town centre and employment at the railway for anyone needing a job."

"And would there be places where we could find lodgings?" Cora asked.

"Is it just you and the girl?" She moved forward in her seat, curious about the young woman and her daughter.

"Yes, and she's well behaved." Cora stroked Emily's hair; the little girl's head was turned so she could gaze out of the window.

"I can see that; there's not been a peep out of her." The woman paused for a moment before saying, "There's always cards offering rooms to let. Just walk up to the town and take a look in the windows."

"And is it far to Willesborough?" Cora recalled the address on the letter. "Can I walk there?"

"It's no distance at all for a young woman like you. Nice village it is and close to the railway works too. Thinking of going there, are you?"

Cora glanced out of the window. The station buildings were approaching. "I have a friend there," she said, not wanting to share any details of her life. Then she stood and reached for her bags.

The train came to a halt alongside a great clanking beast bound for towns in the opposite direction. Faces of passengers heading for Folkestone and Dover peered back at those in the train from Hastings and Romney Marsh. They glimpsed each other and fleetingly wondered about their lives before turning away. Cora took Emily's hand and followed the other woman as she stepped out of the carriage. They didn't say goodbye and the stranger, knowing exactly where she was going, soon wormed her way through the crowds and vanished.

"Ashford. Ashford! The train on platform two will be departing for Dover at ten past one. The next train to arrive on platform one will be leaving for London at one forty-five."

Cora found herself standing beneath the station canopy with its scalloped edges. The passengers moved past her as one, all flowing towards a wooden bridge. She and Emily followed, mounting the steps and crossing the tracks to another platform, then paused to give her ticket in before moving through a side gate.

The road outside the station was busy with people on foot, horseback and in small traps like the one they had travelled in earlier. There were carts laden with goods, and a couple of covered horse-buses. For a moment, Cora felt stunned, unable to think what to do next or how to move on. This was a far cry from the empty headland at Dungeness.

"That lady said Ashford was a nice town," Cora said to Emily. "Let's find a boarding house and leave our bags there, then we can look for somewhere to have a nice drink and a bun."

They walked away from the station forecourt. To the left there was a mill, in the same brown brick as the houses and railway works they had passed earlier. In the other direction, there was not only another enormous mill, but also homes of red brick with decorative features and, further away on a slope, shops and houses which appeared to be more tightly packed together. The high ground was topped with a slim church tower; this was clearly the town centre.

They had been walking for a few minutes when Cora spotted a house with a sign offering rooms to let. She looked it up and down, noting grubby windows and tatty curtains, and decided to continue her search. "There's bound to be plenty," she said to her silent daughter, who trailed at her heels. "It looks as if Ashford is a busy place, what with all these trains coming and going."

It was the third boarding house which at last met Cora's approval. Smaller than the first two, and fronting the road leading to the town, it was set slightly back from the pavement with a narrow strip of grass between iron railings and a red-brick facade. Within that scrap of land there were tulips, their bulbous heads in orange, yellow and red. The last of the daffodils were dying off, and most had been dead-headed, showing this to be an establishment where someone was taking the trouble to keep it in good order. In the corner of the front garden, and spilling over the pavement, was a cherry tree laden with pink blossom. "It's beautiful. Really beautiful." Cora murmured her appreciation.

She stepped up to the front door, lifted the brass knocker then rapped it soundly. Footsteps could be heard in the hallway and a girl opened the door. She wore a grey dress and a white apron; her hair was mostly hidden under a mob cap and she was pushing back stray strands while standing looking at Cora and Emily.

"It says you have rooms," Cora said, nodding towards the sign in the front window. "How much for two nights, for me and my daughter?"

"Just wait a minute, please," the girl replied. "I'll fetch Mrs Browne."

Cora stepped into the hall and let the door close behind her. She placed the bags at her feet. It was dark once the door was closed but the hallway smelled of polish and the space was tidy.

A moment later an older woman came through; her pace was brisk, shoes tapping on the tiled floor. When she spoke, her tone was friendly: "Good afternoon, I hear you are looking for a room? For you and your daughter? I'm Edith Browne."

"I think it's for two nights, maybe longer, three or four. I need to find lodgings. Yes, just me and my daughter, who is no trouble." Cora paused, aware she was babbling. Never having stayed in a boarding house before, she wasn't certain of what to expect and realised she hadn't introduced herself. "I'm Mrs Cora Parkins. Pleased to meet you, Mrs Browne. And this is my daughter, Emily."

"It will be one and six a night, or one and tuppence if you are happy with the small attic room with just the one bed." Mrs Browne rightfully assessed that Cora had little money to spare. "Sixpence for breakfast and a cup of tea in the evening."

The sixteen shillings Cora had in her purse needed to be spent wisely. Not wanting to go to the bank and withdraw any of her money held there, her choice was easily made: "I'll happily take the small room and a breakfast, ta."

The girl was loitering in the shadows of the hallway and stepped forward. "Mary, take Mrs Parkins' bags and show her room six please," Mrs Browne ordered. "There's a scuttle with some coal in it for the fire; it's thrupence to refill it and Mary will clear the grate every morning."

Cora tried hard not to show her horror. *A penny here and a penny there, how on earth am I going to keep hold of my shillings when we need to put food in our bellies as well?* She lifted Emily onto her hip and followed Mary up one set of stairs and turned towards another leading to the attic.

"There's an indoor lavatory at the end there!" Mary announced, visibly swelling with pride to be working in such a fine place. "And a chamber pot under your bed."

Cora looked down the corridor to the door leading to a room with its own lavatory in it. She longed to peep in but placed her boot on the stairs and followed Mary.

Although the room was small, with low eaves, it was clean and warm. Cora smiled her approval. The bed had crisp sheets, a thick blanket and an eiderdown with a faded pattern of trailing roses. Walls were papered in a patterned flock of cream and beige; the curtains at the small dormer window were a brown floral pattern. Relief flooded over her weary body when she saw the bed, which appeared so snug, and Cora knew she needn't be burning coal to keep the chill off them once they were under the covers. Tears came to her eyes. They were unexpected and she wanted nothing more than to sink her face amongst those roses and sob for her lost husband and the three little boys left behind at Dungeness. But that was for later when Emily slept; now she had to think of caring for the needs of her little girl.

"Thank you, Mary," Cora said. The girl smiled and turned away.

Cora unwrapped the last of the sandwiches and placed the packet on the floor next to where Emily had flopped on a rug. Then she stepped to the window, curious to learn more about the town. The view revealed the street previously walked along, and Cora was sure if she were to open the window and lean out then she would see the railway station. Instead, she looked across the street to open ground with tracks leading towards the church. There were the backs of houses with a jumble of outbuildings, vegetable plots, and a couple of tethered ponies. The houses were slate or tile topped, and above them all was the slender grey church tower, ornate with turrets which would not have appeared out of place on a royal palace. She could see the clock and windows, seemingly too large for the tower, and while she took in the details the hour chimed: two o'clock.

Turning to look down at Emily, an intense feeling of love flooded through Cora's body. The little girl's face was pale and her eyes listless. She had barely eaten any of the sandwich. "Why don't you have a sleep?" Cora suggested, as she lifted her daughter onto the bed and pulled her boots off, before placing the covers over her. Then she sat, stroking Emily's back, waiting for the child's body to relax and her breathing to slow.

Before she could return to the fascinating view from the window, there was a tap at the door and Mary was standing there with a tray in her hands. "Mrs Browne said you might appreciate this," the girl said. There was a cup of tea and a slice of fruit cake, along with a beaker of milk for Emily.

"I've not had a cuppa all day," Cora exclaimed. "We were going to find a tearoom, but my daughter is exhausted. Ta, ta very much."

An hour later and Cora woke. She had settled in the armchair, pulled a rug over her and succumbed to the sleep her body desperately needed. Emily was stirring and looking around the room. "We've come to Ashford," her mother reminded her. "Come and sit with me; the nice lady has given you some milk." The church clock chimed three o'clock and, with her daughter on her lap, Cora pondered on how to spend the rest of the day.

By the time quarter-past had sounded across the town, Cora was buttoning their coats and fretting about the state of their boots. "They were all right for the shingle, but we'll need smarter ones to be going about the town in," she said while tightening Emily's laces. "But at least we have decent coats." The oversized boy's coat donated to Emily on that first day they stayed at Dungeness had been replaced by a far more presentable grey one with a belt.

Mary was once again hovering in the hallway. "How would I get to Willesborough?" Cora asked. "Is it far?"

"Depends if you walk or take the horse-bus," Mary replied. "I don't know if your little girl would want to walk there. It would be no trouble without her."

"She has to be with me. So, the horse-bus?"

"It goes past here every hour." Mary went to the hall window as if expecting to see it. "It leaves the station at half-past so it's here not long after."

"We'll go and wait then." Cora opened the front door. "Thank you."

"We lock the front door at half-past nine," Mary informed her. "Mrs Browne keeps a respectable lodging house and doesn't encourage the types who stay out late."

"I'll be back long before then!" Cora found herself smiling. What did Mary think she and Emily would be doing in a strange town at night?

The street was quieter now. Delivery boys with barrows and the cumbersome carts pulled by heavy horses were finished with their work for the day. Now schoolboys walked in small groups, calling to each other, darting about, and squabbling. Emily watched them, following their every movement with her grey eyes. She said nothing.

The horse-bus pulled up, and Cora handed over another tuppence. They sat up high, eager to see more of the town. It took them along the same street, until they came to a crossroads. To the left there seemed to be the high street, with shops and inns standing side by side and the church tower still visible above them all. But she was to see no more of the town, as the horse swung to the right and took them down a narrower road, where they passed flat-fronted Georgian homes, some of them three storeys high and all of them elegant. The road veered further to the right and a bridge took them over a wide river flanked by mills. The homes were now humble cottages and terraces. Before long they were leaving the town and looking across the fields.

Ashford was barely behind them when the bus passed an impressive grammar school, with boys, some of them in long trousers, spilling out through its gates. A bridge took them over railway lines and again there were cottages along the roadside. Then a wooden painted sign announced they were in Willesborough. *Mary was right; it was no distance and perhaps if we can find somewhere to eat, then Emily wouldn't mind walking back. And we can put the tuppence towards some new boots, or nearly new ones at least.* She spotted some small shops selling the essentials, including a café with its door open to reveal tables covered in lace cloths. *That looks all right, and perhaps not too pricey with its being out of the town.*

The horse-bus drew to a halt not far from an inn, with a small chapel on the opposite side of the road. Cora went to move in her seat, but the driver looked back and called: "Not yet, missus. Your stop is further on. Church Road you want and this ain't the right church."

"Ta," Cora replied, but he had turned away and was encouraging the horse to move on.

There were more fields and, when the cottages again filled the roadside, an impressive smock mill rose behind the rooftops. The next time the horse slowed, the driver twisted in his seat and gave a nod.

With Emily trailing behind, Cora climbed down and thanked the driver: "Ta very much. If I want to return by horse-bus when would I need to be waiting?"

"I'll pass again in twenty minutes; I don't go much further," he informed her. "Or again at quarter-past five, and quarter-past six; that will be the last of the day."

They were now opposite Church Road. Cora could see the spire of St Mary's Church directly in front of her. "Darn, it's a bit of a walk," she muttered. "Oh well, at least they have pavements here in Willesborough!" She took Emily's hand, and fixed a smile on her face. "Come on, Em, we'll be there in no time. Near the church, I was told."

They passed cottages and houses of various sizes and ages, mostly sitting in their own plots of land, rather than fronting the road in terraces. There was a school: a pretty building of grey stone, now empty for the remainder of the day. In the land between the properties, chickens pecked at the ground, a pony grazed in its paddock and small vegetable plots were prepared for fresh growth. A woman stepped out from an open doorway with a checked cloth in her hands and proceeded to shake the crumbs from it. 'Hot Dinners and Teas' was displayed on a sign at the window.

"Excuse me," Cora called out, while walking towards the woman. "Will you be able to give me and my little girl a dinner in half an hour? We need to call at the rectory and could do with a hot meal before we walk back to Ashford."

"Bless you, dear," the woman replied, her voice was soft. "I was going to finish up, but you can't go walking back there with no food in your bellies. I've got some pie left, and I can fry up the cold potatoes. There's plenty of cabbage and it cooks in no time. But the rectory – it's not by the church; you need to turn back, and you'll find it up there on your right."

Cora gazed along the lane. "I've done enough walking today but if coming down here gives us a hot meal then I won't complain!" She lifted Emily onto her hip and said, "We'll be back in half an hour."

The rectory, a flat-fronted brown-brick house with sash windows, was set back from the road and partly hidden by a privet hedge. Cora paused, nervous of its Georgian splendour, having never seen such a fine rectory before. She walked up to the door, conscious of her scruffy boots, then readied herself with a bright smile and rapped on the door. Before long, footsteps could be heard in the hallway and the door opened. Cora found herself faced with a woman of perhaps thirty years. She was dressed in a plain grey dress with a subtle stripe to the material and a decorative white collar at the neck. Her shoes were well-polished and not the type to wear walking over fields, or on a shingle landscape. Her hair was a nut-brown and swept back into a neat bun. Cora put her hand to her own face and tucked a stray curl behind her ear.

"Good afternoon?" the woman said, her tone questioning.

"Hello. Good afternoon," Cora began. "I'm sorry to bother you. I'm Mrs Parkins, Mrs Cora Parkins. I've got a letter of recommendation, because I've heard you need someone to help look after your baby. I was told to come and see Reverend Tibbs and his wife."

Chapter Sixteen

A baby lay on a soft woollen blanket. She wore a matching dress, cardigan and knitted booties, all in a delicate cream. Her chubby hand clutched at a wooden rattle and a cloth ball rested at her side. When Cora entered the front parlour, the baby rolled from her back on to her front and gave a toothless smile.

"This is my husband, Reverend Tibbs," Mrs Tibbs said. "And my daughter, Alice."

The rector was sitting in an armchair beside the fire, with a book on his lap and a cup of tea on a side table. He wore a slight frown on his rounded face, not recognising the newcomer as one of his parishioners

"Nice to meet you. I'm Mrs Parkins," Cora introduced herself.

"Good afternoon," the rector replied. "Have you come to see me? Shall we step through to my study?"

"I've come to see you all..." Cora faltered. "I've got a letter. It was the vicar at Dungeness who told me you need someone to help look after your daughter, and he thought I might suit you."

"Frederick read my letter and sent you!" the rector exclaimed. "He sent you from Dungeness! My dear girl, how exceptionally good of you to come!"

"I call him Vicar," Cora offered. "But yes, he knew I was in need of some work and he said to come and see you." She held out the letter originally sent from Reverend Tibbs to his friend at Dungeness, telling him the news of his parish and family in Willesborough. "He gave me this letter, so you knew... so you knew I wasn't just some woman turning up without anyone to vouch for me. And he wrote you a message; you can see it here on the envelope."

"Sit down, Mrs Parkins." The rector gestured towards an armchair. "I'd like to see it."

Cora seated herself in an upright chair placed within the bay window. She pulled Emily onto her lap. Mrs Tibbs said nothing. *If I was back at Dungeness, someone would have offered me a cuppa by now,* the young widow thought. She immediately admonished herself: *that poor woman is ill, not that she looks it, but she must be if she can't look after the baby.* Cora watched little Alice reach for the ball and her face crumple when it couldn't be reached. The clock on the mantelpiece ticked and its rhythm seemed to fill the room. Emily slipped off her mother's lap and sat on the floor watching Alice.

"My dear, this young woman is a survivor from the *Northfleet*," Reverend Tibbs addressed his wife. "One of the few. She has lost her husband and seeks the means to support herself and her daughter."

"I don't know that the few shillings we can offer will be enough," his wife replied. "It's not a live-in position, you know."

"No, but she has some compensation and the money will earn her a little interest in the bank. It may well pay for a room for her and the little girl."

"I don't need someone all the time," his wife pointed out. "I was thinking of mornings only. I cannot watch the baby and keep an eye on the maid when there is so much to be done. It is far too demanding for one person to cope with."

"It's a large house for one maid," her husband offered.

"We've just Iris living-in and a girl on a Monday to help with the laundry," Mrs Tibbs explained. "Later in the morning it becomes easier though: Alice has her nap for at least an hour. Then in the afternoon I take her for a walk in the pram, but there's parish work to be done as well."

"It's all too much for you," her husband said. This was clearly a well-worn topic. "If you could have a rest in the afternoon, what a tonic that would be for you."

"But it's not a full-time job," she replied, her tone petulant and not in keeping for a woman of her age.

"You say yourself it is," the rector reminded her. "And there is no reason why Mrs Parkins cannot do a little sewing. Think of all the washing and ironing... This young woman isn't too proud to lend a hand wherever it is needed. It's too much for the maid. Far too much."

Cora said nothing while awaiting the verdict. Her arms were tight around Emily, who had returned to her lap. She glanced around the parlour, from the clutter of ornaments on the mantelpiece, to the oil paintings depicting rural scenes displayed in heavy frames. A log shifted a little in the grate and she saw Mrs Tibbs tense. The baby began to fret over the ball which slipped from her grasp, and she rolled herself to the edge of the blanket. Mrs Tibbs was immediately on the floor, fretting over Alice straying onto the rug; she rolled her daughter back. The ball was now out of reach and Alice spun again. Mrs Tibbs muttered something about the baby being wilful. *It's her nerves,* Cora thought. *The reverend's wife has trouble with her nerves.*

"Where are you staying now?" Mrs Tibbs asked.

"We have a room in a boarding house for two or three nights," Cora told her. "I'm going to look for lodgings; either here in Willesborough, or in Ashford."

"And what plans do you have for your daughter?"

"Plans? If I can find work looking after another child then she will come with me. Otherwise I'll have to advertise for someone to look after her." Cora paused, and then continued, "I've been looking after three little boys at Dungeness."

"It's in the note, dear." Reverend Tibbs held it out to his wife, and she took it.

The clock continued to sound every second. Emily slid off her mother's lap and shuffled towards Alice. Cora shifted in the chair. She moved her feet a little, trying to hide the worst of the scuffs on her boots. Emily reached out and pushed the ball towards Alice.

"I am expecting a Mrs Cole to call tomorrow," Mrs Tibbs announced. "She is an older woman with plenty of experience and is the sister of Mrs Barker from Sevington."

"I'm sorry, I didn't know," the rector replied.

"It was arranged this morning," his wife persisted.

"If you have something organised, then I'm sorry to have wasted your time," Cora began. "I'd like to find another job looking after children. It's nice for Emily and I'd rather not be separated from her, not after what she's been through. I'll look at the cards in the shop windows and see if I can find something."

"I suggest you call back tomorrow afternoon at two o'clock and we'll let you know," Reverend Tibbs suggested. "This may not suit Mrs Cole and I can see you are a capable young woman."

"I'll do that then. Ta... thank you." Cora stood and spoke to Emily, "Come on then, say goodbye to the baby girl; she's lovely, isn't she?"

Despite the uncertainty over her future, Cora slept well under the soft blanket and thick eiderdown in the attic room of the boarding house. She woke early and could hear the unfamiliar sounds of movement within the rooms: a cough, a low voice, the closing of doors and the creak of the stairs. Emily was still asleep when her mother rolled out of bed to use the chamber pot and then stood at the dormer window. The glass was covered in moisture, so she opened it a little and peered out at the street scene below. There were a couple of smart gentlemen in bowler hats and black frockcoats. *They look like bank managers,* Cora thought, *I wonder why they are up so early and not sitting down for breakfast? Perhaps they are catching the train somewhere.* Boys with satchels filled with newspapers ran past, calling out to each other and kicking at loose stones on the road. A horse and cart rumbled by. There was a chill in the air and, as the church clock struck the half-hour, the open window was pulled back into place.

A knock on the bedroom door announced the arrival of the maid with a jug of warm water, and Emily woke. Cora busied herself with preparing for the day, first helping her daughter into a dress and woollen socks. The little girl was subdued but seemed content to stand on a chair and look out of the window while Cora pulled at the fastenings on her light corset and then secured the buttons on her dress. "We'll go into the town this morning and look for some smart new boots," Cora said as she tied their laces. "And perhaps I'll treat us to a bun. That would be nice, wouldn't it?" Emily watched her laces being tied and wriggled her feet a little but said nothing. Her face was pale and grey eyes sad.

A few minutes later they were standing at the entrance to the dining room unsure of what to do next. There was a young woman, covered in a white apron, serving tea; she turned and spoke to Cora: "Sit down wherever you fancy, and I'll be with you in a minute."

Cora smiled her thanks and chose a small table by the window. She seated Emily on a chair; the little girl's face was level with the tabletop, but there was no cushion to raise her. They each had a bowl of porridge with honey drizzled over it. "Open wide," Cora said, as she spooned the creamy mixture into her daughter's mouth. "We can't be making a mess here. And when my tea has cooled, I'll share it with you." After the porridge there was bacon, an egg and a slice of bread. Emily nibbled at bread dunked in the egg yolk. Conscious of her pennies and shillings, it was a relief to see a substantial breakfast was provided and they need not be wasting too much money on food during the day. Cora felt a knot in her stomach every time she thought of her purse of coins and feared the expenses she would endure over the following days.

It was with some excitement that Cora walked up the hill towards Ashford town centre, with Emily's hand in her own. They followed the route the horse-bus had taken the previous day, keeping the church tower on their left and roadside houses on their right. There was an odd scent to the air and a brewery tower, spotted the previous day, gave a clue as to where the smell came from. As if to confirm Cora's thoughts, a dray cart rumbled past with 'Lion Brewery' painted on its side. The street was busy with pedestrians, horse-drawn traffic and, in the distance, animals being herded to the market.

They came to the crossroads and turned into the end of the High Street. It was wide with tall buildings flanking either side, many of them three storeys high, and most displaying goods for sale in their windows or advertising services. There were market stalls set up in the centre and traders called out to offer their wares such as fruit and vegetables, fresh bread and pies, and all manner of household goods. Not everyone had a stall: a girl passed by with a basket of fresh watercress and a man carried a tray on which he displayed his knife-sharpening tools. The tempting aroma of bread and pastry mingled with a winter's worth of body odour and tobacco smoke on old coats and shawls. Women called out to young children and chatted to one another; the men's voices were lower. Cora realised the accents were softer than those in her hometown of Gravesend, yet the scene and the people were much the same.

Keeping to one side of the street, they walked slowly, often pausing to look in shop windows, or to gaze up at elegant Georgian or decorative Victorian facades. The road narrowed and, with the market now behind them, a side street beckoned. The church spire loomed closer, and medieval buildings were snug between modern counterparts.

Suddenly the church, seemingly elusive before, was revealed as an alleyway opened up before them. The tower with its decorative turrets stood proud, looking as if it had come from the pages of a child's book of fairy tales. Jostling for position due to the size of the windows, was the clock: it was small, almost too small for one keeping time for the whole town. Beneath the tower, like skirts splayed out from a narrow waist, the nave and aisles stretched from east to west, as well as jutting to the north and, Cora assumed, the south. This north-facing aisle made a grand porch, with its own large decorative window above.

"We'll come here on Sunday," Cora said, half to herself as Emily was absorbed with the robins, wrens and finches gathered among the small trees and shrubs in the churchyard. "I'd like that. We've not been to a proper church for some time." Religious services at Dungeness had been rather unusual, being performed in an open shed, formerly used to house a lifeboat.

Turning away from the church, with some reluctance, they faced the rear of the town's medieval and Tudor buildings. Kentish pegtiles hung from the walls, as well as the rooftops and dormers. Windows were all shapes and sizes and none of them in any order. It made a pretty scene, but there were boots to be bought and Cora led Emily back to the shopping area.

Wandering further along the High Street, they paused frequently and while Cora took in the details of the buildings, Emily watched the people of Ashford pass by. A shop with smart shoes and dainty boots was hastily rejected as being 'too posh for the likes of us' but when they turned around and crossed to walk past the shops on the opposite side, there was a cobbler's with a large selection of second-hand shoes. "Look at these," Cora said with glee. "All repaired and made to look as good as new!"

The door to the shop was open and they walked in, feet tapping on a red brick floor. To one side wooden shelves lined the walls, displaying the shoes and boots for sale. On the opposite side there were the many other items on offer: laces, polish, shoe trees, brushes and cloths. The cobbler himself was at the rear of the shop, and barely looked up from his repairs. There was a pleasant smell of leather, wood shavings and tobacco smoke from a pipe.

A woman stepped forward to serve. Her face was round and smiling, her hair beginning to grey under her mob cap. "Good morning; I've not seen you in here before. How can I help you?"

"We've not been to Ashford before," Cora replied. "Not until yesterday at least. We both need some decent footwear for the town." She lifted her skirt a little to show the offending boots which were good and sturdy for walking the shingle but not for caring for a baby at the rectory, if only she were lucky enough to be offered the position.

"Goodness!" The woman bent down to look. "A lovely young woman like yourself shouldn't be wearing scruffy things like that. Where have you been in them? Working on the fields?"

Cora laughed. "Me in the fields? I've barely seen a field, not growing up by the river in Gravesend! No, I've been minding some children and living at Dungeness."

"Dungeness? Is that the place with all the stones I hear about? No wonder you're wearing boots like that, and the little girl has ones only fit for a boy! Look at the pair of you with your pretty faces and beautiful hair – we can do better than that for you.

"Ta, we need something a bit more ladylike, although these were all right for where we were." Cora reached for a pair of dark brown boots with laces. The style was plain but far slimmer than those she wore and with a low heel of about an inch. "These look as if they would fit."

"Just what I had in mind for you!" The assistant gestured to a bench. "Sit yourself down and we'll try them on."

Ten minutes later and Cora was leaving the shop with Emily. She wore the brown boots and found herself walking taller, with more confidence. Emily's were black leather with flat soles and buttons at the side, the toes were rounded and the flap where they fastened had pretty scalloped detailing. The old ones were in a bag, hanging from Cora's wrist. New footwear was smart for walking about town, but there were woods, fields and streams in the area and the heavy boots would still have their uses.

It wasn't long before they were passing a broker's shop with second-hand clothes on a rail outside. Cora peered through the window at shelves, baskets and hanging rails. A selection of children's clothes caught her eye. There was a small dress in light brown with a check of darker stitching. The hem was straight and the collar still white. She stepped into the shop and lifted the dress from the rail.

"I've changed the collar on that one." A woman approached them. "It had a stain and the rest was still in good order. It would suit your little girl, don't you think?"

Cora held the dress in front of Emily. It would be a little loose, but the length was perfect. She thought of the baby Alice in her cream knitted outfit and was sure Mrs Tibbs would look kindlier on them when she noted the smart new boots and Emily in a pretty dress. Before she paid, Cora's attention turned to a woman who was holding up a shawl in a dove grey colour; it seemed so soft and perfect for when the weather became milder and winter coats were not needed. But it wasn't to be, and to have another item of clothing would be another penny or two wasted. Cora turned back to the counter but before her pennies had been exchanged for the dress, she became aware that the shawl had been replaced on the shelf and the customer had left. She whirled around, the prized item was claimed, and four pence given for both items.

If I don't impress Mrs Tibbs, then I'll be all the more smart for the next job I go for, Cora thought. *These pennies on smart clothes and boots won't go wasted. We need to look the part, me and Emily do.* Her spirits were lifted by the new sights and sounds of the town centre and the thought of dressing up before heading to Willesborough. "Let's get a cup of tea and a bun," she said to Emily. "Perhaps we can get talking to people in the tearoom and find out where it's best to get a place of our own to live."

Chapter Seventeen

It was with some trepidation Cora raised her hand to the brass knocker on the front door of the rectory in Willesborough. *It would be a challenge looking after the baby. No, not the baby, she's a dear little thing and very placid. But that Mrs Tibbs doesn't want me, and I have a feeling I won't do anything right. Not in her eyes.* Indecision raced through Cora's mind. There were times on the long walk to the village that she felt like turning back in order to seek employment in the town. *But what if I don't find work this week, or next, and I won't get decent lodgings with no money coming in, and I can't afford to keep handing over my shillings to Mrs Browne.* By the time she was approaching Church Road and the spire of St Mary the Virgin was in sight, it was clear that the choice would lie in the hands of Reverend Tibbs and his wife. Willesborough was such a pretty area with the smock mill and the church, and the little school. The countryside was close at hand, and if she could find rooms nearby it would be a pleasant place to raise Emily.

"Good afternoon, Mrs Parkins." Mrs Tibbs answered the door, with a smile fixed on her face. "Do come in."

With the soft grey shawl around her shoulders and her new boots, Cora entered the rectory feeling more confident than she had thought possible. Emily appeared pretty at her side; her hair, warmed by the sunshine, was a gleaming copper, and the new dress suited her very well. If the little girl didn't smile, then most likely Mrs Tibbs wouldn't notice; she would be more impressed by a clean face and hands, and a dress without patches or a ragged hem.

"Thank you, Mrs Tibbs."

Again, they were taken to the parlour, where Alice lay on her blanket on the floor. This time her outfit was a pale pink and white knit. She turned to follow the visitors with her eyes. "I usually put her up in her cot at two o'clock for an hour," Mrs Tibbs said. "But I thought it best if you meet each other again."

"She's a lovely baby," Cora said, kneeling beside Alice and speaking in a sing-song voice, "Hello little Alice. How are you today? Are you getting sleepy?"

The baby chuckled. Emily squatted beside Alice and watched her rounded face with fascination.

"We'd like to give you a month's trial," Mrs Tibbs announced as Cora seated herself in a chair. "I've reservations about you bringing the girl, but we won't pay enough for you to leave her elsewhere and she seems to be well-behaved."

"She's a good girl," Cora confirmed, "and will play nicely with Alice."

Mrs Tibbs gave a nod and a small smile. "We need to discuss your hours. Alice wakes at about seven o'clock in the morning but she's happy in her basket for a while after I've changed her nappy and fed her. Iris starts cooking breakfast at eight o'clock and of course I need to keep a close eye on her."

Cora murmured her agreement, while not understanding why the maid couldn't be left to go about her chores.

"And that's when Alice becomes a little difficult," Mrs Tibbs continued. "You'll notice she needs a firm hand and that's what I expect from you. She gets a little fretful waiting for her breakfast and I find it's best ignored. I don't want her to become a child who has learned to whimper and mother will come running with a cuddle."

184

"You'd like me here at eight o'clock to feed Alice her breakfast," Cora confirmed. She thought of Mrs Tibbs' nerves and continued, "Then you and Reverend Tibbs can start your day in peace, and no doubt he likes to talk about parish matters with you."

For the first time her new employer gave a smile containing some warmth, and Cora felt she had pleased her. Mrs Tibbs clearly wanted to be supportive to her husband. "It's always useful for the rector to have a woman's perspective," she agreed. "We'll eat in the dining room and you will be in the kitchen with Alice. You may of course feed your little girl at the same time. It will be good for Alice to learn from the example set by such a docile child."

"Ta, thank you." Cora corrected herself. "If we are to be here by eight o'clock then Emily will appreciate some breakfast."

"Then you can dress Alice – I'll show you the nursery in a minute and we'll put her down for a sleep – and afterwards you may sit with her in the kitchen where there is a pen, a rug for her to lie on, and an armchair for you. Or on a warm day the garden is very pleasant and the air healthy. At a quarter to ten, you may take Alice for a walk. You'll find she soon falls asleep in her pram and on a fine day she could stay outside. There's nothing better than fresh air to help a baby sleep. Most likely I'll have a few errands for you while you are out but do enjoy a walk if the weather is fair."

"And when she wakes, there will be a nappy to change and a feed?" Cora questioned, although she felt confident with the routine already.

"I'll feed her here in the parlour, and perhaps you'll appreciate that time with your own daughter. We have puzzles and bricks and books in a box under the stairs; all too old for Alice, of course, but useful when children come to visit."

For some reason, Cora couldn't imagine other children visiting the rectory, but she smiled and gave her thanks. Mrs Tibbs moved onto dinner time and the afternoon sleep, now long overdue. It was at this time Cora could take her half-hour break, before helping with some ironing or sewing.

"Is there anywhere Emily could have a nap?" Cora ventured to ask. "After dinner when Alice has hers?"

Mrs Tibbs considered this for a moment before replying, "There's a small bed in Alice's room. Perhaps…?"

For the first time Cora felt truly welcome in the rectory. "That would be wonderful." She got up from her chair, knelt down and spoke to Emily, "Do you hear that, Em? There's a little bed upstairs for you to nap in when we come to look after baby Alice. Isn't that kind?"

Emily turned to her mother and gave a small smile, putting a hand out to rest on Cora's lap. Alice, who had been absorbed with looking into Emily's face and watching her curls bounce about under her little cap, screwed her face up and her eyes filled with tears. Cora quickly reached out for the baby and scooped her up. "Shall we take her up to bed now?" she asked.

Seeming to be a little taken aback, Mrs Tibbs agreed. She led the way up the staircase, with its smooth bannister rail in a dark wood, and polished brass stair rods holding a runner of carpet in place. There appeared to be five bedrooms upstairs, as Cora suspected the sixth door would lead to an indoor lavatory. It was that small room which she felt the most curiosity for and longed to press on the door and take a quick look. Instead she followed Mrs Tibbs into a back bedroom and passed Alice into her mother's arms.

There was a basket on a low stand. This something Cora had only heard of before; the people she knew provided a drawer for the baby and then a place in their own bed or with siblings. To have a small item of intricate wickerwork for the soul use of a baby was a wonderful piece of luxury. The room was plain, with a pine chest of drawers, a small bookcase and a washstand; the decoration came from a repeated pattern of small daisies on the wallpaper, and floral embossed stripes on the curtains. Cora went to the window and held a section of thick material in her hand; she drew it across while gazing out at a long garden with an orchard at the end.

"What a lovely garden you have," she said. It would be wonderful to explore with Emily while Alice lay on a blanket under the trees.

"My husband is fond of tending his vegetables," Mrs Tibbs replied. "And when autumn comes you will help bottle and store the fruit."

"I'd enjoy doing that," Cora said. She turned to watch Alice being placed in the basket.

"Look dear, there's the little bed you can sleep on," Mrs Tibbs spoke to Emily for the first time. Emily gazed up at the rector's wife and went to the low child-sized bed. She ran her hand over the climbing rose pattern on the quilt.

"Not now," Cora said. "Perhaps next week; or whenever Mrs Tibbs would like us to come and look after baby Alice."

Having left Alice to fall asleep, they returned to the parlour. "If you can start tomorrow at eight o'clock, and work until... shall we say half-past four? I'm sure I can manage after that." Mrs Tibbs didn't sit down again, and it was clear Cora was being dismissed. "I have a meeting tomorrow and didn't know what to do with Alice, so that would be useful. You can both eat a breakfast and midday dinner with us. We eat frugally, but you will have a nourishing meal."

"I'd like that, but would you mind if I took Friday off? I could help on Saturday instead," Cora suggested. "I need to go to the bank and look for rooms for me and

Emily. We are in a boarding house at the moment, but I'll start looking here in Willesborough." She paused, concerned that Mrs Tibbs would think her ungrateful for the work, and added, "This is my first day in Ashford, you see. I've had no time to arrange anything."

"That will suit us very well," Mrs Tibbs agreed. "I'm sure we'll manage for one day."

Fancy leaving without being offered a cup of tea, and for the second time! Cora reflected as they wandered back along Church Road. *Oh well, at least Mrs Tibbs was a little friendlier this time and I was offered the job. It won't be easy with her looking at my every move an' I'm going to have to watch my language. I'll be expected to talk proper in front of the baby.* She looked at Emily; the little girl seemed so tired and needed a nap. "We'll go and see that nice woman who serves hot dinners and hopefully she can feed us and perhaps there'll be a rug you can lie on, or even my shawl." With the promise of a good meal, Cora felt renewed energy and increased her pace. She swept Emily up into her arms and walked towards the church of St Mary the Virgin and, more importantly, the prospect of gratifying their hunger at the nearby tearoom.

Before long, the cottage with 'Hot Dinners and Teas' written on a sign at the window was in sight and Cora was walking up the stone path, through a pretty garden with tulips, grape hyacinth and forget-me-nots. To the side of the house there was a willow with clusters of dangling yellow-green catkins and a flowering cherry spread its branches above a tatty lawn between the cottage and road. The front door was ajar, and Cora pushed it open, with Emily almost asleep on her shoulder.

The room they entered was no more than the front room of a home, now set up with five groups of tables and chairs. A bench stretched out in front of the window and thankfully the table before it was empty. She gave a quick smile to the elderly couple seated near the kitchen door, then lay Emily on the bench and placed her shawl over the child.

"What a darling," the elderly woman said. "What pretty hair."

"Emily's a good girl," Cora replied. "We have walked all the way from Ashford, so no wonder she's tired. The horse-bus can take us back there. I can't carry her all that way."

"Of course, you can't." The woman pushed the last of the dinner onto her fork. "You're just a slip of a thing yourself." She placed the food in her mouth. Her husband said nothing.

It felt good to sit down, just close enough to place a steadying hand if Emily were to stir. Cora felt herself relax. She realised how worrying the prospect of finding work had been, and Mrs Tibbs certainly hadn't put her at ease. These tearooms were a good find and no doubt she would treat herself to a cup of tea and a bun on a regular basis when working nearby. Cora imagined pushing Alice along in the pram; it seemed as if tables were set out in the garden during warmer weather and they could spend a pleasant half hour there. But although she had only met the reverend's wife twice, it was clear Mrs Tibbs would not approve. Gazing at the scuffs in the wallpaper and the worn matting on the floor and curtains, which were clean but ragged, Cora recalled the neat and airy rooms in the rectory. If she were to bring young Alice here, then disapproval would certainly be made known to her.

"Hello!" The woman who had so kindly cooked a meal for Cora yesterday came through from the kitchen. "What brings you back to Willesborough?"

"I've got myself a job!" Cora announced. "And I need a decent meal before I go back to the boarding house."

"It's cheese and bacon bake today. A meal for you and a couple of spoonsful for the little one?" She began to collect the used plates from the other table. "Let me get myself organised and you can tell me all about it once you've eaten. You're looking a bit tired if you don't mind me saying."

"Nothing that a cuppa won't cure," Cora replied.

"We can soon remedy that, and some milk for your little girl when she wakes?"

"Ta, ever-so. She doesn't eat much at the moment, but if I can get some milk in her then it will do her good."

"Ida, we'll have a pot of tea," the man at the other table interrupted.

"Of course, I wouldn't let you go without your tea, would I?" Ida bustled off towards the kitchen.

What a lovely little business, Cora reflected, *and such friendly people.* She found out that Ida and her husband owned this little cottage near the church and made a small income from serving dinners or a slice of cake to local people, usually accompanied by a pot of tea. It was nothing fancy and brought in enough money to put food in their stomachs, coal on the fire, and keep the cottage in good repair. As well as that, it seemed as if it gave them pleasure too. The day before, Ida's husband had been digging over the vegetable patch; he had given a cheery greeting and a wave.

Soon, Cora had a pot of tea before her and by the time she was pouring her second cup there was a steaming mountain of cheesy potato slices with chunks of ham and onion, with carrots on the side. "Before long Bob will have all sorts of vegetables growing," Ida commented as she put the plate in front of Cora.

"I'll enjoy that," the young woman replied. "I never had a garden for growing vegetables, just a small yard. And there wasn't much soil for growing them at Dungeness."

"Dungeness – that's a strange old place," Ida remarked. "Is that where you've come from?"

"I was just staying there," Cora told her. "No, I've come from Gravesend, by the River Thames. I'm liking the look of Ashford and Willesborough though."

"I'm glad of that!" Ida glanced towards the older couple who were preparing to leave. "I've been on my feet for hours. How about I pour myself a cup of tea and you can tell me about this new job of yours? I could do with a break before Bob's back in the house and leaving mud everywhere."

Cora tucked into her dinner while gazing out of the window. Emily was sleeping soundly. After a few minutes, Ida drew up a chair next to her and they spoke about the new position at the rectory. Cora was careful not to confide her impressions of Mrs Tibbs, and Ida appeared to share the same respect for the rector's wife.

"I don't want to be taking lodgings in Ashford and paying for the horse-bus every day," Cora said. "And I need to find somewhere soon because I won't earn enough to pay out for a boarding house. I'll take a walk through the village and see if there are any cards up in the shop windows. There's bound to be someone offering a couple of rooms to let."

"You want a widow who has more space than she needs," Ida commented. "Now let me think, there's someone who comes in here once or twice a week. I'm sure she was talking about being lonely because her daughter and son-in-law were moving out." Ida paused, as if recalling the conversation. "That's right. He works on the steam engines and they've got their own house in Newtown now. With one baby and another on the way, they were needing a bit more space."

"Do you know where she lives?"

"Not exactly, but if you go back to the main road and turn right there's a row of cottages not far from the old quarry. Once you're there, there's bound to be someone who can tell you. Her name is Maisy, Mrs Maisy Birch."

"I'll do that." Cora pushed the last mouthful of potato and ham onto her fork. "I'd better wake Emily up and then we'll walk along to see Mrs Birch. Imagine if I manage to get a home and some work all in the same day!"

The row of four red-brick cottages were the last on the road as it narrowed and continued its way to other villages and towns unknown to Cora. There was a man repairing a front gate; he paused and watched as she approached.

"I'm looking for Mrs Birch," Cora said. "I was told she lives here, but I don't know which one."

"Number three," he replied.

"Ta." Cora walked past and pushed on the gate of the third cottage: a plain home with just two windows, one above the other, and a small open porch to the right. The slate roof was in good repair, the windows clean and the front path looked as if it had been swept that very morning. She rapped on the door; it was painted black like all the others in the terrace. Cora waited, and hoped she would find Mrs Birch at home.

Chapter Eighteen

The curtain at the window moved a little and the face of a middle-aged woman peered out before the material fell back into place. Shortly afterwards the front door was opened.

"Can I help you?" Maisy Birch gave a tentative smile. "You caught me having a doze in the armchair."

"Hello Mrs Birch," Cora replied. "Ida from near the church sent me; she thought you might have a couple of rooms to let? It's for me and my little girl here."

"Just the two of you?"

Cora moved her hand a little, so her wedding band showed. "I'm respectable, you've no need to worry about that. Yes, it's just the two of us; I was widowed recently."

"I'm sorry to hear that, dear." Her voice was gentle as she continued: "You're too young to be left on your own. Is it the one child you have?"

"Yes. Emily."

"You caught me by surprise," Mrs Birch admitted. "I wasn't expecting anyone to come asking. My daughter and her family only moved out two days ago and I was thinking about putting a card up in the post office window, and now here you are. Come in and we'll talk about the rooms. Would you like a cup of tea?"

"I wouldn't normally refuse, but I've just had a hot dinner and three cups!" Cora replied as she followed Mrs Birch into a narrow hallway.

They passed by a steep staircase and walked through an open doorway to the kitchen. The table was in the centre of the room; a tray held the teapot and a couple of cups and saucers, alongside the sugar bowl. It made a welcoming sight. Mrs Birch gestured for Cora to sit down, and Emily snuggled into her mother's lap. The room was dark, as kitchens often were in these houses, the rear window being small, and light further blocked by outbuildings in the yard. Washing, strung between one scullery and the next, ensured the view was restricted, but Cora assumed there would be a strip of land beyond the yard. In the kitchen, a neat range sat in the fireplace; cupboards and shelves filled the alcoves either side of the chimney breast. A clothes rack hung from the ceiling and an armchair nestled in the space beneath the staircase. A small dresser stood on the wall between the kitchen and front room, crammed with pretty pieces of patterned china and ornaments of birds and animals. The room appeared to be newly decorated: a dark green wallpaper embellished with acorns and oak leaves adorned the walls. There was little space, but Mrs Birch had made a fine job of displaying hanging plates and small oil paintings in any place they could be squeezed. Barely an oak leaf or acorn could be shown in its full glory, they were so bombarded from all sides.

"I use the front parlour for my bedroom and have the two upstairs rooms to let," Mrs Birch explained. "When it was my daughter living here, we all ate together, but I think it's only fair a lodger has their own space. My son-in-law arranged for a small stove to be fitted upstairs; it has a hot plate on the top, but no oven. I was thinking of a single young woman, you see. Someone out at work." She glanced at Emily.

"I'll be going to work," Cora informed her. "I've been offered a position at the rectory! Looking after the baby. We wouldn't be finished until half-past four, and on a nice day I'll take Emily for a walk or maybe we'll have to get some shopping."

"At the rectory?" Mrs Birch was clearly impressed. "I must say that you seem like a decent young woman and it would be nice to know there's someone else in the house."

"Of course, it would be," Cora agreed. "It can be lonely on your own."

"I'll take you up to the rooms, and you can see if they'll suit you." Mrs Birch seemed to be taking a liking to the young widow, although she still voiced her reservations: "It may not be ideal, so have a proper think. I want to keep the kitchen as my space, but you can go down the alley between the houses and use the scullery. There's a sink of course, and the copper for your washing. It would mean a fair bit of going up and down the stairs at times and perhaps that won't suit you." She stood to lead the way. "Well, you can see for yourself."

Just as Cora had been told, there were two rooms upstairs. The front one had a small double bed, a chest of drawers and a washstand with a mottled mirror hanging above it. To the side of the small cast iron fireplace there was a fitted cupboard with more than enough space for their humble collection of clothes. The bedroom was free from any ornaments and the wallpaper a pale beige with delicate climbing roses. "How lovely," Cora said. "This would be perfect for us." A sense of well-being settled on her, which increased when she looked out of the window to see trees, fields and the spires of two churches, one of them being St Mary of Willesborough.

The second bedroom had become a living room with a narrow table and chairs set by the window, and a couple of armchairs against the opposite wall. There was an oval rag rug on the floor; Emily sat herself in the centre of it and explored the strands of colour. The cupboard and shelves on either side of the fireplace had ample space for food, crockery and cooking utensils and the small stove with its hotplate would be perfect for cooking meals for just the two of them. The walls were again decorated with flowers on a beige background, and it seemed as if the woodwork had been repainted recently.

"This was my daughter's when she was younger, and then of course it became their living room," Mrs Birch informed her. "I've done my best to make it nice for a lodger, and it has the furniture, but you'll need to provide everything else."

Again, Cora walked to the window and this time she peered over the top of the scullery to the privy and a long, narrow garden. Beyond the garden, the ground rose to a wooded area, and to the right there was a small quarry.

"I've got some money in the bank," Cora informed Mrs Birch; there was a hint of pride in her voice. "I was given compensation after my husband was… lost. I'll be able to pay you a deposit and buy everything we need. The rooms would suit me if you're agreeable?"

"You seem respectable and I'm happy to have you lodge with me," Mrs Birch replied. "As long as you can cope without a proper kitchen, and you're happy to use the alley to reach the privy and scullery."

"I'm sure I'll manage very well," Cora said.

"The kitchen is my own area, and I like to keep it that way." Mrs Birch was apologetic.

"Of course, you do." Cora ruffled Emily's hair; the little girl was still exploring the colours on the rug. "Listen, Em, we're going to come and live here; we'll have a bedroom and this back room too. Aren't they pretty rooms? And we can see across the fields from the windows."

Emily looked back at her mother and her face crumpled, the tears began to well up in her eyes. "Johnny," she said.

"Oh sweetheart, we couldn't stay there. We have to find our own home." Cora reached down and lifted Emily into her arms; she turned to Mrs Birch, and said, "It's been a difficult time; I'm sure we'll both settle in very soon. Have you thought about how much money you'd like every week?"

"I was thinking of three shillings, and extra for the coal."

"That's a fair price," Cora replied. She would be eating some of her meals at the rectory and there would be interest earned on her money in the bank. "Would it be all right if we moved in on Friday morning? I start work tomorrow, but Mrs Tibbs said I could have Friday to get the things we'll need. I can give you the three shillings now, and perhaps sixpence for the coal?"

"I'd appreciate that," Mrs Birch said. She led the way downstairs. "Very nice to meet you, Mrs Parkins. I'll show you the privy and garden tomorrow, and no doubt you'll see my daughter over the weekend."

"Ta very much, Mrs Birch. And I'd like to meet your daughter." Cora gave a wave as she walked through the gate. The horse-bus was due, and it would be a treat to take a ride back to the lodging house after such a long day.

The church bells were ringing the hour when Cora knocked at the rectory on Thursday morning. Mrs Tibbs answered the door as before and gave a brief smile, before informing Cora, "In future you can walk around the side and go in through the scullery." She then led the way along the wide hallway and through to a large kitchen.

With its modern range, floor to ceiling cupboards and a large central table, the rectory kitchen made an impressive sight. The ceiling was high, and a window faced out to the side showing an attractive area with mature trees and a gravel path leading to the back of the house. The pantry door stood open, revealing a tempting array of bottled fruit and vegetables, as well as tins and packets. The maid was at the stove stirring a pan of porridge, while bacon and eggs waited on a plate to the side, as well as a loaf of bread.

Alice lay in a playpen, still in her long nightdress. When she saw the new arrivals, the baby immediately let the rattle drop from her hand and rolled over, as if to show off her prowess before giving them a big smile.

"Hello Alice, what a happy girl you are." Cora reached out to touch the small hand. Then she greeted the maid. "Good morning, I'm Cora Parkins."

The maid, a painfully thin woman of about forty years of age, with strands of mousy hair showing from under her mob cap and a pristine white apron covering her plain grey dress, glanced at Cora. Her face remained expressionless.

"This is Mrs Turner. Iris Turner," Mrs Tibbs informed her. The maid turned back to the range and took the kettle off the hob. "You may call her Iris. Mrs Parkins, as you will be caring for Alice, then I think it is more suitable if we call you Cora."

"Of course. The boys I was looking after at Dungeness always called me by my Christian name."

But Mrs Tibbs had no interest in the Rose boys or anything other than her domain. She strode through the kitchen, and out to the scullery, so Cora scuttled after her.

"You and your daughter can put your coats here," Mrs Tibbs instructed. "There's a boot scraper at the door and a good coir mat. Ensure you use them, please."

In the kitchen, Alice was beginning to fret. "May I pick her up?" Cora asked.

"She can go in her highchair," Mrs Tibbs replied, "and your daughter can sit next to her. You can see how difficult it is for me; I left her for a moment, and she is complaining. I do hope you can manage the two of them."

There was a cloth bib on the back of the highchair and another on the chair next to it. *How kind that she thought of Emily,* Cora reflected as she lifted Alice. *Or did Mrs Tibbs think more of saving her rugs and cushions from the porridge spills, rather than the new checked dress?*

Alice gave a huge smile when the bib was tied at the back of her chubby neck; she knew breakfast was coming. "We're going to eat our meals at this big table," Cora told Emily, while placing her onto the kitchen chair. "Won't that be lovely? I'll feed the baby and you must try hard to keep clean."

Mrs Tibbs surveyed the scene, which met her approval. "I can see you're a capable young woman, Cora. I need to tidy myself up before I take breakfast with Reverend Tibbs so please ask Iris if you are unsure of anything. After breakfast, Iris will take some warm water upstairs so you can wash the baby. Her clothes are laid out."

"And then I'll bring them both back here?" Cora checked. It was a lovely room with the heat coming from the range and plenty of space for both the children. "You said there was a box of toys for Emily under the stairs?"

"That's right, and I think you will find this space is ample. It is some distance from my husband's study so he can work in peace. I like to do the housework with Iris, but I thought you could take care of cleaning the nursery." Mrs Tibbs moved towards the door and turned to her daughter, "Now Alice, do eat your porridge nicely; it doesn't do to be greedy." Then as an after-thought: "The garden should be pleasant this morning, but don't forget the boot scraper."

Cora looked towards Iris; the maid was watching her employer leave the room. She raised her eyebrows and gave an audible 'tut' once it was safe to do so, then reached for a couple of small bowls and began to ladle the porridge. Iris made eye-contact when she placed the children's porridge on the table but said nothing. A further bowl and a jug of milk was pushed towards Cora, who gave a cautious smile and received a baleful glare in return. When the children were fed, and their hands and faces wiped clean, Iris replaced her apron with a frillier version before serving Reverend and Mrs Tibbs in the dining room. She said nothing to Cora apart from a brusque 'ta' when asked if the dirty dishes should be placed in the scullery.

"Come on baby, let's get you dressed." Cora lifted Alice from the highchair, then turned to Emily and said, "Up we go, and you can help me, just like a big girl."

The hallway was probably the most elegant space Cora had ever seen. She had been in dance halls and theatres with Stanley, and although those areas were highly ornamental, they were often rather tatty too and the air would be thick with tobacco smoke, cheap perfume and stale sweat. Here in the rectory, there was no overcrowding of bodies; it was quite the opposite with just two adults living in a house which could easily be filled ten times over. Then there was Iris who, no doubt, had a room tucked under the eaves somewhere. The space here in the hallway felt almost as big as Mrs Birch's whole house. Cora's shoes tapped on the tiled floor and the sound echoed through the airy space, then up the staircase. She placed her hand on the wooden bannister and walked up the stairs. The day before, she had followed Mrs Tibbs and felt far too overwhelmed to take in the details. Now the polished woodwork, pretty wallpaper and rural scenes captured in oil paint could be examined in detail.

No wonder Mrs Tibbs must help the maid! I'd think they would need half a dozen maids to look after a beautiful house like this. There was some movement and the rector appeared at the doorway of the dining room. *Lord, I don't want him to catch me dawdling, although he seemed like a nice enough man and I'm sure it was him who said I should have the job.* She continued up the stairs and onto the spacious landing.

In the nursery, Cora opened the curtains. "You're a lucky girl, Alice. look at your beautiful garden." Emily was at her mother's skirts. "There's a little stool. I'm sure you could stand on it and watch the birds in the trees." Cora placed Alice in her wicker basket and arranged the stool so her daughter could stand and gaze out of the window. The little girl was soon absorbed by the activity in the sky and within the treetops.

Alice and her wet nappy claimed Cora's attention; she scanned the room, noting a pile of freshly laundered terry-towelling squares, muslin liners and a jug of warm water on the washstand. "Let's put you in a nice clean nappy and see what clothes your mother has left out for you to wear." Cora smiled at the baby and spoke in a sing-song voice; she was rewarded with a contented gurgle.

When they retraced their steps to the kitchen, the pattern of the day within the rectory was following its set path, which was to become familiar over the following weeks. Mrs Tibbs now donned an apron and had a basket of cleaning cloths, brushes, waxes and a feather duster at her feet. She gave a weak smile. "So much to do in order to keep a home like this as it should be," she said. "The church gives us these beautiful homes, but not the income to manage them. No doubt they expect us to have independent means."

"It is a beautiful home, Mrs Tibbs," Cora replied. "The most beautiful I have ever been in."

"Yet sometimes I think it would be preferable to live in a smaller cottage and to have less responsibility..." Her voice trailed off, and when she spoke again, it was brighter: "But now I have you, and Alice will soon learn not to be fretting for her mother. I can dust and polish without constantly turning to wipe the dribble from her chin – do ensure she always has a fresh bib as the dresses stain so easily."

"I will," Cora tried to reassure the rector's wife. "I've found them in the top drawer, and she has a clean one. Her nappy is fresh, and I'll put Alice in the playpen then go back for the bucket of soiled nappies, which can be soaked in the scullery."

"You have it all in hand." Mrs Tibbs sighed. "Do ask if you need anything and remember the box of toys under the stairs for little Emily. All I expect is that my husband is left in peace; he does his correspondence and writes his sermons in the mornings and you know how the sound of a child's cry can distract one."

"We'll be in the kitchen and then go out for our walk. It's a lovely sunny day, isn't it?"

"How bright and cheery you are," Mrs Tibbs reflected, placing her hand in the basket and selecting a soft cloth with which to dust a mirror.

Feeling rather sad for the woman with the beautiful home, kind husband and lovely baby girl, Cora gave a brief smile which was unseen by her employer. "You girls can stay in the kitchen," she said, "But mind you keep out of the way, Emily. You can watch the baby while I go back for the nappies and then we'll see what's in the toy box."

On the Dungeness headland, not that far away, the two older Rose boys were trudging along the path to their lessons with Mrs Jamieson. Their father was staying at home that morning and when they returned, he would have a hot meal waiting for them. Whilst Jacob was at work, eight-year-old William would take the responsibility of caring for his younger brothers. Their father spoke of finding someone else to look after them, but they all knew that there could be no replacement for

Cora and Emily. At a time when the Rose family were at their lowest, the little girl and her mother had brought a bright light into their home and they had begun to heal. The boys were too young to understand, but they had played a part in Cora's beginning to accept the loss of her husband, bringing pleasure back into her life again. What they did know was that their father was noticeably quieter once more and he was missing the company just as they did. In Willesborough, as Cora pushed the pram along to the main road, and looked in the shop windows, she thought of the family at Dungeness and for a moment allowed her thoughts to dwell on them.

Chapter Nineteen

There was a small knot in Cora's stomach as she ate her fried bacon and egg at the boarding house. The breakfast was much appreciated, but her thoughts were full of the day ahead. She was eager to be leaving Mrs Browne and her room in the attic and set up home in the Willesborough cottage. Usually so patient with her young daughter, Cora urged her to eat the soft egg and squares of bread, while her thoughts were on the first task of the day. She needed to go to the bank and withdraw some money, and after much deliberation had decided that five shillings would be enough for crockery and kitchen pans, as well as a couple of blankets. Mrs Tibbs was preparing a parcel of sheets, towels and rags for cleaning – a generous donation which was to be collected later in the day.

I'll need brushes, and some polish, and soap, and perhaps a bowl or basket to carry our dirty dishes from the backroom and down to the scullery, and a basket for my shopping… Cora's mind raced. *I'm bound to forget something and it all needs doing before the shops close, although I'm sure Mrs Birch would understand and lend me anything I might need, although I'd rather not have to ask.*

Relieved to see Emily eat her last mouthful, the chairs were pushed back. "Ta, Mary, that was lovely," Cora called out to the maid as they left the dining room. "I'm going to the bank and then we'll be back for our bags."

Mrs Browne had suggested that Cora leave their belongings in the hallway and then take the horse-bus to Willesborough after she had been to withdraw her money. Mother and daughter, with the precious bank book secured in Cora's handbag, set off for the town centre, following the directions given by Mary. At this early hour, the delivery boys were busy with their pushcarts and satchels filled with newspapers. They called out to one another, exchanging the reports of the day. In contrast, gentlemen walking into the town, or down the road to the station, kept their eyes on the path ahead and merely nodded to passing acquaintances. There was a chill in the air, but with the promise of warmer spring and summer days to come. Nervous of how to conduct herself in the bank without the support of the kindly solicitor, Charles Scott, Cora walked briskly, pulling Emily along.

"Vicarage Lane, that's the one, between the graveyard and the allotments," Cora said, mostly to herself, before turning to cross the road. This was a new route into the town, taking them to the south side of the church, and past a red-brick police station. "Come on, Emily, we're almost there and, when we've got some money, we can buy the things we need for our new home."

Terraces of cottages were replaced with taller homes, shops, and a tavern. Children played in the street, their faces grubby and clothes stained. A woman stepped out of her doorway and almost walked into Cora. "Mind where you're going," she snapped. The woman's basket was held in front of her, as if ready to be used as a means of ploughing her way through the shoppers. Stepping to the side, Cora just missed some horse droppings. A boy riding a chestnut pony passed by, forcing the pedestrians to side-step again.

A road junction took them into Bank Street, a wider road, with long terraces of matching buildings displaying sash windows, decorative details and ornate doorways. Yet still the lowly side of life could not be ignored: a ragged woman was begging for food, while a tramp still slept on a blanket in an alley, seemingly oblivious that the town had awoken. Cora walked along, scanning the buildings for the emblem of the Pomfret, Burra and Simonds bank. The tension in her stomach increased as she approached the bank, with its tall door standing open, and a brass plaque on the wall stating its name.

A wealth of wood in the form of panelled walls, desks and cabinets gave a sense of grandeur inside. Male clerks in black morning coats and trousers, plaid waistcoats, burgundy cravats and high collared shirts, stood about looking haughty. *How different it was in the little bank in Lydd,* Cora reflected. *Perhaps I could make do with the shillings I have left in my purse and not bother these important men.* A woman bedecked in layers of brocade, feathers arching from her hat, and soft cream gloves, glided into the bank. Cora moved to the side and allowed her to pass.

"Good morning, Madam." A young man approached just as Cora was about to flee, his voice was friendly, not nearly as serious as she would have imagined it to be. "How may I help you?"

"Oh! I've brought my bank book and I need to..." What was the word Mr Scott had said she was to use? "I need to... withdraw. Yes, withdraw some money out. Five shillings."

"Of course, Madam. Come this way..."

It took only a few minutes for her bank book to be examined, the columns filled in and for Cora to be leaving with five shiny new coins in her purse. Her body relaxed as she retraced her steps and returned to the boarding house, before setting off for Willesborough.

By the time the church bells had rung the half-hour, Cora and Emily were standing at the roadside with the bags at their feet. They faced the south, waiting for the first sign of the horse-bus, and before long it could be seen labouring up the road between a mail cart and a flock of sheep. A gentleman astride a black gelding overtook all three at a fast pace, and in the other direction, heading towards the railway station, there came a smart trap followed by a lumbering cart. The sheep were turned and herded towards the market; Emily clamoured to be held in her mother's arms so she could watch the animals until they were out of sight.

"There's another railway station which brings in sheep, and cattle and all sorts of animals," Cora told her daughter. "That would be a sight, wouldn't it?"

From the direction of the main station, there came a low drawn-out whistle and great long sigh as the engine released steam. Then the horse-bus was pausing at the roadside and Cora busied herself with handing over tuppence to the driver. She lifted first the bags and then Emily into the coach and stepped up to join them.

They sat on a bench at the back and, as the horses picked up speed, Cora glanced back at the boarding house, the view down to the station and across the roofs of the roadside houses to the Lion Brewery. Already its chimneys belched the odour of brewing hops. "I like Ashford," Cora said to her daughter, "but I won't miss the stink of that brewery."

The route between Ashford and Willesborough was becoming familiar, as they turned their backs on the turreted church tower and the town centre, before heading towards the river and the corn mill. "Look out for the railway tracks next," Cora said to Emily. Then a few minutes later: "Now, let's see if the donkeys are in their field." Before long, she was pointing out the church, "Do you see Reverend Tibbs' church, with its special spire, like candle snuffers one on top of the other?" Finally, the horse-bus slowed, and Cora was saying: "Out we get, Emily, there's Mrs Birch's cottage: our new home!"

Throughout the journey, Emily spun her head and gazed at whatever her mother showed her. Or found her own amusement in the birds flying overhead, the rabbits scampering over the fields and the spider crawling along the wooden frame holding the canvas roof above them. But her eyes remained serious and no words passed her lips. *She were like this when we first arrived at Dungeness, It doesn't matter; it will all be fine in a day or two, and I'll be scolding her for chatting too much!*

Cora couldn't keep the grin from her face when she knocked on the door of the third cottage in the terrace of three. Those two upstairs rooms would make the perfect home for her and Emily, and a trip to the local shops would bring the items needed to fill the cupboards. By the end of the day she could see them seated at the little table eating a meal cooked on the stove.

"Good morning, Mrs Birch," Cora gushed, as soon as the door opened. "I hope we're not too early, but we have to leave our bags and go to the shops before they close for half-day."

Mrs Birch looked down at the pitiful collection of two bags, "Are the rest of your belongings being sent on?"

Cora followed her gaze, and when she replied her tone was more sombre, "We don't have much. Me and Stan, my husband, were emigrating when I lost him. All the things we had: the teapot, the pans, the carriage clock, they all had to go. There's a box with Emily's books and toys to come from Dungeness, and a few bits of clothing. Not much. Nothing much at all."

"You'll soon make a home here," the older woman replied, her expression serious. "I can see you're determined. You can't replace a good husband, but a few pots and pans are easy enough to come by."

"We'll take our bags upstairs and go along to the shops straight away." Cora reached for her belongings and stepped into her new home. "I hope we won't be no bother, coming and going all day."

Upstairs the sun was shining into the backroom; it cast rays across the windowsill and the table, then lit up the colours on the rag rug, immediately engaging Emily's attention. Cora noted the full coal scuttle by the stove, the curtains hanging straight and clean at the windows, and the glossy paintwork covering life's dents and scuffs on the doors and skirting boards. "Isn't this lovely?" she said to Emily, who didn't look up from the coloured tufts of rag which were all-absorbing to the small child.

Moving through to the bedroom, Cora emptied the bags onto the bed and busied herself with hanging dresses on pegs in the cupboard. *There's plenty of space for summer clothes, and something smarter to wear to church on Sunday.* She closed the door on her one spare dress and the two belonging to her daughter. In the chest of drawers, underclothes and nightgowns were arranged and, in the deepest drawer at the bottom, Cora placed her thick shawl and their cardigans. The sturdy boots, exchanged for newer ones on their first full day in Ashford, were left wrapped in paper and put at the bottom of the cupboard.

"Come on, Emily," Cora called. "We'll go to the hardware store, because there will be no dinner if we haven't got no plates or pans, and we mustn't eat with our fingers. Imagine if Mrs Tibbs got to hear of it!"

Several hours later, when the sun had almost completed its path for the day and now warmed the bedroom with a soft golden light, mother and daughter sat at the table in the backroom and tucked into fried potatoes with cold ham and pickle. Exhausted, but satisfied, Cora looked across at the small stove and the new kettle on its hotplate. "We'll have a cup of tea," she told Emily, "and then you can stay here, and I'll take these dishes down to wash in the scullery." It wasn't ideal having to go along the alley between the houses and into the extension by the back door, and it would have been good to have a stove with an oven for baking bread, but Cora was already taking pride in the home she was creating within these two rooms.

It was chilly in the scullery, and the light dim. The door leading through to Mrs Birch's kitchen was closed with a strip of pale light seeping beneath it. Cora poured the last of the hot water from the kettle into the stone sink, knowing it would cool quickly. She washed the plates, cups and cutlery, then put each item back in the enamelled bowl she had carried them in. *If I take them back upstairs to dry, then I'm not leaving Emily for long at all,* she decided. Cora retraced her steps through the yard, opened the gate to the covered way, and glanced back at the privy. *I'll bring Emily here before it gets dark; there's no need to use the chamber pot any more than we must.*

With the clean crockery left in the bowl on the table, Emily was scooped up by her mother. "I'll take you down to use the privy; we got spoiled having an indoor lav at the boarding house, and that one at the rectory – it's a bit special, isn't it? But this will do for us and there's not many people posh enough to have a fancy one with flowers painted on it." The little girl wrapped her legs around Cora's waist and gazed at her, listening to every word, her grey eyes wide. Yet she said nothing, and her expression remained serious.

Back down the stairs they went, taking care with each step as they were steep and the tread narrow.

They left the house by the front door and turned into the covered way. The privy was a small lean-to on the end of the scullery, with a tiny window facing away from the last rays offered by the evening sun. Although they couldn't be seen in the dusky light, Cora knew slugs lurked in the corners between the damp brick walls and the stone floor. She was careful to remain in the centre of the space and hoped they knew to stay in their own murky area. The wooden seat had a crack in it which threatened to give a vicious pinch if not carefully negotiated. One of them was sure to fall foul of it before long. Yet none of these things mattered compared to the fear imposed by the huge metal cistern fixed to a couple of bent brackets on the wall. It leaned forward, threatening, at the very least, to drench her with water. Even as Cora sat beneath it, something fell upon her shoulder: a slither of rusting metal, a dead spider or merely a smattering of dust? She brushed it aside, none the wiser in the gloom, before reaching for a square of newspaper on a hook. A moment later and poised in the open doorway, she leaned forward to pull the rusting chain hanging from the cistern. A sharp tug was followed by the *kerdonk* of the mechanism, and the rushing of water. Cora retreated swiftly, darting back into the yard, her heart pounding. Emily was once more in her arms and clung on as they retreated through the gate with the sound of gushing water still in the air.

Cora took her daughter to the bedroom and sat her on the bed. "Oh darn, I didn't think to buy a bowl for the washstand," she remarked, looking at the marble-topped cupboard. "Never mind, we've had a dinner and a supper, so I've done well. I couldn't have carried any more back from the shops." There was a dish in the other room which would do nicely, and she wiped Emily's delicate skin clean before putting her into a nightgown.

The little girl cuddled up to her rag doll and listened to stories of make-believe characters and animals in faraway lands, while her eyelids dropped and breathing slowed. Then Cora kissed her on the forehead and went to sit in the armchair. She thought of Stanley and their home in Gravesend. *If only we could have lived in a little cottage like this, we'd have been truly blessed.* She imagined her husband digging over a vegetable plot while Emily played under an apple tree. Her thoughts moved to the barren landscape at Dungeness and Cora pondered upon how it would change once the summer came; she wondered about the three little boys and if they would run free on the shingle while their father worked. In her mind's eye, a small auburn-haired girl ran at their heels and she shook the thought away. *It's just me and Emily now, and she's going to have a lovely time here in Willesborough.*

It was getting dark and Cora realised she had no oil lamp. It would have to go on the shopping list for Monday morning. There was a chill in the air, so she retreated to the bedroom and prepared to go to bed under the smooth sheets and thick blankets provided by Mrs Tibbs. The following day would be spent at the rectory looking after Alice. Then it would be Sunday, a day of rest, and she wondered what it would bring for her and Emily.

Chapter Twenty

Sunday morning saw Cora and Emily strolling along Church Road to St Mary the Virgin. Recalling the fairytale turrets of the church bearing the same name in Ashford, Cora was a little regretful not to be walking to the town. "We must go to Reverend Tibbs' church," she said to Emily. "What would he think if we weren't there?" Although it was not the wrath of the kindly rector she feared, but that of his wife who would be sure to notice their absence. It was another fair day and it seemed as if the sun always shone on Ashford; not one April shower had fallen since their arrival. The church bells rang out and the air was scented with blossom. "It really is a lovely place, isn't it?" Cora continued, knowing that her daughter would not respond, but wanting to share her feelings.

The young widow felt certain her decision to move to Ashford was a good one. All the time the images of the three little Rose boys and their father were held at bay, then her future seemed promising. If her thoughts were allowed to dwell on how they might be coping, or what they might be doing, then the guilt Cora felt about leaving weighed down upon her young body. She wondered if it would have been wiser to have waited a little longer to see what changes the spring brought to her life at Dungeness. But that was not to be and, walking past the school, she brushed away pictures of the boys running on the shingle banks and their father tending the light. Looking down at her daughter – at the shine of her hair and the dear little upturned nose –

Cora felt satisfied that in coming to Willesborough she was able to provide a better life for Emily.

The church was substantial, built of Kentish ragstone under a tiled roof. It appeared to be traditional in style other than the unusual spire, which Cora studied as she approached. "It seems to start, and stop and start all over again," she said, more to herself than her daughter, who had no interest in such a thing. "It's as if they built it one way, changed their minds and added in some little windows, then started again. I wonder what's there, right where those windows are? Perhaps the bells? I'd like to go up there and take a look." But Cora thought of Mrs Tibbs, imagining her disapproval, and knew better than to ask the rector.

Local people filed along the path and through the church porch, to the open doorway where each was greeted and handed a hymn book. The bells now resonated through the centuries-old walls and the air was filled with the familiar smell of a building that never quite recovered from the damp. Shoes were polished, hats were straight and if Reverend Tibbs' parishioners did not have an outfit solely for Sunday best, then they did their utmost to look respectable. Coats were brushed, dirt was sponged from hems of skirts and trousers, and many of the women had posies of spring flowers on their hats or pinned to the lapels of their coats. Cora recognised no one and, with Emily held tightly against her, she followed them into the church. She seated herself in a pew towards the back, with the little girl on her lap.

In the afternoon, Emily slept between the blankets and sheets donated by the rectory, while Cora settled herself at the table with some sheets of thick writing paper and a pen and ink borrowed from Reverend Tibbs. She gazed out of the window, across the scullery roof, and along the strip of garden to the flowering trees at the end. How long had it been since she had last picked up a pen and written anything more than a quick note? Cora's mind took her back to the damp room in Gravesend, where Stanley's overalls dried by the fire and the carriage clock sat in pride of place. Occasionally, not often at all, she had sat at the kitchen table and laboured over a few words, taking pride in a neat loop or an upright line, but despairing of her spelling and grammar.

She dipped the tip of the rector's pen into the ink and dabbed it on a scrap of paper ensuring the excess ink was let free and was not going to spill onto the pristine paper. Cora raised her eyes to the wall and allowed herself a moment to follow the trail of flowers on the beige background. Then she placed the nib on the paper and slowly formed the first words of her letter. The pen was of good quality and gradually neat lines formed. Cora began to relax and when the task was complete, she felt a rare pride in her accomplishment.

> *3 Sand Quarry Cottages,*
> *Willesborough*
> *Ashford*
> *Tuesday 8th April 1873*

Dear Ada and Reuben,
Me and Emily have found a nice place to live in a village called Willesborough, near Ashford. We have two upstairs rooms in a cottage. They came with furniture and a nice little stove to cook on.
Please can you send the two boxes of our belongings which are packed up in the old storeroom.
Ashford is a nice town. We both got smart new boots and Emily has two dresses! We have to look decent because I got work from the vicar's friend,

Reverend Tibbs. I am looking after his dear little baby. It is a girl baby called Alice. They are ever so posh. I miss the boys and I hope Mr Rose has found someone to look after them. Someone who won't go running off.

Thank you for everything you did to help me and Emily.

From your friend,

Cora

Satisfied with the result, Cora pushed the letter aside, ensuring it was fully dry before folding it. Then she started on the envelope, frowning a little as she wasn't certain of the exact address. "I'm sure it will find them," she murmured, writing just three lines on the envelope: *Mr and Mrs R. Roberts, The British Inn, Dungeness.* The following morning, Cora wheeled Alice's pram to the post office and bought a stamp which she stuck onto her carefully addressed envelope. She pictured it arriving at Dungeness, the postman placing it on the bar top, and Reuben then putting it on the parlour table for Ada to open. The scene was so familiar, and tears threatened as the letter slipped into the postbox. Taking a deep breath, Cora placed her hands on the pram, spun it around, and walked back to the rectory at a brisk pace.

A week passed in which Cora became accustomed to the routines of her new role: she learned that Iris, the maid, would never utter more than a tut, a sigh, or occasional word; she watched Reverend Tibbs go about his duties serene and generous with his time; she saw Mrs Tibbs fret over the home and become nervous around her daughter. The days were not difficult, and Alice was a delightful baby, but Cora gained none of the pleasure to be had from caring for the young Rose boys. In their home by the lighthouse she had been welcomed as one of the family. At the rectory she was the paid-help, careful to watch her speech, conscious of her hem being ragged and of any dirt on Emily's hands or boots.

At the end of the week, Cora had seven shillings in her pocket and was able to buy some more items for her rooms in Mrs Birch's house. Here she felt content, appreciating the attractive home and village location. If it was a bother to walk downstairs and through an alleyway to reach the scullery and privy, then the sun pouring into the back room in the morning, the comfortable bed, and the long garden with fruit trees at the end all gave pleasure.

Walks took Cora and the children past the church, and into the countryside where the River Stour split in two and then joined at the corn mill, becoming a pool before flowing onwards. The church spire at Sevington, belonging to another named St Mary's, was in the near distance, and she vowed to walk there one Sunday with Emily. Other times she explored further along the road where they lived with Mrs Birch, pushing the pram past the area with the sand quarry, and then onto a place called Lacton Green with pretty cottages, medieval houses and an oast house.

The small shops in Willesborough had everything Cora needed, and she planned to treat herself and Emily to a hot dinner in Ida's home near the church once a week after work. If her role at the rectory left her spirits a little low at times, then Cora couldn't think of a nicer place to live than Willesborough, with the town of Ashford nearby and countryside all around her.

"Cora, there's a parcel come for you," Mrs Birch announced on a Monday afternoon, a week after Cora had posted the letter to Ada and Reuben. She was standing in the hallway when Cora came back from work.

"That will be some clothes and toys from Dungeness," Cora replied. She turned to Emily who was trying to squeeze past the box in her haste to scamper up the stairs. "Look Em, this has come from Ada and Reuben. It's got some clothes and books and toys in it. Do you remember your bricks and the puzzle Reuben got for you?"

"Johnny?" the little girl queried.

"No darling, not Johnny. He can't come to us in a package!" The smile fell from Cora's face and she lifted the box. "I've got to do the washing, but let's see what's in here and take something out in the yard for you to play with after your nap."

Mrs Tibbs allowed her to settle Alice for an afternoon sleep and go home early to do her laundry on a Monday. In return Cora was to work occasionally on Saturday morning, or even mind Alice during a church service on a Sunday so Mrs Tibbs could concentrate on her parish duties. She took the box upstairs, with Emily clambering up behind her. It remained unopened while the little girl was placed in the bed with her rag doll. "There's no point in exciting you now," Cora said, before placing a kiss on her daughter's forehead. "Not when there's chores to be done."

In an hour most of the wet clothes had been squeezed through the mangle, then pegged on the line in the yard. On Cora's return to the house, Emily was beginning to stir in their bed, her eyes heavy and cheeks flushed. In the back room, Cora began to pick at the knots in the string of her parcel until it fell away, and she could lift the lid on the box. A letter was laid on top of the clothes, which in turn covered the toys. Her heart leapt in anticipation and Cora swiftly unfolded the thin pages, soon recognising the swirls of Ada's handwriting in black ink.

The British Inn
Dungeness
Friday 11ᵗʰ April 1873

Dear Cora,

We have been wondering how you are and hoping for a letter every day. Reuben and I are pleased to read that you found a job and home so quickly. You are a nice young woman and deserve it.

Constable Wilde has been to see us; he was looking for you and sorry to hear you had moved away. He has some news, and it is not something I can write in a letter. Don't go getting your hopes up, Cora. There can be no happy ending for your husband after all these weeks, God bless his soul. I am coming to Ashford on Saturday and if you could meet me off the 9:40 train then we can talk about it. I will stay with James overnight in Lydd so I can leave early and we can have as much time together as possible. Reuben says I am to come to Willesborough to see your lodgings as he wants to be sure you are settled nicely. If Saturday does not suit you then please write to me by return.

Your affectionate friend,
Ada Roberts

Cora was reading the letter for the second time when Emily came into the room. There was something to be told and clearly it was news of Stanley, but no hope that he had been found alive after nearly three months. Her slim body chilled and her throat tightened. *They must have found a body. But they wouldn't know for sure… How could they after all this time?* Emily was delving in the box, pulling out her bricks and books, and Cora knew that she must find the strength to push the images away and to think only of the little girl. She took a book and settled in the armchair, with her daughter on her lap, and began to read. The words flowed and the child's delicate finger followed the familiar lines and images. But while birds and fairies adorned the pages, Cora only saw the water washing around her ankles and heard the shouts and screams as the *Northfleet* lurched towards the end of her journey.

The streets of Willesborough were quiet early on Saturday morning when mother and daughter walked into Ashford. They waved at the milk cart and nodded to the men walking in to work a half-day, but the women and children were in their homes, perhaps sitting around the table with a large brown teapot in the centre and a pan of porridge on the hotplate. An early morning mist settled over the fields and, as they neared the town, the rooftops loomed above it. It was a peaceful world they wandered through, yet Cora was anxious to be on time for the train carrying Ada, and her head whirled as she wondered what news came with the landlady of The British Inn.

"I'd love a cup of tea," Ada said, as they walked out of the station gates and veered to walk up Marsh Road. She had Emily's hand in her own and, as yet, nothing had been said about the purpose of her visit. It was too soon.

"There are plenty of nice places for a cuppa and a bun in the town," Cora replied. "But you've got something to tell me, and I don't want to be getting all upset with people looking on. There's some open ground just along the road here where we can sit and have a talk."

"Fair enough." Ada turned to Emily. "You've got her looking lovely, with new boots and a nice dress. She couldn't be sitting about at the rectory with those old boots on her feet."

"They were good enough for Dungeness though," Cora reminded her, "and I was grateful for everything we were given. Emily was pleased to have her books and the bricks."

They walked past Mrs Browne's boarding house and Ada gave a nod of approval before they crossed the road to an area of open ground with mature trees. A wooden bench under an oak tree beckoned them, and the women sat there, with the backdrop of the town centre behind them. "It's nice and quiet at the moment," Cora said. "But you see over there, past the boarding house, that's the brewery and I don't think I could ever get to like the smell coming from those chimneys; you can't see them but there's a tannery and corn mills down by the river behind it. And there's another railway station just for the livestock market; they've got their own platforms and everything. It's ever so busy there when the animals go to market. The town has its own market, of course, separate from the other one, and some lovely buildings. Oh Lord, Ada, I had to go to the bank and I've never been anywhere so posh in all my life." She paused, knowing there was something far more important to be said, and hoping her friend was ready to tell her.

"It's a lively place," Ada agreed. "And perhaps that's best for a young person." She looked towards the brewery, and then to the station, before continuing, "Constable Wilde came looking for you the day after you set off for Ashford. He had some news, but we couldn't do anything until we heard from you. There's another body needing identifying."

"Identifying?" Cora repeated. "But it's been so long."

"It's not that simple. This man was washed up just days after the incident and buried as unknown. It was only recently when someone worked through all the files, they matched him with your husband."

"Matched him?" Cora echoed.

"There was a photo."

"But they stopped taking photos. It was too upsetting after all that time in the sea." Cora frowned, trying to remember other conversations with Constable Wilde.

"They did stop. But this was taken when he'd not been in the water that long," Ada reminded her. She reached out and took Cora's hand. "It's been nearly three months and there wasn't much hope that Stanley was going to turn up safe. All the survivors came to port in Dover, apart from those who ended up at Dungeness."

"I'm glad he wasn't in the water for too long."

"And now you can visit his grave and say goodbye."

"Where is he?" Cora asked.

"At a little place called Capel-le-Ferne on the hills above Folkestone. The constable said you could travel by train to the town and someone will take you along to Capel. It's a steep hill for a young child to manage."

For a few minutes they sat in silence, allowing Cora time to think about the news. Questions flooded her mind, and with them a sense of acceptance, then relief to know she could properly mourn her husband. Finally, she asked, "They took a photo of him, the body, but how can they be sure it was Stanley? How will I know it really is him lying there?"

"Because they need to show you the photo."

"Show me?" Cora's voice was high, and Emily turned, alerted to her mother's despair. "What do you mean, show me?"

"Constable Wilde has sent it to the police station here in Ashford," Ada told her. "We need to go there to view it, and you must say if it is your husband. They are expecting you this morning. So perhaps we can have that cup of tea and then walk along." She paused and placed her hand on Cora's arm. "It won't be easy, but you'll have me with you, or at least to keep an eye on Emily."

"No." Cora's voice was firm. "It's only two minutes away, the police station. We'll go now and then I can begin to put Stan to rest."

Chapter Twenty-One

The oak table was wide and well worn. It hadn't seen a tin of polish for a long time, if ever. A shaft of light fell upon one corner, emphasising the grain and a deep scar across the wood. A buff-coloured envelope had been pushed to the centre of the table by the policeman, who had seated himself opposite Cora. He now gave it a further nudge. "When you are ready, Mrs Parkins, here are the photographs of the man we believe to be your husband. Take your time."

Cora nodded. Reaching forward, she slid her fingers into the opening and felt the sheen of the paper on her skin. With her heart pounding, she pulled the contents free of the envelope. There were three photographs, all in various shades of grey. The images in the centre were clear, albeit with a few marks or speckles; they faded towards the edge and a neat band of white framed them. One showed a head and shoulders image; the eyes were closed, the lips slightly parted, and there appeared to be a bruise to a cheekbone. *He wouldn't like his hair brushed like that,* Cora thought as she studied the picture of her husband's face. The second revealed the whole body of a young man laid out on a bench, wearing just his vest and long-johns; his limbs were straight and there was no sign of injury. The third image was a close up of a group of three moles on a forearm: a pattern familiar to her.

She turned away and faced the policeman. "That's my husband, Stanley."

"Stanley John Parkins?" the policeman looked at his notes.

"That's right," Cora confirmed. "He looks peaceful, doesn't he?" She pushed the photographs towards him.

"He does, Mrs Parkins." The images were replaced in the envelope. "I'll arrange to have the death certificate sent to your address."

Cora nodded her understanding and gave her details.

"That will be all then." The policeman stood. "I'll see you back to your friend. Perhaps you can go and have a cup of tea somewhere. Give yourself a moment to… to… well, it's not been an easy day for you, and no doubt unexpected after nearly three months.

Cora gave a small smile. "Thank you for your understanding." They left the room and returned to the reception area. "It was him," she told Ada. The older woman merely nodded, and they left the police station in silence, then walked to the town centre.

It was comforting to be in the tearoom. Sitting in the shadows beside a tall potted plant, Cora felt as if she could hide away and allow Ada to take care of Emily for a short time. The tea came and she sipped at it, liking the sensation of warmth running through her body. Gingerbread and fruit cake were placed on decorative plates, which in turn were set on layers of lace and linen cloths. Cora discovered, to her surprise, that she was ravenous, and the cake was devoured. Her mind was on those first weeks at Dungeness when she had fought against anyone who suggested that Stan had not survived. She reflected on the times when those first doubts had crept in, until an acceptance came. "It's almost a relief," she admitted to Ada, when the plates were empty, and teacups drained.

"I hoped it would be," Ada replied, "but the words had to come from you. Now let's take this horse-bus you speak of and you can show me your new home."

The journey to Willesborough encouraged conversation as Ada saw the sights which were becoming familiar to Cora and Emily: the mill and the river, the railway tracks, the windmill and church spire. Once in the village, they paused at the bakery to buy pies for dinner and a loaf of bread. "We don't have an oven, only a hot plate," Cora explained as the bread was wrapped. The next stop was the greengrocer's for vegetables, and the shopping basket was left at Mrs Birch's cottage before they strolled along to see the church and countryside views beyond it.

"There's the rectory," Cora said, as they passed the elegant house set behind a hedge.

Ada gazed at the Georgian house, taking in the details. "Blimey, Cora, I never dreamt it was so posh! Not in a village like this. Imagine you walking up to the front door like Lady Parkins!"

"The front door!" Cora let out a laugh. "No, it's the back door for me and only after I've checked my boots for mud!"

"That's one thing you don't have to worry about at Dungeness," Ada remarked.

"The mud?" Cora replied. "No, I suppose you don't. But there's not much of it on the pavements. I have to watch out on the lanes though."

The next place of interest to point out was the school, and then Bob and Ida's cottage, where teas and hot meals could be enjoyed. Soon they were at the church and skirted the graveyard to look out over the countryside. "Emily loves to see the lambs," Cora said. She held her daughter up high to watch the newborns gambol about on the rough grass. "We've been for a walk over there, by the stream. There's a mill, can you see it?"

"It's a lovely place," Ada replied. "I can see why you like it here."

It was while they looked out towards the river that Ada spoke of Stanley. "Do you feel ready to see your husband's grave?"

"I'd like to do that," Cora said. "It sounds like a nice place, up on the hills. We can take some flowers. Emily won't understand and there's no need for her to try to, but it will do no harm to take her."

"It will bring you peace."

"I'm sure it will," Cora agreed.

No more was said, and the pies beckoned, so the two women and the little girl returned to the cottage. They spoke of other matters: people they both knew, the success James Roberts was making of his public house, The Dolphin, and life here in Willesborough.

"Now, Cora, there's things that need to be said before I go back home, and I think they are best talked over face to face," Ada said. They were sitting on an old bench at the end of the garden. Emily was searching for insects amongst the gnarled roots of the apple trees. "You've got a lovely home here, there's no doubt about it. Those rooms are better than the old store would have been even after Reuben had made the improvements we spoke about."

Cora nodded and waited. Tears were already threatening as she knew within the hour Ada would be back on the horse-bus, and any plans to visit Dungeness were many months away.

"You've got yourself a decent job, with the rector and his wife. Some might say better than looking after those three boys and an old widower."

"Mr Rose isn't that old," Cora objected. "He really isn't. He is just a bit serious and that makes him seem older. And the boys were no trouble at all." Her words flowed with passion, revealing her feelings towards the little family living beneath the lighthouse.

"Exactly!" Ada gave a broad grin. "You've got a good job, but that Mrs Tibbs will always be on the look-out for your faults. You've told me yourself how you have to be careful to speak proper. Jacob and the boys were so fond of you, and he didn't watch over you, and make a fuss about everything. But never mind about all that; you don't need me to point out what a lovely family they are. There's something else on my mind."

Cora waited, knowing Ada wasn't going to hold back with her words.

"It's Emily."

"Emily?" Cora glanced across at her daughter. She was wearing the new dress bought in Ashford on their first trip into the town; it was clean and fitted nicely. The boots had been polished that morning and her auburn curls shone in the sunshine. "What's wrong with Emily?"

"You know very well what's wrong," Ada replied. "I love that little girl as if she were my own grandchild and I saw her come to life after the terrible time she'd been through. You can put her in a nice dress and wipe her face clean, but the girl isn't talking. She doesn't look unhappy, I'll grant you that, but there's something wrong and it needs to be said."

"She's not backward." Cora felt her body tense. "You know that; Emily has had a lot of change and will soon become used to being here."

"I'm sure she will," Ada agreed. "But she settled in once before. That little girl loved the boys - playing and chattering away as if she was their sister. And you took that away from her. She lost her father and there was nothing anyone could do about that, and now she's lost those little boys. What next, Cora? I've not met the rector's wife, but I don't trust her. You can't be sure of someone who suffers from her nerves like she does."

The tears began to well, and the first began its slow descent on the young widow's face; she didn't brush it away. "It's nice here," Cora defended her choice. "But it will take time to settle properly. I was lucky to meet you and Reuben, and I'm so grateful for everything you did for us. Perhaps we can visit, and Emily will see you are not so far away. And if I write to Jacob, then she can see the boys too. We'll leave on an early train and hire a pony and trap… and stay overnight if you'll have us." But even as she said the words, the whole trip sounded difficult.

"It's early days," Ada admitted. "But I won't pretend I'm not worried about the girl. You keep a close eye on her and if she's not chatting away in another month, then I think it will be time to ask yourself why. She's getting tired, so why don't you put her down for a sleep, and we'll have a nice cup of tea before I catch the horse-bus back to the station."

Cora stood and bit her lip a little in an attempt to keep the tears at bay. "Come on Emily," she said. "Time for a sleep. Ada has to go, but we'll visit her soon."

It was only three days later when concerns for her daughter were again at the uppermost of Cora's mind. Alice had been placed safely in the playpen while Emily sat nearby with some picture books. In the scullery, Cora laboured with the clean nappies which needed to be wound through the mangle. Iris was making a sponge cake and occasionally throwing baleful glances towards the children. Alice let out a squeal and threw her rattle out of her playpen; it slid across the floor and the baby let out a huge screech of delight. Emily picked up the rattle and was about to return it, when Cora called out: "There's a good girl, Em. Say 'ta', Alice."

Unbeknown to those in the kitchen, Mrs Tibbs was about to enter. "Mrs Parkins," she called. "You may have encouraged the boys from Dungeness to throw

229

toys, but it is not suitable behaviour for Alice. What is appropriate for boys who roam about on the beach and shingle ridges is not right for a young lady."

"Sorry, Mrs Tibbs." Cora came to the door of the scullery with a wet nappy in her hand. "I don't think, I mean I don't want to be rude, but I don't think it was a game. I wouldn't let Emily throw, and the same for Alice." The water from the nappy was dripping onto her apron, but she daren't turn her back and return to her task. Cora waited. She noticed the children were quiet now, and Alice's face was turning pink, a sign that she was about to start crying unless comforted.

"I can't deny that your daughter is well behaved," Mrs Tibbs replied. "But if she were to speak then I have concerns regarding her vocabulary. You must try, and try extremely hard, to improve your speech. Ta is not appropriate; I wish Alice to learn to say 'thank you', and later 'thank you kindly'. Manners are everything."

"I've been trying," Cora attempted to defend herself. "It just slipped out, what with me doing the washing and then the rattle goes flying… And Emily does speak; she has lots of words. She's just feeling a bit shy at the moment."

"Let's hope for her sake that she is not backward," Mrs Tibbs replied. "She's a good girl and no trouble to have about the home."

Backward. The word flew about in Cora's head. *Backward. I've never thought of such a thing. I'm going to have to make her talk. Be a bit sharper with her. I can't have anyone else talking about Emily and saying she don't have enough words. I'll have to make her talk and I don't know how…*

Her thoughts were interrupted by Mrs Tibbs, who was not done with the subject. "There are plenty of classes for young women who want to better themselves. I suggest you ask your landlady or a girl from the village to mind Emily once a week and you must go to elocution classes."

"*El-ow-cooshon*?"

"It's the art of speaking correctly," Mrs Tibbs informed her. "Lessons would benefit you and your daughter immensely."

"Oh. I never thought of doing something like that..."

"I *hadn't* thought." Mrs Tibbs' tone was sharp. "We'll discuss this at the end of your month's trial." She spun and left the room.

Alice began to wail. Cora tossed the nappy towards the bucket in the scullery; it landed on the edge and the bucket tipped over. Metal hit the stone floor with a clatter. Iris smirked and Cora flashed a scowl in her direction. *I don't know what Iris has to look so pleased about. I've never seen anyone so miserable and she don't speak so why ain't she being sent to el-ow-cooshon lessons?* She untied her apron and slung it on the hook behind the door, then reached for Alice.

With the nappies pegged out on the line, Cora placed the baby in the pram and wheeled her around the side of the house and onto Church Road. When they were out of sight of the rectory windows, Cora lifted Emily, so she perched on the edge of the pram. The little girl held the handle tightly and smiled as they moved along. The pram was high, with a pair of huge wheels at the front and two smaller ones at the back. Alice had pulled herself up and sat beneath the great black hood, but in time she would become sleepy and lie down.

They wandered past the church and along a narrow lane towards the mill stream before Cora turned and retraced her steps. The sun was warm and a cup of tea in Ida's garden beckoned. Alice was asleep by the time the pram was being manoeuvred along the narrow garden path, over which the leaves of the spring bulbs now flopped. The pink petals on the flowering cherry were fading fast and had scattered themselves on the grass. *Mrs Tibbs wouldn't like this. She'd be fussing about the path needing a sweep and sayin' it was time to cut the leaves back from the daffs and tulips.* Cora straightened her back and smiled to herself as she left the pram by the doorway and walked in with her daughter. "Hello, Ida, a pot of tea for me and some milk for Emily please; we're sitting outside with the baby."

After a while Emily slipped off the chair and began to explore the garden, looking back every so often for reassurance. Cora pondered on the prospect of elocution classes. She knew that there were women like Mrs Tibbs, vicars' wives or those with their own income, who wanted to improve the lives of the poor. They were setting up classes and schemes to help the needy and uneducated. Cora had attended her local school, but she had known plenty of girls who were required at home to help their mothers with younger siblings and rarely attended classes. Once she was strong enough to turn the mangle or carry a sopping wet bucket of clothes, there had been no school for her on a washday. She thought of Mrs Birch, who was pleasant but kept herself to herself, and knew she couldn't ask her to look after Emily. *I'll find out about classes first, because it seems like I have no choice, and perhaps Ida here would know of a girl who could watch Emily. I hope I won't have to walk into Ashford, I don't fancy coming back at night when the class finishes.*

There were two letters placed on the bottom stair when mother and daughter returned home that afternoon. Cora picked them up and was easing the seal of one apart as they walked up the stairs. The paper inside was crisp and folded once; she opened it to reveal a neat frame of boxes and, within these, the loops and lines of words in ink. It was Stanley's death certificate; Cora's only record of her life with him. All other papers had been lost at sea. Feeling numb, she placed it in her top drawer underneath her spare corset and bloomers.

"I wonder who this is from," Cora said to Emily. "I don't recognise the writing." She pulled out a piece of cream paper from the second envelope and, with her finger running along the lines, began to read.

Lighthouse Cottage
Dungeness
Monday 21st April 1873

Dear Cora,
I'm sorry to hear from Ada that your husband's death has been confirmed. It is very sad news. I have business in Ashford on the morning of Monday 29th April. My plan is to come by train on the Sunday morning, and stay overnight in Ashford, returning on Monday afternoon. I would be honoured if you would allow me to accompany you to the churchyard in Capel-le-Ferne on Sunday morning. I hope you consider me a friend and these things are best not done alone. Please reply by return.
Yours sincerely,
Jacob Rose

"Emily!" The little girl turned, surprised to hear such joy in her mother's voice. "Emily, look at this. A letter from Mr Rose – Jacob. He's coming to Ashford and we are going to see him! He'll come with us to… to… Never mind where. Won't that be nice?"

Chapter Twenty-Two

Emily and Cora stood on the footbridge spanning the railway tracks and waited for the train to come in from the Hastings line. The little girl wriggled with excitement when they spotted the trail of smoke belching out, then she clung to her mother as a long low whistle was emitted. As it approached the platform, the engine and carriages took shape, until all the details could be seen: the curve of the boiler, the brass pipes, the carefully painted lines, and the face of the driver through a small window. The wheels were turning slowly now, and smoke licked around the station buildings: the painted fascia boards, cast iron canopy supports and the wooden bridge on which they stood.

Through an open doorway, there was a flash of red hair. "*Jay-cu, Jay-cu,*" Emily squealed. But it was too soon to know if it was him, and the moment was gone.

The engine eased to a halt and a stream of white steam gushed out at platform level. Emily hid her face in her mother's shoulder. They waited on the bridge, looking for a glimpse of Jacob; soon they were waving madly, and he was looking up at them. They ran down the steps to meet him on the platform.

"Hello, Em, aren't you looking pretty?" Jacob crouched before the little girl, then stood and spoke to Cora: "And I hope you don't mind me saying, you're looking well. It's good to see you, although I understand it won't be the easiest of days."

"It's better than not knowing, and always wondering," Cora replied. She noted that Jacob was dressed a little smarter than usual, with a tweed waistcoat, a fresh white collar and smart cravat. His hair had been trimmed recently and his cap matched his waistcoat. Cora didn't comment on his appearance: it wouldn't be right.

"Shall we take the train to Folkestone, and stop there for a cup of tea?" Jacob asked. "I hear it's a bit of a trek to the church on the hills at Capel-le-Ferne."

Before long, they were sitting in a carriage and Cora was pointing out the spire of Reverend Tibbs' church, and then all the familiar sights were left behind them. They sped through the countryside with fleeting views of villages, farms and the ruins of an ancient castle. The train stopped at a couple of stations; more passengers got on and a few disembarked. "They must be going for a day trip to the seaside," Jacob suggested. When they passed through woodland, the views became limited as the train continued along tracks set in deep cuttings. Then the scene opened up again, and it was clear they were entering the outskirts of a town. "I spoke with the porter at Appledore," Jacob told Cora. "He suggests we get off the train at Folkestone Central, as there is more likely to be someone who will be standing by with a trap. But first we'll have that cup of tea, as Capel isn't much of a place and I imagine there will be nowhere to eat on a Sunday. And afterwards, how about fried fish and chips near the harbour?"

He had planned it all out, and Cora was grateful. *I'd have felt all of a dither coming here on my own with Emily. It all looks so busy and getting into a trap... heading off to some village on the hills... I can't say I'd be happy about it.* She couldn't express how she felt, and although they were visiting Stanley's grave, there was a feeling of excitement about the prospect of fish and chips. "You've thought of everything," she said. "What a shame the boys aren't here to share it."

"I couldn't bring them," Jacob replied. "I have business to see to in Ashford tomorrow, but I've promised them a trip to Hastings in the summer."

"They'll like that," Cora replied. She wondered what he had to do in Ashford but didn't like to ask.

Their conversation was cut short as the train arrived at Folkestone Central. Jacob busied himself with helping Cora and Emily off the train and then spoke to a porter enquiring as to where they might buy a cup of tea. A few minutes later, they were sitting on wooden chairs at the edge of the platform with cups of weak tea and rather mean slices of bread pudding. "I hoped for better than this." Jacob gave a rueful smile.

"It's a Sunday, and I suppose all the local cafés will be closed; the day-trippers will all be down on the beach, not sitting at the station," Cora reflected. "At least we've been told there will be fish and chips at the harbour, as well as a horse-bus to take us back here when we're ready."

Jacob had given the porter a penny to engage a boy with a horse and trap. He was to take them up the hill to Capel once they had drained their teacups. Impressed at Jacob's ability to plan the day, Cora wondered about his life before he lived at Dungeness. It was easy to believe he had always been on the stony peninsula, but she knew that wasn't the case. Strangely, she didn't like to appear nosy and concentrated on helping Emily with her milky tea.

They didn't linger over their drinks and were soon settled side-by-side in a trap, with Emily secure on Jacob's lap. The road out of Folkestone was steep, at first lined with terraced houses and then occasional cottages. Before long, they were looking back over the town, across the rooftops to the sea. The hill they travelled up was one of a range making an attractive backdrop to the town, but for travellers it made the journey difficult: their position in the cart was perilous as the road zig-zagged to the summit. But once they reached the top, the view was breathtaking.

"Oh, my goodness, look at that!" Cora pointed to the rolling landscape and cliffs, which could be seen across the glittering sea. "Is that France?"

"It is!" Jacob replied. "Amazing, isn't it?"

"It really is," Cora agreed.

The ground levelled out as they approached The Valiant Sailor beerhouse and the trap was turned inland, passing by fields with cattle, sheep and crops. As they travelled higher, the land was open, but the English Channel could no longer be seen. From the trap, they spotted farmhands working on the land and passed the occasional cottage. Emily pointed to birds of prey soaring high above them. The little girl was mesmerised by all she could see.

When they reached the place of worship, it was not set within the heart of a small community, as they imagined, but down a dead-end track, surrounded by trees with long trunks and windswept canopies. The church was ancient and squat; built of flint, under a tiled roof, and a tower barely higher than the ridge.

The boy driving the trap pulled up by the lychgate. "I'll wait here for you," he said. "There's nothing much to look at."

Cora led the way through the gateway and paused to scan the graveyard. Her eyes ran over ancient tombstones, crooked headstones and wooden markers. She saw ragged grass, dried by the warm sunshine and winds which swept by unhindered. Jacob stood behind Cora, allowing her to take her time. When she spotted a mound of fresh soil, he held back, knowing this was her moment alone with her husband.

The grave had a wooden cross, which Cora knelt before to read the inscription: *Unknown. Lost at Sea 26.1.1873.* "But how am I to know?" she murmured, looking towards two other mounds of disturbed soil.

She moved from one to the next, noting they were named. There were no other new graves. "This must be his," Cora thought, returning to kneel on the dry grass near the marker.

"Hello Stan. It's me, Cora. We didn't think it would be like this, did we? We were meant to be in Tasmania, or at least nearly there, by now." She raised her face and gazed past the stone wall, across the field of ripening hay, and frowned a little. The dream of a new life had been short-lived. Just four weeks from when Stan suggested it, to when it ended as the *Northfleet* was hit. "Now it's just me and Emily, and she's not happy. I know that, and I promise you that I'm going to try to get her talking again. We've got a nice place to live. It's homely, and you'd like Ashford, Stan. But I'm not sure about this job of mine and I don't know how to fix it. I'll think of something though." Cora heard Emily laugh and she turned; the little girl was doing something with Jacob, looking at the flowers or searching for insects in the long grass. But this was her time with Stanley, and she faced the grave. "I think of you every day; you're always here with me, in my heart. And I'll make sure Emily knows all about you. And I will look after her... and I'll come up here again and have a little talk with you. But I have to go now, Stan. There's a lad waiting with a trap and it took us a long time to get here."

"Ma." Emily was standing behind her. In her little hand there was a small bunch of daisies, buttercups and grass-heads, already wilting.

"That's lovely, Em." Cora took them and placed them on the disturbed ground. She stood and took her daughter's hand, then stepped away from the grave.

They walked towards Jacob, who was waiting at the lychgate. Cora gave a half-smile. "Ta," she said. "They was just as good as roses or lilies."

The journey back to Folkestone was mainly taken in silence. Cora's mind was full of the churchyard on the hillside, and Jacob respected her need to dwell on memories of her husband. Emily laid her head on her mother's lap and fell asleep. Moving by trap down the steep hill was just as nerve-wracking as going up, although the views across the valley where Folkestone had evolved were spectacular. As they neared the harbour, Cora spoke to Jacob: "I didn't think I'd see him laid to rest, and I'm grateful for you coming with us. I'd have struggled to do all this... find a trap and everything. Now you promised us battered fish an' chips, so I'm going to make sure we all have a nice time and go home remembering a lovely day, but not forgetting my Stan either."

They rounded a corner in the trap and to their pleasure the harbour was before them. It made an attractive picture, with fishing boats riding on the high tide, their ropes creaking, little flags fluttering, and all cosied-up within a high-walled area. On the harbourside there were huts, piles of crates and neat coils of rope. Women in vast aprons were selling fish directly from boxes on the ground, while men were loading the catch into wooden wagons for transporting to markets and shops in the area and further afield. They called to one another, bantered with customers, and hurried the carts away before the fish were lost to the herring gulls. "Bugger off," one woman screamed at a bold gull. "You gotta watch 'em all the time," she called to a passer-by. But the birds didn't care; they knew the game and screeched at one another in the sky as they took their chance at snatching scraps of food.

"Look at that!" Cora pointed towards the railway track. "It's not going over there, is it?" They watched as a steam train crept along and crossed a viaduct before coming to a halt at the station on the harbour arm. "I wouldn't want to go over that, would you?"

"It's the quickest way for us to get back to Folkestone Central," Jacob told her.

"Blimey! I'd rather walk!" Cora replied.

"Then we shall walk. But first, are you hungry?" Jacob asked. "There's a hut selling fish and chips over there, and I thought we could wander along to the Marine Gardens. It will be a lot quieter, and I'm sure we'll find a tearoom so we can finish off with a nice cup before we go back to the station."

"I'm starving," Cora replied. "And I like your idea of going to the gardens afterwards. Is that the place up on the hill with the big houses?"

"No," he said. "It's by the beach. You are thinking of The Leas, and that's for the upper classes to go walking. They won't let the likes of us go there."

Jacob led the way to the fish and chips stall, and before long they were picking pieces of battered cod and crispy chips from within the folds of newspaper. Emily shared Cora's meal and ate with relish. Then fingers were wiped on handkerchiefs, and they left the harbour scene behind them. Walking to the west, they approached an area of open greens, flower beds and terraces of tall houses.

"Are we allowed to walk here?" Cora asked. She had noted the fine ladies, with layers of lace, skirts of beautiful fabrics and pretty shawls. The men were dressed in formal black or a more comfortable tweed, with starched collars, well-trimmed facial hair, and top hats or bowlers. "They're ever-so posh, aren't they?"

"They might be posh," Jacob reassured her, "but we are allowed here, and do you see them look at your beautiful hair and wish theirs was so pretty? And I shouldn't like to be wearing all that lace; it would have got in the way of eating fish and chips!"

Cora let out a burst of laughter. "Imagine them eating from newspaper at the harbour. But they are not to know that we were, and you're right about all that lace!" She straightened her back a little and walked beside Jacob, with Emily running ahead.

*

"Something has come to my attention." Mrs Tibbs spoke to Cora after their midday meal. "Iris shall look after the children and we can talk in the parlour."

"Now?" Cora asked. She was wiping Alice's face.

"Yes." Mrs Tibbs sailed from the room.

Cora glanced at Iris, whose expression was sullen. "I'll be back in a minute," she said to the children, forcing her tone to sound bright.

Mrs Tibbs was sitting in her usual armchair. Cora stepped towards the upright chair by the window. "Do sit down," the rector's wife said. She paused for a moment, looking towards the vase of flowers on a side table and then at the headlines in the newspaper, before returning her gaze to Cora. "It's so important to be seen as respectable, don't you agree?"

"Respectable?" Cora repeated.

"Especially when you are married to a man of the church, or indeed if you work for such a family."

"Of course, Mrs Tibbs." Cora looked down at her clean boots, then at her neat nails. There was a mark on her skirt, and she recalled Alice grabbing at her spoon and then the gravy-soaked potato flying off it. She had been going to sponge it off but had been called to the parlour.

"And you a widow. A newly widowed young woman… God bless the soul of your husband."

"Thank you." Cora bowed her head a little.

"I thought you should know that you were seen courting on Saturday," Mrs Tibbs informed her. "I suggest, my dear, that you think carefully of liaising while you still wear a mourning band and choose carefully while you are in our employment."

"Courting?" Cora repeated, unable to think what Mrs Tibbs meant. Her thoughts spun about, so unexpected was this suggestion.

"You were seen with a man at the railway station."

"I weren't courting… wasn't courting," Cora replied, unable to keep the shock from her voice. "I was accompanied to visit the grave of my husband, Emily's father. That's hardly the place to go courting."

"Nonetheless, you were seen with a man and not everyone is as understanding as myself," Mrs Tibbs reminded her. "Take care, Mrs Parkins, for I should be sad to have to let you go."

"I understand," Cora replied. But as she said those words, her disbelief was replaced with a quiet fury. *How dare someone spy on me and go telling Mrs Tibbs such dreadful lies, and why should I have to tell her what I was doing on a Sunday when it was my day to do as I pleased! Whoever said such a thing must have seen Emily was with me, and did they think I would take my daughter courting?* She said nothing else and merely stayed seated, waiting to be dismissed to the kitchen.

"There is no need to say any more," Mrs Tibbs replied.

Cora stood and as she did so, recalled a time, not so long ago, when Jacob had held her in his arms at the top of the lighthouse. He had made her feel safe for that moment, although it was only days afterwards when she had fled Dungeness and begun a new life in Ashford. Cora thought of Ada and Reuben and how they had treated her as a member of their family. Then she thought of her silent daughter and the three little Rose boys.

"Mrs Tibbs," Cora began. The older woman stared at her; there was no compassion in her face. Cora knew however long she remained in this home then she would never be anything but a servant to the family.

"Mrs Tibbs, if you don't need me here on Saturday, then I'd like to take Emily to visit our friends at Dungeness."

"I do need you," came the reply. "We agreed that you would work occasionally on a Saturday."

"Very well."

"But you can have the following Saturday off."

"Thank you very much," Cora said, as she left the room.

Chapter Twenty-three

The trek from Lydd to Dungeness was difficult underfoot once the track changed to shingle. Cora stumbled in her old boots, thinking of the pavements lining the streets of Willesborough. For Emily, it seemed as if she were born to navigate the stony ridges. She scampered ahead, pointing to the gulls and pulling at her mother's hand. Her skin glowed with the exertion and her eyes were bright. And if her hair was a wild tangle, as the wind whipped it about, then it didn't matter at all: Mrs Tibbs wasn't looking on!

It was the middle of May and, where the landscape had been almost bare of any plant life, tiny wildflowers now grew amongst ragged grass, while pale green lichens took on an intricate beauty amongst a stony backdrop. Brambles had sent out fresh shoots creating a trip hazard for the unwary and woody broom was a flash of arching yellow flowers. Emily squealed and pointed at the goats who had wandered further than the shelter of their pens. In the distance there was a man with a sack, and Cora wondered if he was collecting rabbits from traps. A group of children played on the slope running up to the old Napoleonic fort and, towards the coast, the sun shone on the lighthouse, glinting on the panes of glass. The beach was mostly empty of boats, but figures moved amongst the cottages: women with pails of water or baskets, young children cared for by older siblings, and old men shifting heavy nets in need of repair.

"Ma!" Emily squealed. "Look. William and Johnny and Frank!" She clamoured to be lifted into her mother's arms, straining her small body and pointing wildly. "It is! It is!"

Cora felt the tears well up, and a sensation of love washed over her, not only for her daughter who had not spoken more than one word at a time in weeks, but for the place which had welcomed her and Emily when they had nothing else in the world. "I can see them!" she cried out, lifting the little girl. "There they are, by the lighthouse. We'll go to see Ada and Reuben and then we'll see the boys. I promise." But at that moment, the tallest boy turned, signalled, then all the three boys were waving and running over the shingle, with little Frank being helped along by his brothers.

"Ma! Ma!" Emily shrieked. "Run! William! Johnny! Frank!"

"It looks like Ada and Reuben will have to wait!" Cora grinned at her daughter who was racing towards the lighthouse.

"Run. Ma," Emily insisted.

Within minutes, the children were together once more, and Cora found tears were pouring down her face. Dashing them away with the back of her hand, she gave each of the boys a big hug and kissed the top of their heads. "Look at you all. I'm sure you've grown in just six weeks!"

"Why are you crying?" Johnny asked.

"I'm not crying," Cora protested, pulling her handkerchief from a pocket. "At least, I don't mean to be. They are happy tears; I'm so pleased to see you."

"Happy tears?" the child repeated. "Emily's not crying, but she's talking, and Pa said she didn't. Like when she first came here."

"He told us not to speak about it," William reminded his brother.

"I'm just saying..." Johnny shrugged.

"It doesn't matter." Cora put her arm around Johnny's shoulders and gave him a squeeze. "What matters is that Emily is smiling and talking now."

"Are you coming to see Pa?" Frank asked.

"Of course!" Cora replied. "But we are going to The British Inn first and, after dinner, we'll come to see you all."

"Pa asked Mrs Jamieson to make a cake!" William informed her.

"How lovely." Tears threatened again. "We need to go now," Cora told them. Emily's face began to crumble. "Come on Em, we'll go to The Brit first and see them all again soon; won't that be wonderful?"

The boys hugged the little girl, turned to face the lighthouse and raced away. Cora could hear them bickering over who would be the first to tell their father that the visitors had arrived. Emily let go of Cora's hand and now she was scrambling along in the direction of the beerhouse, aiming for the kitchen. As they reached it, she brought her small fist to the door and knocked on it as hard as she could.

"I seen William and Johnny and Frank!" Emily blurted out as Ada opened the door.

"Did you?" Ada picked up the little girl. "I bet they were happy to see you!" She grinned at Cora. "Come on in. I can't tell you how glad we are that you've come to stay with us."

Cora stepped into the kitchen. It was as she remembered: the basket of clean tankards and glasses on the side, the kettle on the hotplate and a loaf of fresh bread in the centre of the table, the smell of fish. "Mmm, dinner smells good!" she said, voicing her appreciation.

But Ada was gone, with a jubilant Emily in her arms. "Reuben! They're here!" Cora heard the door of the bar open, and the familiar smell of tobacco smoke and ale flowed through into the home.

"Already?" Reuben called. "Blimey, they must have raced across the shingle, and with no backstays."

Then they were back in the kitchen and Emily was in Reuben's arms, with a huge grin across her face. "Hello Reuben," Cora greeted him. It seemed as if she had never left.

"Hello Cora, love. Thank God you came visiting. Ada was missing the pair of you, I can tell you." He reached over and put his arm around Cora's shoulder. "Where's your bag?"

"I left it outside, by our room," she looked towards the back door and the covered area leading to the old store.

"That's not your room, not anymore," he said, going out to pick up the bag. "Come on..." Reuben headed out of the kitchen and through a doorway leading to a further lobby area. This was where the family had their bedrooms and an area Cora had rarely ventured. "No need to keep a room for a son who has his own home in Lydd now," Reuben said, as he opened a door. "Someone's been keeping me busy, as you can see."

Cora walked into the space she knew to be James' and stopped to gaze at the transformation. The walls were freshly papered in cream with trailing roses, and the curtains were a dark pink. There was a single bed and an additional one for a small child, a chest of drawers and a washstand with a mirror. In a box on the floor she saw a wooden puzzle, some picture books and a pair of cloth dolls. Cora felt the tears forming again. "What's the matter with me?" she asked, reaching for her handkerchief. "It's lovely, Reuben. I've never seen anything so pretty." She went to the window and peered out to see but miles of shingle ridges, and the occasional goat. Emily had wriggled out of Reuben's arms and was looking through the toy box.

"It's a pleasure to have you here," Reuben said. "I'd better get back to the bar and I'll see you at dinner time, which shouldn't be long now."

An hour later, both Cora and Emily had cleared their plates of fish pie and it seemed that an afternoon sleep was the last thing on the little girl's mind.

"I'm sure three boys and their pa are waiting to see you," Ada commented. She saw Cora look towards the pile of dirty dishes. "Go on, it's been lovely to see you, and the clearing up will be done in no time."

"Ta, Ada. It was lovely." Cora reached for Emily's hand. "Come on, let's go and see the boys. It's warm enough to go without a coat, fancy that!"

Long before they reached the lightkeepers' cottages, the door to one of them opened and three boys spilled out, calling for their father to follow. Jacob appeared, with a smile on his face. *He looks younger every time I see him. It must be that he is coping now, and the summer makes everyone a bit happier. His eyes crinkle around the edges when he smiles, and they don't look sad no more.*

Emily ran ahead, in the best way she could on the stones, determined to be with the beloved family, and shouting their names one after the other: "William! Johnny! Frank!"

"Hello Jacob," Cora said. "Look at her! I don't know what Mrs Tibbs would say with all this shouting and running about!"

"I don't think the rector's wife would be very impressed!" he replied, with a grin. "We'll have to be glad she didn't come with you."

"Oh Lord, imagine that!"

Emily was at Jacob's legs babbling away about something, her words all mixed-up. He crouched down to listen and, at that moment, Cora felt she couldn't be happier to be with all her favourite people in one day.

As that thought settled in her mind, it was replaced with a feeling of horror. *What have I done, leaving these boys and their pa to go and sit about in a posh house and have lessons in speaking proper?* She pushed it aside, just as she had done with the earlier tears, and gave herself a stern talking to. *Now don't go getting soppy over them. It's no life stuck out here with the reminders of what happened, not when we can be in Ashford with all them smart buildings, the countryside and nice little schools for Emily when she's bigger.*

"Pa said he'll take us all up the lighthouse," William announced. "But Johnny and I will have to be very careful, as you and Pa will be looking after the little ones."

"Not me!" Frank scowled. "I'm bigger than Emily."

"You'll hold my hand or stay behind," Jacob told him; his voice was stern.

"Or Cora's hand?" Frank pleaded.

"And Emily can go with your pa?" Cora suggested.

"Shall we go now, or let them play out here for a while and we'll have a cup of tea?" Jacob asked.

The children decided for themselves – a ball was produced and soon they were running, kicking and throwing it about, in some form of a game which was unique to those who didn't have a grassy field or a road to play on.

"Shall I make the tea?" Cora asked, and then suddenly felt a bit shy. *I mustn't walk in and make myself at home, like I never left them.*

"I won't say no to that!" Jacob replied. "There's a Victoria sponge on the side, but perhaps for later?"

"With jam," Johnny added, as he raced by.

Cora walked into the living area of the Roses' home. It was so familiar, yet different: the blanket thrown over the back of Jacob's armchair was new, and Cora wanted to reach for it and feel if it was softer or thicker than the one it replaced; the central table had been moved a little, almost tempting her to push it back into place; the teapot into which she spooned tea-leaves was new, causing her to wonder if the old one had been broken. She wanted to walk in and find it all as it had been, but this wasn't her home or her workplace. It was unreasonable to feel like this and she knew it. Cora poured the boiling water into the pot and admired the sponge cake on its cut-glass plate. *Stop being foolish and enjoy your day with them,* she silently scolded herself, before walking outside with two cups and a smile on her face.

An hour later, and the climb to the top of the lighthouse had begun. "At last you'll see Dungeness at its best!" Jacob had said, when they started on the first set of wooden stairs.

"I think I already have," Cora replied. Sitting by the cottage, sheltered from the breeze and with the sun on her body, she had relaxed more than she thought possible.

When she reached the top of the last ladder, with Frank just a couple of steps ahead of her, Cora held his waist as he clambered through the trap door. As they surfaced from the gloom of the tower, her first impression was how bright it was in the lamp room. Then the heat wrapped itself around her, its intensity almost stifling. The roof did little to shield them from the sun's rays which beat down upon the headland through a cloudless sky. It came as a contrast to the stale dampness they had become used to as they rose through the various levels to the top, where small windows allowed only narrow shafts of sunshine to penetrate.

Cora pulled her body through the hatch and faced Jacob. He grinned at her, "Perhaps I should have warned you it would be a bit warm!"

"Blimey! I thought Dungeness was always cold!" she replied. "But you've got a hothouse up here; you could have lemon trees and grow tropical plants, like they do in those glasshouses I've heard about!" Cora breathed in the warm air and felt it on her skin. For a moment she recalled the vision of life in Tasmania where the sun would always be warm and fruit abundant on the trees. She looked across at Emily, whose tiny hand was held by Jacob, and then turned towards the sea.

"It's gone," Jacob said, recalling her distress on the first trek to the top of the lighthouse. "There was a storm, perhaps three weeks ago, and afterwards we saw the ship was no longer there."

"I'm glad," Cora replied. She couldn't express her thoughts any further but knew, now Stanley was buried, it only seemed right that the *Northfleet* had settled on the seabed.

The fishing boats were coming in, and with them the gulls. Cora gave her attention to the activity on the beach and concentrated on the children's chatter. Finally, she moved to stand beside Jacob and gazed over the shingle ridges, now showing patches of green plant growth amongst the shades of grey and brown.

"There's Lydd," he said, pointing towards the church tower and rooftops. "It's too far, isn't it? Too far to walk to school or to get some shopping."

"It is," Cora replied. "But you have everything you need here."

"But I went to school," he persisted. "It doesn't seem right keeping the boys here; I wonder if it's the best thing for them?"

"They seem happy enough," Cora said. "Reuben told me there has been some talk about a school being built here at Dungeness. A proper school, with teachers!"

"The vicar mentioned it to me last week," Jacob replied. "I worry that it won't be soon enough for William though, he'll be nine at the end of June."

Unsure of how to respond to this, Cora said nothing. She crouched beside the younger children and pointed out landmarks; it turned into a game of I-spy, which occupied them for a while. Then they moved away from the heat of the lantern-room, allowing their feet to find a way onto the rungs of the ladder. Jacob closed the trap door and for a moment they were in darkness.

Sitting at the central table in the living room, Cora found she had become accustomed to the small changes in the home. When the children slid from their chairs and emptied a box of bricks onto the floor, Jacob returned to the subject of his sons and the concerns for their education. "If it happens at all, then I can't see a school being built in time to be any use to William. And who would want to come and teach here?"

"If it's made of wood with a tin roof then it won't take long," Cora suggested.

"Vicar said the church in Lydd are going to plan it and oversee the construction. They say it will be of brick or concrete block," Jacob informed her. "It's going to be a big task getting all the materials here by cart."

Cora pondered over this. "I can't imagine it," she said. "What about the vicar? Would he teach the boys when they get older?"

"He'll do a few mornings, but it's not the same as school..." Jacob said. "I'm probably worrying over nothing though. It won't take long to build, and when it's ready a lot of my problems will be solved. In another year, all three could be out having lessons for the day, and I could get a local woman to come in to do the washing and cook us a hot dinner. We'll manage until then."

"I'm sure you will," Cora agreed, although she couldn't quite see how he coped at the moment. It wasn't right to leave William to look after the little ones so much, and it seemed that there had been no one employed to replace her.

"Listen, I don't know if I should say this, but it's better said in person than by letter." Jacob paused and topped up Cora's cup of tea; he glanced at her and then looked away. "I know you have a lovely home in Ashford, and everything I hear about the town and the village you live in… well, it sounds a darned sight better than being stuck out here. But there's that Mrs Tibbs and she sounds like a right stickler, and I'm sure one baby girl is easier than three boys but..."

"You're right," Cora agreed. "There's nothing wrong with little Alice, but I'm always having to watch myself." She recalled being summoned to the front parlour having been seen with Jacob, and felt the colour rise in her cheeks. "I'm sure I'm going to have to look for another position and I don't want to leave Emily if I have to work in a shop or a café."

"It's not my business to talk about Emily." Jacob watched the little girl for a moment; she was chattering away and leaning against Johnny while he helped her build a tower with wooden bricks. "But she seems different from when I saw her two weeks ago."

"She loves being with the boys."

"What I'm trying to say," Jacob persisted, "is that there's a local girl who is going away to work in service at the end of July. She'll be helping me out regularly until then, and you can see I need it. Come again, perhaps in another month, and if you wanted to come back then we can talk about it. Perhaps it would be the best solution, and this way you have no need to rush into any decision."

Chapter Twenty-Four

"Good evening, Mrs Parkins." Mrs Staples spoke slowly, her tone clear and crisp. It rang out in the back room of the chapel.

"Good evening, Mrs Staples," Cora replied. Her voice was rushed; she had been forced to run most of the way. Emily hadn't settled; the little girl seemed to know her mother was planning on slipping out for the evening.

"We missed you last week."

The two other young women looked on. Cora knew they were glad to have the attention shifted from themselves and she didn't blame them. "My daughter… she had a fever an' I didn't like to leave her."

"My daughter had a fever and it seemed unwise to leave her."

"Yes, Mrs Staples."

It was dim in the room: the evening sunlight slipped through small windows, framed with heavy curtains in a dark green flock material; the partially panelled walls and the doors to the chapel, scullery, and a storeroom were all stained a dark brown. Cora glanced at the other women, both unmarried and about twenty years of age. She gave a slight smile and they acknowledged it with a flicker of their lips. Like her, they stood upright, their eyes alert and hands fiddling with the material of their shawls. Mrs Staples had never invited them to sit during any of the three classes Cora had attended.

"We'll start with you, Mrs Parkins." She was handed a piece of thick paper by the teacher; the print was large and beautiful with elaborate curves and loops. The page was embellished with flowers and leaves on the corners. "This is by Christina Rossetti. I will read it first, and then you, Mrs Parkins, will take your turn.

Unmindful of the roses,
Unmindful of the thorn,
A reaper tired reposes
Among his gathered corn:
So might I, till the morn!

Cold as the cold Decembers,
Past as the days that set,
While only one remembers
And all the rest forget –
But one remembers yet."

Cora scanned the lines as Mrs Staples read; she frowned at *reposes* and *morn*, words unfamiliar to her, then noted the pattern of the rhymes. Her attention moved to the title of the poem and she felt her body stiffen and chill. Mrs Staples stopped reading and there was silence in the hall. The words blurred and shifted like the tide on a calm day. Cora blinked and they came back into focus, but she couldn't bring herself to read them.

"Come along, Mrs Parkins." The voice of the teacher was brusque: it demanded a response.

"It's the title *One Sea-Side Grave.* It don't sound like it's about the sea, but the title says it is," Cora attempted to explain her confusion.

"That is the joy of poetry, Mrs Parkins: to explore the meaning of it and learn to appreciate its form. Now from the first line please – *Unmindful of the roses.*"

"*Unmindful of the roses,*" Cora began. She thought of Stanley's grave, not a seaside grave but a hillside grave. "He doesn't have roses."

"He doesn't have roses?" Mrs Staples repeated. "I was led to believe you could read the lines. Start from the top again."

"I don't think I can read about seaside graves or any kind of graves," Cora babbled. "How can there be corn and roses and all sorts if the grave is at sea? I can't do it Mrs Staples, not reading about graves. I'm sorry." She stepped forwards and handed the paper to Mrs Staples, who took it without speaking, then the young widow turned and fled from the room.

Once out on the street, Cora leaned against the wall of the chapel. The evening was warm, and a soft light was cast upon red brick walls and rooftops of slate and tiles. *Oh Lord, what have I done now? That Mrs Staples weren't to know about what happened and all those people lying there with the ship. Now she'll tell Mrs Tibbs and she'll be complaining about me again. I should go back in, but I can't face it. Perhaps I can write her a note explaining.* She pictured her words on a sheet of thin writing paper. *No, I can't do that; she'd only say my scribbles aren't good enough and have me going along to more lessons. I'll just have to try harder to talk proper. I'll listen to the rector and Mrs Tibbs and try to talk like them.*

Voices were coming towards her, and Cora didn't want to be seen loitering by the chapel, so she pulled her shawl into place and stepped out from the shadows onto the pavement. She walked briskly past shops and homes. Willesborough was a village of three parts: there was the area not far from Ashford then, separated by a few fields, it began again ending by Sand Quarry Cottages. The third was past Reverend Tibbs' church and an old house called Boys Hall; here the housing was under the name of South Willesborough. Unable to face going back to her rooms, and knowing Emily would be sleeping, Cora turned and walked past the rectory to the church. Before long she was peering through the trees and across the lawns to the country house built in Jacobean times. She wondered about the people who lived there and if the staff had to have elocution lessons

A couple of figures appeared from the side of the house and strolled along the front driveway towards the gates. Aware it was becoming dark and it may not be wise to be wandering the country lanes, Cora changed direction and scurried back to Church Road where cottages fronted the street and the area felt safer. With the disturbing title of the poem still on her mind and the first line playing over and over, she passed the rectory, turned at the top of the road, and was soon nearing Mrs Birch's home.

Although the sun had now set, the sky was still light, and Cora could see Emily curled up in the bed. She sat beside her and stroked the little girl's hair. It had been three months now since they had come to live in Ashford, and two months since they had visited Dungeness. "I must ask Mrs Tibbs if she would allow me to have an extra day off work so we could go to Dungeness for two nights," she whispered to Emily. "You'd like that, wouldn't you? If we don't go soon then you'll forget how to talk, and I know you'll want to chatter if you see the boys."

Emily was over two-and-a-half-years old now, and never spoke freely. She said please and thank you when expected to, and would say the occasional word to Alice, who was now a competent crawler. Cora reflected on those first days at Dungeness when Emily had fallen silent but had soon been interacting with the other children and forming new words every day. She knew her daughter wasn't backward but noted how other people looked at her with sympathy when they saw that the child barely spoke.

"I know what we'll do," Cora whispered to the sleeping child. "We'll go to Ashford on Saturday and look for some nice picture books. Some with birds like the vicar had; do you remember how you used to sit on the floor of his wooden home and look at his books?"

Feeling pleased by her plans to encourage Emily to talk, Cora left the sleeping child and moved through to the back room. She busied herself with the teapot and kettle, then settled in the armchair. The room was almost in darkness, but she lost herself in thoughts of visiting Dungeness and seeing her daughter thrive in the company of the three Rose boys.

To step into the horse-bus, knowing they were heading for the town, gave Cora's spirits a much-needed lift. She held Emily on her lap and soon they were looking at the familiar shops and homes from a higher perspective. Then came the sheep and cattle in the field between the village and the town – always a delight for the little girl. Next Emily was pointing at the donkeys, a favourite for her, and it was almost as if they were going on a daytrip, rather than along the road to Ashford. The little girl wriggled, pointed, and smiled, bringing pleasure to her mother who was determined the outing would be a success. Before long, the road was lined with tall buildings and the horse-bus stopped at the end of the High Street.

"Ta very much," Cora said, as they stepped down. She could hear a change in her voice; it sounded younger, less burdened by responsibilities.

It was the middle of the day, and the wide street running through the centre of the town was crowded, both with people and stalls, odd tables or even individuals with boxes of assorted trinkets. The best of the fruit, vegetables, and meat had already sold, but Cora was not looking for food. She had been to her local butcher when the shop in Willesborough first opened and had a small piece of stewing beef on the cool slate in the scullery. She had also filled her basket in the bakery and greengrocers, and the food was stored in one of her cupboards. The market traders still called out to customers, but unless she saw a stall with books, then Cora was determined not to buy anything unnecessary. She kept to the side of the street and walked past the pavement displays belonging to the shops, which vied for attention with the market traders.

Outside the tall buildings, there were tables of clothing for those in service: from frilly aprons for serving dinner, to overalls for gardeners, and smart black dresses and trousers, all neatly folded. Kitchen pans and utensils were randomly displayed in wicker baskets and household linen - sheets, tablecloths, and napkins – were arranged on a long bench. From new items to second-hand, Cora passed the racks of clothing without even pausing to take a closer look until she came across a selection of second-hand books.

It was whilst browsing through her third box of children's items, she turned to spot Emily holding up a book in a genre of its own, having no place amongst those for children or adults. It was a bound manuscript of sheet music pages, once used for composing and now taking on a new life as a lively bird embellished each page. The creatures were plump and colourful, each one full of character and cheer; some clung to the lines or staffs as if clutching a branch while others flew freely on the page. If their colours were a little brighter, and their expressions a little bolder than the birds Emily watched in the garden or on the beach, then this could only enhance her pleasure in them. She lifted the pages with a care beyond her two and a half years, while babbling away in childish wonder.

"How much do you want for this?" Cora asked the shopkeeper who hovered in the doorway.

"It's a funny old thing; I was in half a mind to put it on the fire," he replied. "Give me a penny and I'll be happy."

"I'll have it for my daughter then," Cora replied.

"She wouldn't like some fairy tales or nursery rhymes?"

"No, this is just the sort of thing she likes." Cora took the penny from her purse and handed it to him. "Come on, Emily. We'll go and get a cup of tea and look at this together."

The little girl held the book against her body with one hand, and with the other she reached for her mother.

*

Cora picked up Alice and returned her to the rug. The baby was eager to crawl across the lawn, to pick up leaves and run her fingers through the grass. She wanted to take a piece of earth or a stone in her pincer grip and feel the texture of it on her tongue. But Mrs Tibbs was ever watchful of a grass stain on the skirt of a dress, or a scuff of mud on the elbow of a cardigan. While Emily roamed under the fruit trees, looking for beetles in the bark or trails of ants in soft soil, Alice was frustrated by the limits to her world and her face began to turn red while tears welled.

"Come on, baby. Let's do some walking," Cora cooed. She swung Alice up high and set the child on her feet, taking most of the weight by holding her chubby arms. The child screeched with delight, and set off at a good pace, determined to explore as much as possible. They headed towards the fruit trees.

A few minutes passed and Cora sensed that someone else had come into the garden. Scooping Alice into her arms, she turned to see Mrs Tibbs.

"How nice to see the children having fun," Mrs Tibbs said, her merry tone giving away none of her true feelings.

"It's a lovely day," Cora offered.

"Perhaps you could put Alice on the rug," Mrs Tibbs suggested. "I'd like to speak to you."

"Yes, of course, but she keeps crawling off and it's a job to keep her on there in one place."

"I hoped her wilful nature would have lessened by now," Mrs Tibbs replied. "I suggest a sharp tap to her hand when Alice places it on the grass, and she'll soon learn. It was your lessons I wished to speak to you about, Mrs Parkins."

Darn, she's been speaking to that Mrs Staples about them lessons on speaking proper. Cora fixed a smile on her face and waited for the reprisals.

"I met Mrs Staples yesterday," Mrs Tibbs continued. "What a good woman she is, to help with cleaning the church and to do her best to offer young women opportunities in life. She tells me you missed one of her lessons and then left before the next had finished. In fact, you ran out giving no explanation!"

Cora felt her face begin to redden. "It was the poem. I couldn't… I couldn't read it. How could I read about a man lying in a watery grave? It was awful to see them words and think of it all."

"Perhaps you could have allowed the poem to offer you comfort?"

"It made no sense at all," Cora tried to explain. "How could there be roses and corn if the grave is underwater?"

"A desire to understand poetry would be something to treasure," Mrs Tibbs replied. "But you are there to learn to form your speech in a more appropriate manner. The subject of the poem is of no consequence."

Consequence. Cora frowned and considered the meaning of the word, and then she realised it didn't matter. She looked at Emily who had stopped playing under the trees and was watching the exchange between the two women. The little girl always paused

261

in her game when Mrs Tibbs appeared. Cora glanced at Alice who had crawled several feet away from the rug then stopped, also seeming to sense the tension.

"I told her you'll be at next week's lesson with an apology and the intention of participating in every session until we see a marked improvement." Mrs Tibbs' tone was sharp as she ended the conversation, "That's settled then. Time for your morning walk, I believe, and don't forget to give a rap to Alice's hand if she strays from the rug."

"I think, Mrs Tibbs..." Cora spoke just as the older woman was about to turn away. "I think this isn't working for either of us. I'll work until the end of next week and you can find someone else to look after Alice. She's a lovely baby and you shouldn't find it difficult to find a girl who speaks nice and can look after her."

Chapter Twenty-Five

Despite it being the middle of summer, the fog rolled in from the sea on Cora's first morning back at Dungeness. Throughout the night, the foghorn had blasted its mournful message to passing ships. While Emily slept, Cora was wakeful, unused to the constant disruption to her sleep. She wondered if Jacob was working on the beach, shovelling coal into the firebox and maintaining the pressure in the boiler, then controlling the steam through the trumpet. He had often said that it may be a dirty job but was warmer than tending the electricity generators outside or the lights in the lamp-room.

"Thank the Lord it wasn't all foggy yesterday," Cora said to Ada over breakfast. "I couldn't have walked here in weather like this."

"You never know how it's going to be when you live by the sea," Ada replied. "The sun will burn it off and I reckon we'll be complaining of being too warm by lunchtime.

Knowing the boys would be at their lessons and happy to be with Ada in the home, Cora kept busy. She donned a vast apron and cleaned the bar area, brushing off all the stools and tables with a stiff brush before wiping them. Then she dusted behind the bar and tidied the glasses.

"We're not in the rectory now!" Reuben said, as he hauled a barrel into place.

"It's good to be useful," Cora told him. "And I don't need to look after Emily." The last time she had checked, the little girl was standing on a kitchen chair, with her hands in sticky bread dough, and chattering away while she worked with Ada.

Later, they walked to collect milk with the fog still snaking around them. Drawn to the sea, Cora and Emily stood amongst the boats on the ridge but a view of the Channel eluded them. The air was still and the sea slapped upon the beach, then dragged the shingle into its depths. It was a sound that had always soothed Cora, and she reflected on her lowest times, while grateful she now had a happier future ahead of her.

"Come on Emily, we had better go for the milk." Cora turned away from the beach. "And after dinner we'll go to see the boys."

By the time dinner was finished, the fog had almost burned away and only the horizon bore the hazy remains. It had been two months since they had seen the Rose family, yet it was clear Emily's enthusiasm for the boys had not diminished. She was calling for them as they approached their home. William opened the door, closely followed by his brothers and a girl of about fourteen years.

"Hello Cora," the girl said. "We didn't know you were coming, at least Mr Rose didn't say."

"I decided in a bit of a rush, and they only got my letter at The Brit the day before I arrived," Cora told her. "How are you getting on with the boys?"

"It's all right, I'm used to children," Connie replied. "There's four younger than me at home. But I'll be leaving in a couple of weeks. I was given a job at a hotel in Hythe, and I'm looking forward to it."

"I hope you like it and you are going to meet an awful lot of different people." From the doorstep, Cora watched the children running about and chattering.

"Look at them," Connie said. "Your Emily looks like their little sister."

Cora smiled, knowing it to be true. She would miss being in Ashford but had made a promise to Stanley that she would do the best for Emily and this was where their daughter was happy. Jacob had once mentioned the five of them becoming a family, and over the past weeks the idea had played on her mind, developing into more of an attractive proposition.

"Has he got anyone else to look after them?" Cora asked. There was no point in her coming and suggesting she had her old job back if he had someone to take over.

"No. I don't know what he is going to do," Connie replied. "But I think he has something in mind."

"What time does he finish work?" Cora glanced up at the lighthouse, wondering if he was in the lamp room, or traipsing up the stairs.

"Work?" Connie replied. "I thought you would know, but of course he didn't say you were coming. Mr Rose has gone off somewhere, and he won't be back until late this evening. He went at first light yesterday morning, before the boys woke."

"He's not here?" Cora never considered that Jacob would be any further than the lighthouse or the foghorn. "Where has he gone?"

But Connie didn't answer; her mind was elsewhere. "It's lucky you came because I'm in a right fix. Ma has twisted her ankle, and Pa went over to Rye to see his brother. I'm needed at home to help but I can't leave these three, can I?"

"You want me to have them?" Cora couldn't help grinning. "I'd love to. You get back to your ma and don't worry."

"That's a relief; Ma will be pleased." Connie reached for her shawl, pulling it from the coat hooks, and stepped outside. She lowered her voice and said, "You asked where Mr Rose has gone. I don't know but this is the second time in a month he's taken himself off somewhere."

The evening came and after a supper of bread and jam, with warm milk, the children got ready for bed. They sat on the rug listening to a story about fairies and goblins, and soon Frank and Emily were becoming sleepy. "Time to get the little ones into bed," Cora said.

"Emily hasn't got a bed," Johnny pointed out. "Not here anyway."

"She can go top-to-tail with Frank and I'll carry her home when your dad gets back." Cora took her daughter's hand and led her into the bedroom. Johnny gave Emily a soft rabbit to hold in bed and she settled down without a fuss. Frank seemed to accept having to share; he fidgeted a little, pulling the blanket so it was tight around him, and closed his eyes.

The older boys were allowed to sit at the table with a puzzle for a while, and both gave Cora a hug before going to bed. Unable to settle in the armchair, Cora made sure the home was tidy. She straightened the rug and plumped the cushions on the armchairs, then went to the scullery and picked up a couple of jugs before going out to the pump.

It was becoming chilly outside, and the sun was dropping below the hills at Fairlight. Its rays were beginning to soften and spread in wings of soft orange and red across the sky. In another hour it would be dark and, for the first time, Cora wondered if Jacob would return that night. *I'll have to sleep in the chair. I'm not going to help myself to his bed, but I might have to take a blanket.* She pressed on the handle of the pump, at first feeling a friction and then the water began to flow. One jug filled, then the other, and she walked back, careful to keep them steady.

The children were settled, and Cora smiled to hear one of them snoring gently. It was becoming quite dim in the cottage. She drew the curtains but didn't light the lamp. With the chores done and the children settled, Cora allowed her thoughts to wander and she recalled the time spent at Folkestone Harbour with Emily and Jacob. Then she thought of the grave in the lonely churchyard and felt regretful she was unable to visit more often. *It's too far, but you're here with me in my thoughts, Stanley. I don't know what's going to happen next in my life, not until I see Jacob, but I'll do my best to keep Emily safe and happy.*

With Stan on her mind, Cora decided to step outside again. She moved between the cottages and outbuildings near the base of the lighthouse. The sun was now sinking fast behind the dark hills; the seabirds had settled for the night and there appeared to be no one else out on the headland. She watched the rhythmic sweep of light catch the tops of the waves and closer by the tin roof of the building housing the foghorn, which was now silent. The light-beam caught the rigging of a sailing ship and the heavier bulk of a steamer; they both travelled through the deep water close to the Dungeness point. Glad to know Stan didn't lie in a watery grave, and that the *Northfleet* was now gone from sight, she turned back to the cottage.

Wishing she had questioned Connie more about Jacob's whereabouts, Cora filled the kettle and pushed it onto the hotplate. Earlier in the day, William had gone to The British Inn with a message to say she was looking after the Rose boys; Ada and Reuben would know she and Emily were safe. The water boiled and Cora made enough tea for one cup, then settled in the armchair, with a blanket covering her, and a shawl around her shoulders. Her imagination wandered to a future where she and Emily spent their days with the boys and their father. In her mind, her daughter grew in confidence every week, and all four children settled with a mother-figure to care for them. It was late and sleep was not far away, causing her mind to become confused: images came of them all sharing the home, and of the time when Jacob had held her in the lamp room. Unsure of where he was, Cora wondered if… but pushed the rambling thoughts away. The niggle persisted: perhaps… maybe in the last two months he had found himself a woman to share his life with. Her eyelids closed and she fell into an uneasy sleep.

It seemed to Cora that she had been dreaming for hours, but it was only ten minutes before the door opened and there was movement in the home. With a pounding heart, and confusion in that in-between time between sleep and awakening, she struggled to pull her mind into focus. Knowing it to be Jacob, and suddenly nervous of him finding her there, Cora clutched the blanket tight against her. The room was almost dark, and she was aware of him fumbling with his boots and jacket.

"Connie, I'm sorry. I thought I'd be back hours ago," Jacob said; he kept his voice low and walked over to the range then pushed the kettle onto the hotplate.

"Connie had to go. It's me, Cora." She didn't know how she squeezed the words out into a rational order.

"Cora! How…?" Jacob exclaimed as he went to the window. He pulled back the heavy curtain and the room was lit by the full moon. There was laughter in his voice as he continued, "It really is you! But what on earth…?"

"Connie's mother needed her and…"

"But she didn't get you from Ashford. You were already here? Why was there no letter?" He sat in the chair opposite. "I'm pleased to see you, don't think I'm not. It's just a bit of a shock!"

Cora saw him grinning as the moonlight fell across his face. She also became aware he was very smartly dressed, with a neat collar and cravat. "It must be a shock," she admitted.

"A nice one. I promise," he insisted. "Is Connie all right, and you... what brings you here?"

"I'd had enough of that Mrs Tibbs and all her fussing, so I've finished with the job and I came here for a few days."

The kettle began to boil, and Cora started to pull herself out of the chair. "I'll make the tea. You've had a shock and quite a walk." She moved to the pot, which was still warm from her earlier brew. Reaching for the caddy, she added a spoonful of leaves and the boiling water. "We came this morning, me and Emily, then Connie said you'd gone out for the day." Cora tried to keep her tone neutral, as if where he had gone held no interest for her.

"I had to go to Ashford," he told her. "I stayed overnight in Mrs Browne's boarding house!"

Cora smiled at the thought of him being there and wondered if he had been in her own attic room. "Emily's asleep with Frank," she informed him.

"Is she really? I thought she would be with Ada."

"I was planning to carry her back." Now darkness had fallen, the thought of taking a sleeping child over the stones no longer seemed like a good plan. "I'd better go now you are here." She didn't want to; Cora wanted to hear his news but didn't like to be too pushy.

"If you want to, then I'll carry Emily. Or let her stay here?" Jacob suggested. "But it's lovely outside. Let's sit on the bench and talk for a while?"

"I'd like that," she said, and smiled even though he couldn't see it.

The seat outside the cottage was no more than a couple of planks on some bricks, but it served its purpose well, as a place to sit, relax, and watch the children play or simply to have a cup of tea in peace and reflect on life. In the daytime, there was a view along the beach front, taking in the fisherman's homes, and the boats. By night, these were in darkness, with the moonlight catching the angles of the cottage roofs, the curve of the underside of the boats and the uprights of their masts.

"You've left Mrs Tibbs then?" Jacob began. "You'll miss the baby."

"I will. But she'll have someone else to look after her. Someone who doesn't have to go to elocution lessons." She waited for a moment, hoping he would suggest she look after his sons again. But he seemed to be deep in thought, and so Cora asked: "Are you needing someone to look after the boys when Connie leaves? Or perhaps you have someone in mind…?"

"I know who we all have in mind," he replied without hesitation. "They've never stopped asking if you and Emily can come back."

"And you?"

"I've never stopped hoping that you would, but I'm not foolish and I can see there's nothing much for a young woman around here. There's not much for anyone."

"Are you still thinking of their schooling?" Cora asked. "Is there any word of a school being built?"

"There's talk of it, and talk of a railway line," he told her. "Imagine that!"

But she couldn't think of a noisy great metal beast belching its steam over the headland, and what would be the purpose of it? "It would certainly make a difference," she conceded. "You'd be in Lydd within minutes." They had moved away from talking about her coming back, Cora realised. Jacob had said he would like her to, and then the talk had turned to trains. "I've still got my rooms in Willesborough," she told him. "I'd happily stay there if you didn't need me, but if there's a place here looking after the boys then I'll come, and I promise I won't go running off again."

"I know that," he said. "You're more settled now. You have seen your husband buried, and sad as that is, it brings things to an end. And you've proved you can look after yourself and Emily."

"I'm not so sure about that," Cora admitted. "She is such a good girl, but only content when here with your boys. So, if you're happy for me to be here then I've got my room at The British Inn, and when Connie leaves, I can start again."

"I don't want you to come back here," Jacob replied.

Cora felt sick. Colour rushed to her cheeks and she was thankful he couldn't see her embarrassment: the moonlight was not cruel enough to reveal it.

"I want you to stay in Ashford with Mrs Birch and look after the boys, and on a Sunday, I want you and Emily to go for walks and picnics with us all. And sometimes I'd like to find a girl to mind all four of the children and we can go to a dance hall or a show..."

"You're not talking sense," Cora managed to say. Her head was spinning. The thought of staying in Ashford and looking after the boys was perfect, and as for all the talk of dance halls... she liked the idea of that too. "I can't stay there, even if they did build a railway line."

"I'm moving to Ashford," he announced with relish. "Me and the boys! That's where I've been today, sorting it all out. I've got a job at the Railway Works, and a nice little terraced house in Gladstone Road."

Cora's mind settled as she digested his news and understood the plan. Jacob wanted a proper school for his sons, and a job where he would always be at home with them overnight. He knew there were better opportunities in Ashford: a town which was growing fast due to the railway. She saw herself and Emily walking down Church Road, then along the lane, past Boys Hall and over the tracks to South Willesborough. Cora need not leave her lovely rooms with Mrs Birch, but would be free of Mrs Tibbs and dour Iris of the rectory.

"Ashford!" Cora replied. "Blimey, there was me almost packed up to move to Dungeness, and I could have passed you on the road there!"

"Does it sound like a good plan?" Jacob asked.

"It sounds like the best," Cora replied. "Especially the picnics and the dance halls!"

Epilogue
March 1874

Reuben took the letter from the postman and was about to put it aside when he recognised the handwriting and noted the Ashford postmark. "Ada," he called, as he opened the door between bar and home.

"In the kitchen," she replied.

"There's a letter from our Cora," he said, walking through and offering it to her. "I know you'll want to read it."

3 Sand Quarry Cottages
Willesborough
Tuesday 17th March 1874

Dear Ada and Reuben,
We are getting married! Jacob and I are getting married on Saturday, April 4th, in the Methodist Chapel, Cudworth Road. I didn't know he was Methodist until he moved to the area, what with there being no church at Dungeness. It will be a small gathering. Just us and Mrs Birch, and a couple of men he works with. Not forgetting the children, of course. You can imagine how excited Emily is! We are hoping you can come. It won't be right without you. The wedding is at 2 o'clock, and afterwards we'll have some sandwiches and a piece

of cake back at Jacob's house. By then it will be my
house as well!
With affectionate wishes,
Cora

"Oh, Reuben, isn't that perfect? Didn't I say we'd have good news from her soon?" Ada gave her husband a hug.

"You did, love," he agreed. "Let the girl know we'll be there, and we can make it into a holiday. Book a room at that nice boarding-house and spend some time with them all."

"What a thing to look forward to!" Ada beamed her happiness. "I'll do it straight away, after this," and she leaned forward to deliver a big kiss, before going to her box of writing paper in the parlour. "You're a good husband. And, as for Cora, I knew she would shine bright, despite all her troubles."

The End

Memorials

Memorials and graves for the victims of the *Northfleet* can be found in the following churches:

An obelisk memorial above the grave in the churchyard of St Thomas' Church, Winchelsea.

Graves in All Saints, Lydd; St Nicholas, New Romney; St Mary le Merge, Capel-le-Ferne; St Margaret's, St Margaret's at Cliff and St Peter and St Paul, Worth.

A stained-glass window in St Nicholas Church, New Romney, commemorates the crew and passengers who died. Angel trumpeters are shown calling them up to heaven from the waves.

About the Author

Romney Marsh writer, Emma Batten, loves to combine her interest in local history with creative writing. It is important to her that historical details are accurate in order to give readers an authentic insight into life on Romney Marsh. She enjoys giving author talks about her journey as a writer, planning unique writing workshops and meeting her local readers.

Still Shining Bright is Emma's eighth novel.

Her first, *A Place Called Hope*, is set in the 16th century and tells the story of the lives of two young women living through the decline of the remote settlement of Hope on Romney Marsh.

Her second novel, *Secrets of the Shingle* is a mystery set on the wild, windswept wastes of the Dungeness peninsula in the 19th century and seen through the eyes of a naive young teacher.

Her third, *What the Monk Didn't See,* is the story of New Romney and the 1287 storm which changed the fortunes of the town forever.

But First Maintain the Wall is set in Georgian Dymchurch. Harry is passing through the village when the seawall breaches and events force him to stay. As an outsider, he struggles to be accepted and a tentative friendship is forged with a young woman who seeks answers to her past.

Stranger on the Point, a sequel to *Secrets of the Shingle,* is the story of a young woman's quest to fulfil her worth as the shadows of WW1 live on. Set in Dungeness and Ashford.

The Artist's Gift tells the story of a fictional character living amongst real life events during the Second World War. Set in Lydd and Dungeness. A sequel to *Secrets of the Shingle* and *Stranger on the Point.*

Inspired by the pub sign for Botolphs Bridge Inn, *The Pendant Cross* introduces West Hythe and Lyminge in Anglo-Saxon times.

For more details take a look at Emma's website:
www.emmabattenauthor.com